7/14

Love with a Perfect Cowboy

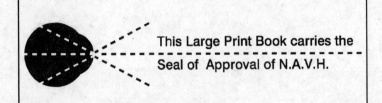

This Large Print Book carries the
Seal of Approval of N.A.V.H.

LOVE WITH A
PERFECT COWBOY

LORI WILDE

THORNDIKE PRESS
A part of Gale, Cengage Learning

GALE
CENGAGE Learning·

Farmington Hills, Mich • San Francisco • New York • Waterville, Maine
Meriden, Conn • Mason, Ohio • Chicago

GALE
CENGAGE Learning®

Copyright © 2014 by Laurie Vanzura.
Thorndike Press, a part of Gale, Cengage Learning.

Thorndike Press® Large Print Romance.
The text of this Large Print edition is unabridged.
Other aspects of the book may vary from the original edition.
Set in 16 pt. Plantin.

LIBRARY OF CONGRESS CATALOGING-IN-PUBLICATION DATA

Wilde, Lori.
    Love with a perfect cowboy : a Cupid, Texas novel / Lori Wilde. — Large print edition.
        pages ; cm. — (Thorndike Press large print romance)
        ISBN 978-1-4104-6823-9 (hardcover) — ISBN 1-4104-6823-2 (hardcover)
        1. Large type books. I. Title.
    PS3623.I536L68 2014
    813'.6—dc23   2014012375

Published in 2014 by arrangement with Avon, an imprint of HarperCollins Publishers

Printed in the United States of America
1 2 3 4 5 6 7 18 17 16 15 14

*This book is dedicated to the
memory of my beloved Daisy.*

ACKNOWLEDGMENTS

This is the last book in my Cupid, Texas series, and I hate to leave the Trans-Pecos region. There's no other place like it in Texas. The people there are a different breed — rugged, independent, hard working and long suffering — molded by the extremes of climate and topography.

While my husband and I were visiting the area, a bigger dog attacked our New American shepherd puppy, Daisy, as we walked her on a leash. We raced her to the local vet, but, alas, there was nothing they could do to save her life, and we had to have her put to sleep. Losing her was so very hard, and I left a bit of my heart in the Fort Davis Mountains that awful day. Most everyone in the small close-knit town heard about our loss, and many came by our motor home to express their condolences. The veterinarian never cashed the check we gave him. I can't begin to express my gratitude for the kindness I was shown and can only hope my books honor the community in the way it deserves.

CHAPTER 1

New York, New York
April 1

Melody Spencer was rushing up Madison Avenue when she spied him.

A tall, lanky man in a black Stetson log-jamming the flow of foot traffic by moseying along at a lamb's pace, craning his neck up at the skyscrapers as if he couldn't believe they made buildings that lofty.

Two simultaneous thoughts popped into her head. One was: *What a hick.* The other was: *I'm homesick.*

Twelve years earlier she had marveled at the towering buildings when she first arrived in the city as a green freshman on a full academic scholarship to NYU. While she no longer stared at the high-rises, she still lived by one motto — *Keep looking up.* Vision, commitment, and hard work were what had brought her to this moment. She was about to receive the promotion she worked a lifetime to earn.

Why else would her boss, Michael Helmsly, have texted her and asked her to come in for a private meeting thirty minutes early on the same day that the creative director was retiring?

She shivered, smiled.

At long last her time had come.

A river of people flowed around the cowboy, some muttering obscenities, others flipping him off, a few glowering, but most not even bothering to acknowledge him at all. He was nothing more than a speck in their obstacle-laden day.

Although one smart-aleck teen — probably a tourist — hollered from a passing taxi, "Why aren't you naked in Times Square, cowboy?"

The man tipped his Stetson at the taxi, briefly revealing a head of thick, whiskey-colored curls and a sense of humor. A navy blue, Western-cut sport jacket hugged his broad shoulders. The crowd obscured her view of his backside, but she would have bet a hundred dollars that tight-fitting Wranglers cupped a spectacular butt.

Cowboys always seemed to have spectacular butts, probably from all that hard riding in the saddle.

He turned his head and the morning light

illuminated his profile — straight nose, honed cheekbones, chiseled jaw. He was freshly clean-shaven, but she could tell he had a heavy beard and that long before five o'clock he'd be sporting a shadow of stubble. In that regard he looked a bit like the actor Josh Holloway, who'd played Sawyer on the television show *Lost.*

A cold jolt of recognition smacked into the pit of her stomach. She knew this man! Had once both loved and hated him.

Luke Nielson, from her hometown of Cupid, Texas.

Her chest tightened and suddenly she couldn't breathe. What was Luke doing in New York City attracting attention like the proverbial fish out of water? What if their eyes met and he recognized her?

Pulse thumping illogically fast, Melody ducked her head and scurried to the far side of the sidewalk. She had no time or inclination to take pity on him and help him navigate the city. He was on his own.

Coward.

She had fifteen minutes to spare. She was using the meeting as an excuse to get away from him. Right-o. And a good excuse it was. She needed those few minutes to compose her thoughts and tamp down her excitement before heading into her boss's office. Cool, calm, and unruffled. That was the image she projected on the job.

Praying that Luke hadn't seen her, she held her breath until she put an entire city block between them. By the time she exhaled, her lungs felt stretched and achy. Okay, she dodged a bullet, onward and upward.

She pushed through the frosted glass door of the building that housed the Tribalgate offices. In the lobby, the security guard positioned at the check-in desk nodded a mute greeting as Melody used her ID badge to swipe her way through the turnstile granting access to the elevators.

Because she was a bit early, there was no one else waiting for the elevator to the thirty-fourth floor. On the ride up, she whipped out her cell phone to text her boyfriend.

Jean-Claude was a top-tier photographer who traveled all around the world, and Melody still couldn't believe he'd chosen her when he had his pick of beautiful, fascinating women. Yes, sometimes he was distant and a bit self-absorbed, but what artist wasn't? He might not be the love of her life, but they had a nice thing going on.

For the last two weeks, she'd been living with Jean-Claude in his Upper West Side apartment across from Central Park. Not to mention that her new residence and illustrious boyfriend had duly impressed her mother, Carol Ann Fant Spencer, when she told her about him, although her mother had immediately made when-are-you-getting-married noises.

It was definitely a monumental step up from her former loft apartment in Queens, although moving in with Jean-Claude had taken a nerve-wracking leap of faith on a relationship that was barely two months old. But her landlord had jacked up her rent, and one night Jean-Claude casually offered to let her stay with him. For once in her life, she plunged in feetfirst without calculating the risks, and so far, so good.

Tomorrow, Jean-Claude was catching a plane to South Africa for a ten-day photo shoot and she wanted to give him a proper send-off.

Dinner 2 nite. My treat. Bernadette's, she texted. *Fingers X we'll have something big to celebrate.*

She waited a moment to see if he would text back right away. When he didn't, she logged on to OpenTable. Since it was early in the week hopefully she could swing a reservation at their favorite restaurant.

OpenTable came back telling her there

were no vacancies at her preferred time of eight P.M. but there was a table available at five-thirty. It was pretty early for dinner, but hey, at least she scored a table. She accepted the five-thirty spot through OpenTable, and then on impulse called the restaurant and asked to have a bottle of iced Dom Perignon waiting tableside.

It wasn't every day a girl made creative director at one of the biggest ad agencies in the country.

Her mother was going to be over the moon when she told her.

Only a couple of executive assistants were in the office. She waved hello and headed for the coffee machine. She poured herself a cup, but drank only half of it, not wanting to look jittery when she walked into her boss's office. With a couple of minutes left to kill, she popped into the ladies' room and reapplied her lipstick.

"Why thank you for this opportunity, Michael," she said, practicing accepting the position. "I do appreciate your confidence in me and I promise you won't be disappointed in my performance."

She smiled carefully. Making sure her upper lip hid her slightly crooked front tooth. She'd learned the flaw-camouflaging smile when she was on the beauty pageant circuit.

14

Why hadn't she gotten veneers years ago? Oh yes, they cost a lot. But with this promotion, she could finally afford them now. Jean-Claude had been nagging her to do it.

She straightened her collar that wasn't askew and brushed imaginary lint off her lapel, and gave herself one last appraisal. She wasn't perfect, not by a long shot, but she looked presentable.

"Here we go, Ms. Creative Director," she murmured, and stepped out into the hallway.

Her boss's door stood ajar.

She poked her head into his office.

Michael sat at his desk, scowling at the computer screen. He looked so much like the *Mad Men* character Roger Sterling that he was almost a caricature, although he possessed none of that character's easygoing, flamboyant ways. Personality-wise, he was more like Don Draper, brilliant, but darkly moody.

He glanced up and his scowl deepened.

Her euphoria evaporated. What had upset him? *Bounce. Don't let his mood throw you.* "Am I too early?"

"Come in," he said curtly. "And close the door behind you."

Squaring her shoulders, she stepped into the room and quietly shut the door. Michael did not ask her to sit down. In fact, he stood up.

Her stomach pitched.

"Jill Jones called me over the weekend," he said.

Jill Jones represented Mowry and Poltish, a chemical company looking to rebrand their image. She and Ms. Jones had had a difference of opinion over the direction of the recent ad campaign, but Melody believed they'd ironed out their differences.

"Isn't Jill sharp? I'm learning so much from her." She struggled to keep her tone neutral. Where was this going?

"Jill's asked that you be removed from the campaign."

What? Melody gulped. "May I ask why?"

He leaned forward, placed both palms flat on his desk in an intimidating gesture. "She says your values aren't consistent with Mowry and Poltish's vision."

She sank her hands on her hips. Yes, she wanted this promotion more than anything in the world, but she had to set the record straight. "Ms. Jones requested a television campaign that essentially claims their new cleaning product is one hundred percent safe. Her idea was to have a mom cleaning a cutting board with their product and then without rinsing the cutting board, cut up raw fruits and vegetables on it and serve the food to her family."

"Sounds to me like you're making a mountain out of a molehill."

"The cleanser should be thoroughly rinsed off. It says so on the labeling. The chemicals could be harmful if ingested."

"Did Jill ask you to make false claims about the product?"

"No, but —"

"It's not your job to police our clients' ethics."

"Yes, but such a —"

"How many times do I have to tell you we're selling the sizzle not the steak? Advertising is about playing on people's emotions, not about bald-faced facts."

"I know that, which is precisely why I objected to Ms. Jones's vision of the ad. Her version would make people feel safe, but it's a false sense of security and I pointed this out. She agreed to allow the actress playing the TV mom to thoroughly wash the cutting board before cutting food up on it. I don't see —"

"That's just it. You don't *see.*"

"See what?"

He shook his head. "Jill says you're difficult."

A heavy weight settled on her shoulders.

She was *not* about to get that promotion after all. In fact, she was being called on the carpet. "So being ethical means I'm difficult?"

"Jill didn't ask you to tell a lie."

She extended her arms out to her sides, palms up. "So I shouldn't have said anything?"

"Never argue with a client."

"Even if I believe the ad they want intentionally misleads the consumer?"

"The truth is rubbery, especially in advertising, and you should know that. There's nothing wrong with bending the truth as far as it will go as long as you don't break it."

"You're telling me that you want me to lie?"

"That's not what I said." He stalked around the desk to stare her down. "The fact that you can't tell the difference between a lie and a creative spin on the truth concerns me."

A hot blast of adrenaline shot through her. Stunned, she curled her hands into fists. "What are you saying?"

"This isn't the first time your provincial *ethics*" — he spat the word with disdain — "have tripped up a campaign."

Taken aback, she placed a palm to her chest. "Specifically, what campaigns are you speaking of?"

"The Palmer campaign for one thing."

"But I only worked on the Palmer ad for a few days," she protested.

"Exactly. Palmer said you were argumentative so I put you on another project."

"I merely pointed out that the campaign they wanted was lewd and suggestive. The insinuation of a ménage à trois featuring their garden hoses was in poor taste."

"And yet, that ad went on to become Palmer's most successful campaign ever. Implied sex sold those garden hoses like hotcakes."

"It also garnered more consumer complaints than any other ad we've ever produced."

"Which goes to prove controversy is a good thing. You seemed to understand that when you first came to work here. The family feud television spot you created for Frosty Bites was not only hilarious, but it was one of Tribalgate's most successful campaigns in the last decade."

"So what's the problem?"

"That campaign was six years ago. What have you done for us lately?"

"I won a Clio two years ago!"

"Which means absolutely nothing. The ad you won the Clio for was cute and attention-getting, but in the end it did nothing to increase the sales of the cars it was advertising. And Hyundai dropped Tribalgate over it."

"All right." She nodded. "I see your point. Message received. I will strive to get over my ethics and infuse ads with more titillation."

He shook his head. "I'm sorry, but no you won't."

"You don't want me to put more sexuality in the ads?"

"You will no longer be putting anything into the ads."

"I . . . I don't understand."

"It's not your fault." His tone softened. "You come from a small town. You're just not sophisticated enough for Tribalgate."

Her jaw dropped. "What do you mean? I've lived in the city for twelve years, almost half my life."

"Ms. Spencer, Melody . . ."

Goose bumps spread over her arm. The left muscle in her eye jumped, a tic she got whenever she was super stressed. This couldn't be happening. "What are you saying?"

"Not to sound like Donald Trump or anything, but you're fired."

Stunned, she stood there, mouth open.

She caught sight of Michael's desk calendar Tuesday, April 1. April Fool's Day. Relief washed over her.

"Oh, very funny, sir." She smiled circumspectly, hiding that defective tooth. "You almost had me going there."

He glowered. "What are you talking about?"

"I've got to hand it to you. It's the best April Fool's joke anyone has ever played on me."

Slowly, he shook his head. "This is not a joke."

The dread was back and heavier than ever. Oh shit. "This isn't a prank?"

"No."

"Are you sure Ashton Kutcher isn't going to jump out of the closet and declare I've been punked?" she asked hopefully, even as she knew she was well and truly sunk.

No joke. He was serious. She'd been fired.

Her boss held out his palm. "Please hand me your identification badge."

Pressing her lips into a straight line, she fumbled with the ID badge clipped to her lapel. She could barely see through the mist of tears welling up in her eyes, but she refused to let him see her cry. She swallowed the saltiness, blinked hard, and passed her badge to him.

Michael took her ID that represented her entire sense of self, stared at someone over her shoulder, and nodded.

She turned and for the first time saw the two security guards standing in the doorway behind her.

"They'll take you to your desk to collect your things," Michael intoned. "After that, they'll escort you from the building. I'd appreciate it if you didn't cause a scene."

CHAPTER 2

Hours later, Melody sat in a pew at St. Patrick's Cathedral, the cardboard box of her belongings clutched in her lap, the gold-plated Clio statuette sticking out of the top, mocking her. Yeah, hot stuff, not so spectacular now, huh?

Whenever she needed a respite from the crazy business of day-to-day Manhattan, she came to St. Pat's. Even when the cathedral was packed with tourists, as it was this afternoon, there was still a reverential hush that soothed her.

After Michael fired her she hadn't known what to do or where else to go, so she'd stumbled in, and once seated, she hadn't been able to make herself get up.

She was going to be okay. She was a survivor. She would get a job with one of Tribalgate's competitors and go head to head with her former employer and she would kick their asses. Temporary setback.

Okay, so she was turning thirty at the end of the summer without having achieved her lifelong goal of becoming a creative director at a prestigious Madison Avenue ad agency, but oh well. She would make new goals.

Yeah, uh-huh, sure.

She'd been a high school cheerleader, but she wasn't buying the rah-rah rallying cry going on inside her head. She had credentials, but it wasn't as if ad executive jobs were low-hanging fruit.

She notched her chin up, but the pain in her heart was sharper than ever.

Fired.

She'd been fired. Never in her life had she been fired. She worked hard and achieved everything she ever dreamed of — valedictorian of Cupid High, homecoming queen, head cheerleader, and 4.0 GPA at NYU. Why then did she feel like a complete and total failure?

Why? Because she *had* failed.

Setting her teeth, Melody hissed out a long breath. Yes, she'd achieved a lot, but in spite of that, life had been one long series of failing to live up to her mother's edicts and expectations — stand up straight and hold your shoulders back; when you gain three pounds immediately go on a diet; avoid carbs at all cost; a minute on the lips,

24

forever on the hips; nice girls finish last; strive, strive, always strive to be the best you can be; keep up, keep up; no excuses; it's all in the presentation; life is a contest; you have to play to win; grab the spotlight whenever you can; and whatever you do, never, ever, under any circumstances trust a Nielson.

All those exhausting rules!

A Latino family, consisting of a mom, dad, and four little girls with big white bows in their hair settled in the pew beside her. The parents knelt and began to pray. One of the little girls canted her head, and studied Melody intently.

Once upon a time she'd been that age — young, inquisitive, and full of dreams.

Melody massaged her throbbing temple. Sometimes it felt as if she had baling wire wrapped around her chest. A memory flitted across her mind. She was four years old, and entered in her first beauty pageant.

Backstage, her mother fussed with Melody's hair, and accidentally spritzed hair spray in her eyes.

"Momma! That burns."

"Don't rub your eyes. You're smearing your mascara." Her mother licked the corner of a Kleenex and dabbed at Melody's face. "Stop squirming and hold still."

That baling-wire sensation had come over her then, squeezing her lungs so tightly that she couldn't breathe. Body burning hot all over, she struggled from her mother's arms and clawed at the cameo ribbon necklace clasped at her throat.

Momma swatted Melody's petticoat-padded fanny. "Stop that behavior. Stop it right now," she hissed. "There is no excuse for panic. You must uphold the family name by beating Carly Nielson. No Nielson has ever beaten either a Greenwood or a Fant in the Cutie Pie Valentine's Day pageant."

But she liked Carly. At preschool, Carly had let her borrow crayons after Melody had left hers out in the sun and they melted in a pile of colorful goo. She didn't understand why she was supposed to hate Carly just because her last name was Nielson.

"I don't care 'bout no stoopid booty pageant." Melody folded her arms over her chest, pooched out her lower lip.

"You paste a smile on your face, young lady, and get up on that stage and win that trophy or I'm going to paddle you so hard you won't remember your own name," her mother threatened.

The baling wire tightened. "I can't, I can't —"

"You can and you will. Greenwood-Fant

blood flows through your veins. Your family runs this town and you will win this pageant. Now get up there and beat the pants off Carly Nielson. No excuses. Win." Her mother glared and pinched her arm.

Melody gulped, blinking back the sting of tears. Somehow, when they called her name, she got up on that stage and did exactly as her mother demanded, completing the routines they'd practiced over and over.

And win she had.

Not only won, but she also had the entire room erupting in a standing ovation.

For her.

In the flush of victory, she should have been happy. Most anyone would have been happy. But as she stood there next to her preening mother, the gold-plated trophy gleaming in the fluorescent lighting of the ballroom of the Alpine Holiday Inn, she caught sight of Carly's crestfallen face and her heart sloshed into her patent leather Mary Janes.

Poor Carly.

The truth hit her. If she won, then someone else had to lose.

Get over it.

That was the first time she remembered the sharp lash of her internal taskmaster whipping her into compliance. Throughout the years that punishing voice had intensified until she devoured her inner Simon-Legree-on-Benzedrine, chewed it, swallowed it, and internalized it, until finally that punishing voice had eclipsed her mother's.

Nothing she ever did was good enough. Nothing ever satisfied. The more she strived, the more there was to accomplish. She climbed and climbed and climbed and for a brief moment — even though she hadn't truly appreciated it — she'd summited the top of the heap.

Only to crash.

Spectacularly.

How could she tell her mother she'd been fired?

Melody started to gnaw on a thumbnail, but then sat on her hands to make herself stop.

Ah. That's why she'd been parked in St. Pat's all day even when her stomach grumbled and her mouth was bone dry and she needed to go to the bathroom. She couldn't face calling her mother.

Enough.

Melody shook off her ennui. No more pity party. Get it in gear. Make plans for a comeback.

She called Jean-Claude for the fourth time

that day to tell him she needed a shoulder to cry on, but his phone went to voice mail again, as it had the other three times. Dammit. She really needed to hear a sympathetic voice right now. Sighing, she finally sent him a text saying she was on her way home.

She nibbled her bottom lip. Jean-Claude had only known her as a winner. Would this shift in her status upset the balance of their relationship?

Only one way to find out. See him face-to-face.

She couldn't emotionally handle the trip up to Seventy-second Street on foot, nor could she see herself taking the subway with the pitiful box in her arms, so she splurged on a taxi. Maybe she should be concerned about saving money at this point, after all she didn't know how long she would be out of work, but anything other than a cab ride felt too much like a walk of shame.

The taxi dropped her off in front of the apartment. She stood on the sidewalk gathering her courage. Jean-Claude should be packing for his trip to South Africa. How would he react to her news? Would he be supportive, disappointed, or, worse, disinterested? Why hadn't he returned her calls or texts?

An uneasy sensation rippled over her.

Jean-Claude could be a bit narcissistic at times — honestly, his obsession with his art was part of his charm — but he'd never outright ignored her. What if something was wrong?

Resolutely, she squared her shoulders, hoisted the box higher up in her arms, and stepped toward the front door.

"Hello, Parker," she greeted the doorman and put a cheery, crooked-tooth-hiding smile on her face.

Parker did not smile back. In fact, he did not automatically open the door for her either. "Ms. Spencer," he said solemnly. "I must speak to you privately."

Alarm bells went off in her head. Had something terrible happened to Jean-Claude? Was that why he hadn't answered her calls and texts?

"Now?"

Parker nodded and opened the door. "Please come with me."

Heart in her throat, she followed him inside the building and glanced around. There were people in the lobby and some standing at the bank of elevators, but she barely noticed them as her pulse pounded harder and louder with every step. A hundred horrible scenarios involving Jean-Claude and some kind of terrible accident sprang into her head.

Parker went to the other side of the check-in counter, opened the door to the storage room, and crooked his finger for her to follow him.

The female security guard on duty at the desk craned her neck around, peering curiously at her as she walked past.

With each step, her chest squeezed tighter and tighter and she clung to the cardboard box as if it were a magical shield that could keep her safe. *Wait a minute. Don't freak. It is April Fool's Day. Maybe Jean-Claude is playing a joke.*

Yes, except while Jean-Claude was beyond gorgeous and a talented photographer, he did not have much of a sense of humor. What if he was giving her an unexpected gift or throwing her a surprise party to celebrate her promotion?

She suppressed a groan. Oh great, just what she needed. A surprise party when she'd gotten fired instead of promoted. Still, it was better than the thought that something terrible had happened to him.

Melody stepped over to the open door and peered into the storage room. No friends gathered to yell, "Surprise." No grinning Jean-Claude to give her a kiss. No brightly colored packages. No ribbons. No bows. No balloons. No confetti.

Good, right?

Except there sat her suitcases and several cardboard boxes closed with masking tape, her name scrawled across them with a black Sharpie in Jean-Claude's distinctive hand-writing.

She shifted her gaze to meet Parker's eyes. "What is this?"

"Your belongings."

"Why are they down here?" She didn't mean to ask the question. It made her look like a complete dumbass, but her world had been knocked off kilter and her mind couldn't fully absorb what she was seeing.

Parker cleared his throat, lowered his voice, and looked at her like she was the saddest thing he'd ever encountered. "Mr. Laurent requested that your things be made available to you on the first floor."

"I don't understand."

Parker lifted his doorman's cap and scratched his bald head. "He changed the access code to his apartment and he re-quested that you not be allowed onto the floor."

"Excuse me?"

"He's evicting you."

Melody blinked. "Jean-Claude is breaking up with me?"

Parker shifted his feet, coughed lightly, politely. "Ahem. So it appears."

"Did he say why?"

"I'm just the doorman."

"I heard him muttering something about an ugly crooked tooth," volunteered the security guard. "But maybe that had nothing to do with you."

She didn't recall dropping it, but the box in her hands hit the ground with a loud smack and she put a palm to her mouth.

People jumped and looked around.

The Clio statuette flew from the box and skidded over the polished marble. The ball that the statuette was holding broke off and rolled across the floor.

It stopped at her feet.

Broken.

Just like her career. Just like her relationship with Jean-Claude. Just like her life.

"Jean-Claude is not getting away with this. He can't simply dump my stuff and forbid me to go up onto his floor. I demand an explanation, dammit."

"Do not put up a fight," Parker said sternly. "Go quietly. It's for the best."

"Best for whom? Jean-Claude?" The bastard. "I deserve better than this." Melody spun on her heel and stalked toward the elevator.

Both Parker and the security guard charged after her.

She reached the elevator first, and frantically punched the up button.

Gawking tenants and visitors to the building stopped, stared, and whispered.

"It won't do any good to throw a fit." Parker closed his hand around her wrist as the security guard moved to block her entry to the elevator door that opened up. "Mr. Laurent has already left for South Africa."

It was all too much to be fired and dumped by her boyfriend in the same day.

Melody pulled from Parker's grasp, flung her arms overhead, and stepped backward until she ran into the cool marble wall behind her. Nowhere else to go.

"Please, Ms. Spencer," Parker said. "I know it's a shock, but you are a woman of dignity. "Please . . ." He sounded desperate now. "Get your things and go."

The security guard reached for the Taser clipped to her utility belt. "I won't hesitate to use this," she threatened.

"Don't make us call the police," Parker bargained, in a kinder tone.

Her legs trembled. *No. Do not collapse.* Her knees gave way.

Slowly, she slid down the wall until she landed on her butt, not giving a damn that she was in a skirt and heels. Numbly, she stared down at the polished marble. How did they keep it so spotless in here? She could see her pathetic reflection in the brilliant shine.

"Ms. Spencer," Parker murmured. "We're going to have to ask you to leave."

Parker. Was that his first name or his last? She had no idea.

"We'll give you a minute to pull yourself together," the security guard added, and steered Parker back to the check-in desk. "But only a minute."

A muscle in her left eye jumped. The cursed tic she got when she was overstressed. She nodded blindly, trying to make the tic go away, but never glanced up. She should snap out of it. This wasn't she. She was an achiever, a survivor, a doer. *Get up.*

"Show's over, folks," the security guard announced to the lobby at large and shooed them off like Central Park pigeons. "Go about your day."

Feet scuffled. The elevator dinged. Voices murmured.

So Jean-Claude had thrown her out. The ass hat. Okay, fine. What next?

She couldn't stay here. But where could she go? Her best friend, Bethany, was married with three kids and lived out in Brooklyn. Her other best friend, Amy, shared a one-bedroom with her boyfriend in Soho. Both would willingly put her up for a night, but she couldn't impose on them for longer than that and what was she going to do with her things?

It was all too much to process.

She dropped her head in her hands and shut her jumpy eyes. Heard footsteps come closer. Was it Parker returning to roust her?

Blowing out her breath, she opened her eyes, and spied a pair of cowboy boots in front of her.

A shiver ran through her, although she didn't know why. Slowly, following the lines of those boots up to firm muscular legs encased in tight-fitting jeans and on up farther to the big gold rodeo belt buckle positioned above the zipper of snug Wranglers, she raised her head . . .

. . . and gulped.

"Melody," he said her name soft and low.

She tipped her chin all the way up and gazed into familiar hazel eyes swimming with sympathy, surprised to realize her eye tic had gone away.

Luke Nielson.

And from the tender, rueful expression on his face, he'd apparently heard the entire exchange between her and the doorman.

Oh God, she even had a Nielson feeling sorry for her. That was some kind of pathetic. Earlier that day all she'd wanted to do was avoid him, now she had an overwhelming urge to throw herself into his arms, bury her face against his broad chest, and sob her heart out.

He was taller than he'd been in high school, having sprouted a good two inches over the almost six feet he'd been then. Even though she was tall for a woman, five-seven and a half, he made her feel petite. His hair was a shade darker and his eyes were a deeper shade of hazel. Or maybe it was just a trick of lighting. He reached down a hand to help her up just as the afternoon sunlight cut through the window casting him in a halo glow. In that heartbeat of a moment, he looked like a knight in shining Stetson. The only thing missing was the white horse.

"Sounds like you've been having a rough day, darlin'," he drawled.

"To say the least," she mumbled.

"C'mon with me and I'll treat you to supper."

Supper.

One of those words she'd dropped from her vocabulary. Since Cupid was a ranching community, back home they called lunch "dinner" and dinner "supper," because dinner was when the hands ate their biggest meal of the day.

Melody didn't know why she sank her small, smooth palm into Luke's big, calloused one. Back home, Nielson and Fant descendants got along like Hatfields and McCoys, but here in the asphalt jungle, well, all bets were off, weren't they?

In New York City, they could be unexpected allies, and it was an oddly pleasant feeling.

He led her by the hand, stopping at the desk long enough to peel a hundred-dollar bill from his money clip and pass it to Parker. "Keep her belongings here overnight."

"Yes sir." Parker snapped his heels together. "But I can't keep them past tomorrow evening."

"That's long enough," Luke said, and slipped his hand to the small of her back.

Any other time, she probably would have bristled at the overly familiar gesture, but today? Well, the warmth of his palm radiating through her clothes felt good and she allowed him to sweep her out of the building.

Her phone dinged, telling her that she had a text. She was so accustomed to living her life tethered to electronics that she didn't even think about what she was doing, simply took her phone from her pocket right there on the street and read the text.

It was a reminder from Bernadette's about her five-thirty dinner reservation.

"You've already got supper plans," Luke said, reading over her shoulder.

"I don't want to keep them." She moved out of the flow of foot traffic, leaned one shoulder against the outside of the building, and stowed her phone into her purse.

"Why not? You've got reservations and I'm hungry. Let's go." He took her elbow.

She pulled back. "It's not your kind of place."

"What's that supposed to mean? No sawdust and peanut hulls on the floor? No cigarette smoke circling the ceiling fan? No stuffed animal heads on the wall?"

"That's not what I meant at all," she said. "The restaurant is pretentious."

"So it's *your* kind of place."

"My boyfriend's kind of place," she corrected.

"The boyfriend who is not man enough to break up with you face-to-face."

"That'd be him."

"Excuse my French," he said, "but the man is a douchebag."

Melody laughed. "So he is."

"I like the sound of that."

"Of what?"

"Your laughter. Let's go eat at Douche-bag's favorite restaurant and say rude things about him."

She shook her head. "I can't."

"Why not? I'm buying."

She surrendered a halfhearted smile. "The dinner was supposed to be a celebration."

"We can still celebrate without him. In fact, I think we'll have a lot more fun without his sorry ass around."

"There's nothing to celebrate."

"C'mon." He chucked her under the chin with an index finger, and she felt his touch clean through the center of her body. "You can't tell me that you were that hung up on him. Major tool like that? No way. You're far too sensible."

The muscles in the center of her chest tightened. "You're right. The relationship was still new, so I'm not devastated. But he sure picked the worst day in the world to pull this stunt."

Luke slanted his head, the brim of his Stetson casting a shadow over his face. "How's that?"

"I thought I was getting a promotion. That was the reason for the celebration."

His mouth turned down. "But you got

fired instead."

She met his eyes. There was no judgment, only sympathy. From a Nielson? She arched an eyebrow. "How did you know?"

"I went to your office building, saw you being escorted out the front door with that box in your hands and tears in your eyes."

Melody groaned and put a hand over her face.

"It's nothing to be ashamed of." His deep voice soothed. "Some of the best people in the world have been fired. Henry Ford. Albert Einstein. Bill Gates. Square pegs who didn't fit into round holes. Cheer up. It simply means Tribalgate didn't appreciate your talent."

Another compliment.

Uneasily, she dropped her hand. "Wait a minute, how did you find me here?"

He shrugged, looked guilty. "Followed you into that church."

"You were at St. Pat's?"

"For hours."

"Why didn't you come up to me there?"

"You looked like you needed to be alone."

"So how did you get from St. Pat's to here?"

"I heard you give the address to the taxi driver."

"You're stalking me?" she asked mildly in

a vain attempt to convince her quaking knees she was not overwhelmed by his intoxicating scent that reminded her of too many things she wanted to forget — furtive rides on his mustang, furtive glances in high school library stacks, the night all hell had broken loose.

He gave a one-shoulder shrug. "I wouldn't call it stalking per se. I needed to talk to you. Looks like it's a good thing I did. You're in over your head."

She held up both palms, bristled. "The last thing I need is some Nielson thinking he's going to save me."

"Don't do that," he chided.

"What?"

"Bring up the family feud."

She straightened. "You're right. This isn't the Trans-Pecos."

He glanced around, and pretended to be startled by the passersby. "I hadn't noticed."

"The multitudinous taxis weren't a dead give-away?"

He chuckled. "I've never seen so much yellow in my life. It's getting close to five-thirty. Do you want to keep those reservations? I still need to talk to you."

"About what?"

"Let's save it for supper." He put his arm around her shoulder and she did not shake him off.

"Okay," she said. "Why not?"

It had been one hell of a screwed-up day. Her family might not agree, but there were worse things in life than having dinner with a Nielson.

CHAPTER 3

At the swanky seafood restaurant, Melody tried to wave away the champagne on ice that was waiting for them at the table, but Luke wouldn't let her.

"Leave it," he told the sommelier, then doffed his cowboy hat and settled it on the seat of the empty chair beside them.

The sommelier sniffed and looked down his nose at the Stetson as if to say, *How did you get in here dressed like that?*

"It costs over a hundred dollars a bottle," Melody whispered.

He lowered his head and his voice. "You don't think I can afford it?"

"That's not the point. Dom Perignon is major celebration champagne. This is no longer a celebration."

"Sure it is," he said easily. "When was the last time a Nielson and a Fant broke bread together?"

"Probably sometime before 1924."

"My point exactly. Our being together is something special to celebrate."

"But then if you count those fruit chews we shared on the picnic table at Lake Cupid, it was fifteen years ago."

His heart slammed against his rib cage, hard and loud. "Are we counting that?" he asked, surprised at how calm he sounded.

She didn't avert her gaze. Brave woman. "Are we?"

He gulped. "Those fruit chews caused a mess of trouble."

"They did indeed."

He was about to tell her how much he regretted all the dark things that had transpired after their midnight teenage rendezvous, but a tuxedoed waiter arrived, and with a bow, passed them leather-bound menus, and the moment vanished.

"Any appetizers?" the waiter asked. "Tonight we have fresh caviar. It is *très magnifique.*" He pressed two fingers to his thumb and kissed them.

"Yeah, go ahead and bring us some of that." Luke nodded.

"Are you sure?" Melody asked. "Have you ever had caviar?"

What? Did she think he was the most backwoods of hicks? "Yes, I've had caviar. Love the briny flavor."

"Okay, just making sure. Cupid is about as far away from the sea as you can get."

"Believe it or not, I *have* been out of the state of Texas."

"But not to New York."

"That obvious, huh?"

She shrugged, dipped her head, and offered up a teasing smile.

The waiter departed.

Luke narrowed his eyes, studied her for a long moment — slender shoulders, delicate but strong, creamy skin unblemished by freckles. A silky blue blouse clung with just the right amount of snugness to round, pert breasts.

She crossed her arms and hugged herself, delineating firm, toned biceps. She worked out. A thin gold bracelet glimmered at her wrist, expensive but understated, just like the woman in front of him, elegant and flawless. Soft blond hair curled gently down her shoulders. Her makeup was muted, except for her lipstick. Her lips were painted a dark, lush color, as deeply red as the inside chamber of a summer rosebud, at once seductive and utterly feminine.

How much she'd changed over the years. Evolved into a sophisticated creature far out of his league. Why was he here?

The sommelier returned to open the

46

champagne. He poured a bit of the liquid into Luke's glass for him to taste and pronounce acceptable before filling both their champagne flutes.

Melody brought the flute to her lips. Those red lips stirred something primal inside him. Once upon a time, quivering in the grips of powerful, youthful lust, he'd claimed those lips, branded them with his own.

"Wait," he said, and extended his glass. "A toast."

"I'm not in a toasting mood."

"Too bad. Change your mood."

"You're bossy."

He ignored that, stared at her pointedly. "To new beginnings."

For a moment, he thought she wasn't going to join him in the toast. That long-standing Fant-Nielson animosity? But then she lowered thick, black lashes, and raised her glass to clink against his.

"To new beginnings," those gorgeous lips whispered as her chocolate brown eyes assessed him.

Damn, but he admired her ability to quickly shake off adversity and move on. Of course, that same quality had left him in the dust, but still, he loved a tenacious woman.

He took a sip of the smooth, bright bubbly.

It was unsettling, sitting here so close to her. Over the years, he'd seen her around Cupid, of course, whenever she came home to visit her parents. They nodded on the street, occasionally shared a brief smile, but never alone, never up close and personal like this.

"Wow," he said, because he did not know what else to say. "This tastes the way diamonds sparkle."

"Poetic. You should be in advertising." Melody stroked a slender finger down the side of her glass, wiping off the condensation.

His gaze zeroed in on her long fingers. Did she have the slightest idea how much that simple gesture affected him?

"Rumor has it that when Dom Perignon took his first sip, he said, 'Come quickly, I am drinking stars,' " she went on.

"No kidding?"

"It's a myth. Actually, the quote was part of an ad campaign."

"What a letdown."

"But the champagne is not." She took a long sip, that lush red mouth closing over the delicate glass.

His tongue tingled to taste her again.

Memory knifed his brain. Back then she tasted of the fruit chews — cherry, lemon, lime, grape. A veritable fruit punch. She sat in his lap, her arms around his neck, their mouths fused, as their bodies rocked together, desperate, hungry, searching for nirvana. He recalled the sharp, aching pressure in his cock and how his fingers slipped under the hem of her shorts past the waistband of her panties, seeking and finding the mystery of her dark, wet heat.

Luke felt a distinct tightening below his belt. *Ah, hell, no. Don't go there.*

She set down her glass and met his gaze, yanking him back to the present. "So, what brings you to New York?"

He inhaled sharply, battled flammable emotions. Swallowed. Sucked in another breath and forced himself to think about his cattle that need branding and inoculating and castrating. Anything to keep from focusing on how much he wanted the woman sitting across from him.

"You," he said hoarsely.

"Me?" She straightened, and a teasing light came into her smart brown eyes. "So you *were* stalking me."

"I was looking for you," he corrected. "It's not the same thing."

"Well, you found me," she said, and took

49

another long drink of champagne. "Not exactly on the best day of my life. In fact . . ." She tilted her head. "You might say this is the worst day of my life."

"I can think of one that was far worse," he said evenly, but every muscle in his body turned to cement. "It was certainly the worst day of mine."

Her eyes clouded. "Yes, you're right, *that* was much worse."

Neither one of them articulated what "that" was, but they both knew. The day the Fant-Nielson family feud encroached on their budding teenage romance and killed it before it had a chance to bloom.

Luke cast around for something to say to shift things, but couldn't think of anything. Luckily, the waiter showed up with the caviar on a bed of ice, and crusty toast points to serve it on.

"Would you like to hear the specials of the day?" the waiter asked as he set the appetizer before them.

"Sure," Luke said.

In a heavy French accent, the waiter rattled off the specials.

"How much is that fish dish you mentioned?" he asked.

The waiter gave him an impervious stare and named a price that was larger than the monthly electric bill of his ranch, the Rocking N, and he almost choked on the water he'd been sipping.

"Let me pay for dinner," Melody offered. "I was going to treat Jean-Claude anyway."

"Certainly not." Luke scowled. It wasn't that he couldn't afford the meal, merely sticker shock.

"We shouldn't have come here."

"What do you mean? It's a great place." He glanced at the waiter's discreet gold name tag. "Right, Pierre?"

"One of the finest in the city," Pierre acknowledged.

"See there." Luke nodded. "I'll have the barramundi and the lady will have . . ."

Melody pressed her lips together as if trying not to laugh.

What? Had he made some kind of social gaffe?

"I'll have the langoustine, please," she said.

"Excellent choice, mademoiselle." Pierre accepted their menus and glided away.

In between sips of champagne, they noshed on the caviar. It felt sort of surreal, eating the height of culinary gastronomy with Melody Spencer, the simple, sweet country girl he'd once kissed on a lakeside picnic table before their world had imploded.

But she was no longer that girl.

She'd moved away from Cupid. She'd grown and changed into an urbane, accomplished woman and he . . . well . . . he hadn't changed one bit. He was still a rough-around-the-edges cowboy. They were so very different now.

"So this Jean-Claude character, was he the love of your life?" Luke surprised himself by asking. He didn't really want to hear that she was madly in love with the guy.

She didn't say anything at first and he studied her face, searching for some sign as to how much she felt for the man who had stupidly dumped her. He hitched in a breath, tried to look like he didn't really care.

"No," she said at last, simply, flatly. "Jean-Claude was not the love of my life."

Ah, well. Ah, hell. His entire body relaxed and it was only then he realized how taut he'd been waiting for her answer.

"If he wasn't the love of your life, why were you living with him?" *Shit, just shut up, Nielson.*

"That's none of your business."

She was right. It was not.

Her posture softened, and even though she owed him no explanation for how she lived her life, she said, "I admired Jean-Claude's artistry and we got along well. We'd only been living together a few weeks, but I could already tell it wasn't going to work out long-term. I just didn't expect —"

"To have the rug pulled out from under you so ruthlessly?"

Her gaze lingered on his mouth. "Something along those lines."

"So you haven't yet met the love of your life?"

"If I had, I'd be sitting here with him instead of you."

Pierre brought their meal, interrupting everything, and by the time he departed, the mood between them had changed again.

That's the way things had always been between them. Mercurial. Mysterious. Mystifying. Maddening.

Melody shifted her attention to her plate, took a bite of her entrée, and made a face of sublime joy, as if she'd just had a most magnificent orgasm.

Damn, he wished he could be the one to put that expression on her face.

"You've simply got to taste this." She leaned across the table to give him a bite of langoustine straight from the tines of her fork. Her chocolate eyes gleamed, her lips glistening from the buttery seafood, and hey, he could see straight down her cleavage.

He should rein himself in, refuse the tasty tidbit, but instead, he leaned forward, his teeth touching her fork, where her teeth had just been. Something inside him unraveled, spooling into a hot mess of desire.

"That's delicious," he croaked, even though he was so bedazzled by her sexy beauty that he couldn't taste a damn thing. Because he couldn't say what he really wanted to say. *You're delicious and I want to eat you up.*

"Told you." She laughed, and in that moment, she looked exactly like the fifteen-year-old girl he'd kissed on that long-ago Fourth of July.

He winced.

She pursed her lips. "Is something wrong?"

"I was just remembering," he murmured.

Her gaze locked with his. "The night you kissed me and fanned the flames of the family feud. I know because I was thinking about it too. How can I not when —"

"Let's not talk about that."

But it was too late. The words had been spoken aloud and the topic lay on the table between them, dark and quivering. The past was a gulf. A chasm. Hell, it was a friggin' abyss. There was no way to get across. No building a bridge. No crossing over. The crater was simply too wide and deep. Grand Canyon–style.

In that moment Luke knew he'd made a terrible mistake in coming here.

"Are you ever going to tell me why you came all the way to New York to see me?" she asked with an uncanny ability to read his mind.

He put down his fork, dabbed his mouth with the white linen napkin. "You heard that I was elected mayor after Joe Thornton retired?"

"My mother did mention something about 'one of those damn Nielsons' taking office," she said. "I guess I didn't pay much attention because I hadn't realized it was you. Congratulations. What inspired you to run?"

"Hell," he said. "We couldn't get anyone to run until I decided to step up to the plate; after that we had Greenwoods and Fants coming out of the woodwork to try and make sure a Nielson didn't take office."

"Small-town politics." She waved a hand and drained her champagne, but did not meet his gaze.

He almost told her to slow down, but

clearly, she'd had a pisser of a day and it wasn't his job to monitor her alcohol intake. He knew this wasn't her normal modus operandi. She was too much of a workaholic to ever become an alcoholic.

"I know it's far removed from your world, but Melody, Cupid needs help and I didn't know where else to turn."

"Help? From me? What's wrong?"

"This drought . . ." Just thinking about the toll the weather was taking on his hometown brought a lump to his throat. "It's not just a long dry spell. We've had plenty of those and survived, but this time, I'm seriously worried about the future."

"Mother did say the water levels in Lake Cupid were dangerously low and water rationing had reached critical level."

"Low?" He shook his head. "Let's just say that the water has receded so much that the pickup truck Pierce Hollister foolishly drove into the lake during his junior year could be driven out of there on parched earth if it would still start."

Her face paled. "The lake is gone?"

"For all intents and purposes. It's nothing but a stagnant mosquito pit."

She put a palm to her heart. "Luke, that's terrible."

"Devastating."

"I had no idea things were that bad."

"It's just the beginning. Farmers can't irrigate enough to keep the crops growing. Ranchers are selling off livestock because they can't afford to feed them. Tourism is our lifeblood and without the lake as a desert oasis . . ." He spread his hands wide. "There's nothing much to attract visitors anymore."

"What about the Cupid Caverns?" she asked, referring to the legendary caverns for which their town was named. Inside the caverns, one of the caves housed a seven-foot stalagmite that resembled the Roman god of love flinging an arrow. That stalagmite had generated a host of myths and fables that the town had capitalized on to encourage visitors.

"The Davis Mountains are a long way to drive just to see some caverns. Especially when Carlsbad is not all that far away."

"Ah, but Carlsbad doesn't have a Cupid stalagmite."

"Cupid is not enough to counter this drought."

"What about the mineral springs?"

"They're in trouble too. The hotels, the vineyards, the botanical gardens, all hurting bad."

"And as mayor, everyone is expecting you

57

to save the day." She summed up his dilemma.

"Something like that, which is why I needed to talk to you."

"Are the phone lines down in Cupid? You could have just called."

Her question wasn't totally rhetorical. Their area of the Trans-Pecos was so isolated that it *was* sometimes difficult to place calls out. "I thought this mission necessitated a face-to-face meeting. Besides, I needed a break from that heat."

All right, so in reality he'd just wanted to see her. What was so bad about that?

"Hmm." She tapped her chin with an index finger. "Things must be really bad for a Nielson to fly to New York to ask a Fant descendant for assistance."

He met her eyes, leaned forward, and lowered his voice. "You have no idea how bad."

A visible shiver went down her spine and she hugged herself. "But what can I do to help?"

"First, let's dispense with the Hatfield and McCoy thing. It's long past time our families buried the hatchet."

"And not in each other's heads?" She smiled.

"This stupid feud has gone on far too

long. Which is one of the reasons I'm turning to you for help. What better way to end a century of hurt than for a Nielson and a Fant to work together to save Cupid?"

"Sounds good in theory," she said. "But what on earth can you and I possibly do to end a drought? Know any rain dance steps you haven't told me about?"

"If I did, you can bet I would have already tried them out."

"So coming to see me —"

"— is a last-ditch effort," he confirmed.

"I hate to dash your hopes, but as you can see" — she swept a hand from her head to her waist and back again — "I'm pretty much of a mess."

A mess was not how he would describe her. Far from it.

He saw a beautiful woman who'd been through the wringer and still managed to pull herself together and come out to dinner with him when many people would be curled up in a fetal position, crying themselves to sleep, but Melody bounced back like a Super Ball.

Her top teeth worried her bottom lip, giving away her insecurity. She was tough and she would survive, but right now she was vulnerable. His timing was for shit.

The sommelier replenished her glass with

champagne and she took another long sip. Fortifying herself in order to get through the evening with him?

"I came to you because you're one of the best advertising executives in the business," he said. "And, granted, the only one I know personally."

"Was," she said. "This morning. Now I'm a has-been."

"Temporary setback. Don't worry about it."

"Easy for you to say, Mayor. Your job is secure."

"The position doesn't pay much. I'm doing it to serve our community, not for the salary. Ranching is still my bread and butter, although, granted, right now it is pretty damn dry."

"*Your* community," she corrected. "I'm a New Yorker."

"Deny it all you want, Melody. Cupid blood runs through your veins. It always has and it always will, no matter where you end up living."

She glanced away, and something akin to regret moved across her face. "I'm still not seeing how I can help."

"We need to come up with a plan for bringing the tourists back to Cupid. We can't control the drought, but we can put on events to lure folks back to the Davis Mountains in spite of the lack of rain. That's where you come in. You've got connections, celebrity friends."

She spread her hands on the table. "I'm not sure what you want from me, Luke."

"I don't know either. That's why I'm here. To brainstorm and see what we can come up with."

"And if I say no?"

"Then I'd say you sure have changed." He leveled her a hard stare. "And not for the better."

"Are you trying to manipulate me?"

He raised an eyebrow. "If asking for what I need is manipulation, then yeah, I guess I am."

"I can't just snap my fingers and make Cupid all better."

"People back home think you can."

"That's my mother's propaganda. She loves to tell everyone how successful I am because it makes her feel good. You've seen firsthand what a train wreck my life is. There's nothing I can do for you. I have my own problems."

"I'm disappointed to hear you say that."

"Manipulator."

"You're right." He held up his hands. "You

don't owe us anything. I just felt obligated to try."

Her face softened. "I'm sorry you made the trip for nothing."

"It wasn't for nothing," he said. "At least I got to have dinner with you."

She sighed. "You're determined to make me feel guilty, aren't you?"

"Only if it works." He gave her his best lady-killer smile.

"All right." She shook her head. "Fine. Let's do this."

"You mean it?"

She snorted. "Stop looking like you won the lottery. I'm not all that."

He stared at her long and hard.

"What?" She put a hand to her mouth. "Do I have something on my face?"

"Are you for real? Don't you get how special you are to our town? When people talk about Cupidites who've gone on to do well, your name is at the top of the list along with Pierce Hollister and your cousin Lace."

"Hmm, former Dallas Cowboys quarterback and a botanist who turned down an offer from the Smithsonian so she could prove the existence of a desert plant that everyone thought was extinct. A plant that has such strong antiviral properties, it could potentially eradicate the flu virus. Let's put

62

them up against a woman who makes her living peddling toilet paper and shaving cream? Sorry to burst your bubble, but I don't even crack the top one hundred most illustrious Cupidites."

"You're just down in the dumps."

"You think?"

"Look, forget that Jean-Claude character. You'll find someone much better suited for you."

Like me.

The second the thought popped into his head, Luke startled. Ever since his thirty-second birthday, his heart had started to feel like the vacant farmhouse off Wolf Creek Road that he passed on his daily drive to and from Cupid. The house stood lonely sentinel at the end of a dirt lane, the only structure in sight on that patch of arid land, unseen by most everyone speeding by on their way to Alpine or Marfa. He wasn't a philological guy and such wistful ponderings had taken him by surprise. He didn't want to be lonely anymore.

And suddenly, Melody was taking center stage in his white-picket-fence fantasy. Right. Like she would ever come back home to Cupid for good. Like his family — or hers for that matter — would ever tolerate him hooking up with Millie Greenwood's great-granddaughter.

Look what had happened when he'd tried it fifteen years ago.

Ah crap, he was setting himself up for a hard tumble down a rocky cliff.

Yeah? Guess what? He didn't give a good damn. He wanted her and that's all there was to it.

CHAPTER 4

Even though the conversation had drifted away from their reckless youth, her cheeks still burned. Why on God's green earth had she mentioned that night at Lake Cupid?

Why?

Because history was a persistent undertow pulling at them, keeping them apart. Tugging him in one direction, her in the other.

She drained the last of her champagne. The candlelight flickered brighter, casting Luke in a hazy golden glow. If they'd been born in another time, another place, to other families, things between them would have been so different.

But fate was what it was and so was the past. No do-overs. No mulligans. No what-ifs.

As it was, she could barely wrap her head around the fact that she was at Bernadette's with Luke Nielson. Never in a million years. Yet there he sat, giving her his patented, come-hither smile and smoldering stare that slid over her like a warm hand. His shoulders were so broad, his arms so strong, as if he could throw her over his shoulder and carry her for miles across the desert if she needed saving.

In a flash of memory, she saw him as the lanky teen he'd once been and not the well-built man before her. They'd been a lot alike, both from close-knit families, each one of three siblings. They were both competitive. He'd been high school class president. She'd been the homecoming queen. He'd had a lawn-mowing business in the seventh grade. By twelve, she'd been running her own franchise of snow cone stands around town. But they were different too. He was deeply rooted in Cupid; she was New York City all the way. He was traditional and down-to-earth. She was modern and creative.

He ordered a bottle of an affordable chardonnay and his selection impressed her. Smooth, easy, humble, light. Completely lulling at first, but the wine finished with a serious kick that sneaked up on her.

Just like the man across the table from her.

She lowered her lashes, studied him surreptitiously, and surprised herself by blurting, "How come you haven't ever gotten married? Smart, good-looking, well-off. I'm sure you have to whack the women off with a stick."

He arched an eyebrow. "Who says I whack them off?"

Embarrassed by the double entendre she'd accidentally started, she glanced away. Wow, this had taken an unexpected turn. "You're a terrific catch. Looks like someone would have snared you by now."

"Thanks for the compliment," he said. "But I could ask you the same thing." .

"I've been busy building a career."

He leaned forward, his gaze holding hers. The way he took notice of her was both flattering and alarming. She wasn't used to having a man's undivided attention. "Tell me about that, Melly."

Melly.

It was his pet name for her in high school. Should she correct him? Tell him she was no longer that perky cheerleader he kissed on that picnic table, the same girl who was once head-over-heels for him, but too afraid of displeasing her family to do anything about it.

Long ago and far away.

She'd changed so much and Luke . . . well . . . he hadn't, had he? He was still easygoing, unhurried, and relaxed, always ready with a grin and wink. A winsome cowboy turned mayor. Nothing wrong with that. Nothing at all. It's just that Melody had bigger plans for her life, redeeming her reputation chief among them.

"I'm all ears," he prodded.

He was easy to talk to. No doubt about it. She told him then about coming to New York and her early days in the business. The waiter cleared their plates, brought Irish coffees and a decadent chocolate lava cake dessert that Luke ordered.

They shared it, bite for bite.

She found herself telling him things she rarely told anyone. Her fears of never being good enough no matter how hard she tried. The conflicts her hometown values caused on a job where having to compromise her standards happened more often than not. How her love of the creative process and New York City made up for those conflicts.

She pressed her palms together. "So there you have it. The ups and downs of a career that is looking pretty bleak right now."

"You're at a crossroads." He reached across the table to lightly stroke his thumb across the backs of her knuckles.

His touch ignited her nerve endings. She sucked in a breath but she did not move her hand away. Oh, this was not good. She needed to remember that. Any decisions she made now were bound to be ones she would live to regret, but her body oozed warmth and her head was spinning and those devastating hazel eyes of his were doing her in.

"No kidding," she mumbled, and finished off her Irish coffee. "Standing at the corner of Walk and Don't Walk."

Luke smiled kindly at her. "You're tough. You'll get through this."

"Easy for you to say."

"Darlin', you're made of rubber. You'll bounce back. I have total confidence in you."

"Do you have any idea how hard it is to make it in this city?"

"You can handle it. I have faith in you."

His words warmed her from the inside out. Or maybe it was the Irish coffee. Probably it was the coffee. But my, my, the man looked prime fine in candlelight.

Her vision was sweetly fuzzy. This was her first time drinking Dom Perignon and she had no idea she would end up so drunk so quickly. The good stuff was the good stuff for a reason. Talk about drinking stars. Then again, apparently she had managed to drink a disproportionate amount of the Milky Way all by herself, not to mention the chardonnay and Irish coffee.

Luke appeared unfazed by the alcohol and amused by her.

At her.

Grinning like a loon, she wriggled her fingers. "Hi."

"You're tipsy," he pronounced.

She pointed at him. "And you're cute."

"I'm getting the check." He pushed back his chair.

"Aw man," she said. "Are we leaving already? I wanted another glass of Dom."

"You've had enough Dom. I'm taking you to bed."

"Ooh, now that's a plan I can get behind. Forget Dom. I'm all yours, Luke." They might not be able to have a happily-ever-after, but this was New York, not Cupid. Nobody knew they were together. Anything could happen. There was nothing wrong with happily-right-now.

Was there?

His face turned the color of sugar beets. "Putting, putting," he sputtered. "I'm *putting* you to bed."

"Putting, taking." She shrugged. "Who cares as long as we get to bed?"

Luke held up a hand for the passing waiter. "Check please."

Dang, he had big hands. And dang, she

was thinking "dang." She'd worked hard to scrub the Texas colloquialism out of her vocabulary. But let her get around a cowboy for five minutes and blam-o, it all came rocketing back.

You can take the girl out of the country . . .

She was having all kinds of thoughts she shouldn't be having about Luke and beds and big hands when the waiter brought the check.

Luke peeled several one-hundred-dollar bills from his money clip and tucked them underneath the receipt.

"Don't you use credit cards?"

"Not if I can help it. I dislike credit."

"Old-fashioned." She clicked her tongue, shook her head.

"You disapprove."

"It was an observation, not a judgment."

"Wasn't it?"

"No."

He raised a skeptical eyebrow. "You spent your whole life trying to get out of traditional, old-fashioned Cupid."

"Yeah." She notched up her chin. "And I did it too."

"I always knew you would. You're the most persistent woman I've ever known."

"Look where it got me." She flung her arms wide. "Fired from my job and dumped by my boyfriend all in one day."

"Neither of whom were worthy of you," he said staunchly.

"I appreciate the loyalty." She hiccupped. Loudly.

The couple at the next table frowned at her.

She giggled, slapped a palm over her mouth, and raised her shoulders. "Oops, sorry. Too much bubbly."

"Don't let those frowners get you down," he whispered, winked.

"Hey, at least I didn't burp."

"There is that." He stood. "C'mon, let's hit the trail."

She pushed back her chair and started to get to her feet, but in the process, caught the tip of her shoe against the chair's front leg. She pitched forward, hit into the edge of the table with her hip.

Stumbled.

"Ouch."

"Here," Luke said in that low, testosterone-laden voice of his, and slipped an arm around her waist. "Lean on me."

She did as he told her, because (a) she was having trouble staying firmly planted on her four-inch stilettos and (b) she wanted to touch him more desperately than she'd ever wanted to touch any man in her entire life.

His body was rock-solid — strong and hard and just *there* — like the Davis Mountains back home.

Her head was spinning from the expensive champagne, from the pressure of his palm at her back, from the fact that being with him felt sinfully taboo. Nothing tantalized more than the forbidden, and a dozen conflicting urges pushed through her. Half of those urges having something to do with getting away from him as quickly as she could and the other half compelling her to press as close to him as possible.

Alarmingly familiar feelings.

And then she did the most shocking thing.

There in the dining room of Bernadette's, as her life was falling in shambles around her, she reached up, slid her arms around Luke's neck, pulled his head down, and kissed him.

The minute her lips touched his, Luke knew the truth of it. He'd lost control. Every fantasy he'd been having about Melody since he'd made the decision to come to Manhattan grew and bloomed.

She sank against his chest, her lips soft as sweet cream butter. "Mmm."

Chocolate.

She tasted of chocolate, delicious and decadent. Everything about her was exciting and different. Her hair smelled of something mysterious, a scent almost electric with possibility and promise, and Luke could have stayed like this until the end of time, his mouth fused with hers, his palm against the small of her back, their bodies pressed together.

A seductive purr hummed over her lips, and a heavy breath drove her exquisite tits straight up into his chest. Through flaring nostrils he inhaled her feminine aroma, the flirty flavor of spice, licorice, and kiwi perfume permeating his olfactory receptors, sailing into his brain, flitting between neurons and skimming over synapses, firing off a timeless male response.

Exotic.

Of course she would smell exotic.

Holy shit! He wasn't prepared for this. Instinctively, Luke tightened his arms around Melody's waist and pulled her closer.

Flaming heat rampaged through his body. It was all he could do not to open his mouth and deepen the kiss. Alarmed, he abruptly grabbed her shoulders and put her away from him.

Her eyes widened. "What's wrong? Didn't you like kissing me?"

"On the contrary," he croaked. "I liked it far too much."

"So what's the problem?" she asked breathlessly.

"You're hurting emotionally and you're tipsy. You're not in your right mind."

"So what? I've spent my entire life trying to do what everyone expects me to do. I'm ready to be spontaneous and impulsive and out of my mind." She puckered her lips and made a move like she was going to kiss him again.

Luke glanced around. Half the restaurant was staring at them. He manacled her wrists to keep her from twining her arms around his neck again. "Wrong place for this conversation, darlin'."

"Where's the right place?"

He steered her toward the door and they stepped out in the flow of heavy foot traffic. It surprised him to see it was dark outside, the lights of the city glowing brightly. They'd been in the restaurant for hours.

Where could he take her? He had no idea. He didn't know New York. Everywhere he'd been was crowded and intrusive. They needed somewhere quiet to talk. He glanced up and down the street and there, like a sign from God, stood the Hilton where he was registered.

"My hotel," he said, pulling her along behind him.

"Ooh. I like the sound of that."

"We're just going to talk," he growled, unable to believe he was actually saying it. "Nothing else."

"Buzz kill."

"Believe me, it's not by choice."

"So why make that choice? Take me, Luke, baby. I'm yours."

He was in over his head. Big-time.

It was dumb, way dumb, to take her to his hotel room, but honestly, he didn't know what else to do with her. It wasn't like he could stick her in a cab and send her home. She had no place to go.

Normally, he was not so impulsive. Normally, he took a long time to make decisions, weighed opinions, and made well-thought-out choices. Normally . . . well . . . when it came to Melody Spencer, nothing was normal.

She was tall and leggy with a figure that wouldn't quit, with long blond hair, a couple of shades lighter than his own, that floated silkily down her shoulders in wide, lush waves. Her eyes were steamy brown, and a guy could tell just by looking that there was something enigmatically intelligent that went on in the brain behind them. It was in the way she delivered her suggestive smile, a quirky tilt of the mouth at the same time she slightly lowered her lashes, canted her head, and leveled him a knowing glance.

Of course, Luke already knew all that from firsthand experience. How was it that he had ever let her get away? Oh yeah, blind ambition had jettisoned her out of Cupid long before he could gather the courage to tell his relatives to go butt a stump and claim her for his own.

He had to think of somewhere else to take her.

Quick.

But a cowboy couldn't think straight amid an assault of honking taxis and screaming police sirens and a mass of human bodies jostling him.

One minute she was mincing along beside him in those ridiculously high heels that made her almost as tall as his six-foot-two height, and the next minute, she let out a little squeal and took a tumble.

He glanced down to see her on her hands and knees over a storm grate; the heel of her right shoe had broken off and was sticking from the grate.

Without thinking twice, he bent and scooped her into his arms, even as people flowed around them.

She let out a soft sigh as her arms went around his neck. Her legs dangled over his arm, the hem of her skirt riding up to mid-thigh, and he saw that her knees were skinned.

"You're bleeding," he said.

"Oh." She blinked, looked down at her leg. "So I am."

He tightened his grip around her. She was even lighter than he expected. He stalked toward the Hilton, a man on a mission. Get her inside. Tend to her wounds.

Then what?

She rested her head against his shoulder, hiccupped again. She was so vulnerable. He'd never really seen this side of her and it tugged at his heartstrings.

Aw, hell. He had not bargained for any of this. Yes, he'd had the hots for her fifteen years ago, but to realize those feelings had not only not gone away, but had morphed into something much hotter and bigger blew him away.

Through the revolving door he carried her into the lobby of the Hilton.

"I can walk now," she said.

"I've gotcha." Truthfully, he was enjoying

this. Granted, probably more than he should, but damn, she felt good in his arms.

Other lodgers stared at them. An elderly lady smiled and nudged her male companion in the ribs. "I remember when you swept me off my feet like that," she murmured.

"It's just a broken heel," Melody explained, and kicked out her foot, waving her damaged shoe in the air.

"Milk it while you can." The woman winked.

The elevator door opened and to make room for others, Luke stalked to the back, his muscles bunched. Someone had already punched the floor where they needed to get off. The smell of her hair, floral and fresh, tangled up in his nose. And he wanted nothing more in the world than to lay her down on a bed and make love to her. The only thing stopping him was that her eyes were bright from too much alcohol.

Who was he kidding? He was none too sober himself. He'd drunk much more than he normally would have because he'd gotten caught up in the excitement of having dinner with her.

Dangerous.

This whole situation was beyond dangerous.

Outside the door to his room, he finally

set her down so he could fish his key card from his pocket. In order to level herself upright on the broken heel, she leaned one shoulder against the wall while she waited.

He got the door open and stood aside so she could enter, his pulse thudding hard in his throat. She hop-stepped inside and he followed, the door closing behind them with a resounding snap. If his family could see him now, they'd have a conniption.

She stopped, kicked off her shoes, and turned to face him. "Well," she said. "Well, well, well."

"Profound," he quipped.

"Can you tell I'm a professional word-smith?" She grinned, fluffed her hair with a palm.

"It's the fourth 'well' that convinced me. You're brilliant and your boss at Tribalgate is an idiot."

Her cheeks pinked. "You don't have to charm me. I'm already aching to sleep with you."

Her words sent blood shooting straight to his dick. It would be so damn easy to unbutton her blouse, strip that pretty blue skirt off her body, waltz her to the bed, and do all kinds of sweet and wicked things to her, but that would cause more problems than it would solve.

"Darlin'," he drawled. "I'm not into pity sex. When we make love it's going to be when we're both stone-cold sober, have our heads screwed on straight, and know exactly what we're doing."

"Aw," she protested, dropping down on the end of the bed, Texas creeping back into her voice. "Where's the fun in that?"

CHAPTER 5

When we make love.

Like it was a foregone conclusion.

Melody gulped, and put a hand to her throat. Her skin burned as hot as a freshly spent firecracker. A smart woman would have turned and gotten the hell out of there, broken heel or not, a place to stay or not, and most of the time, she was a smart woman.

But her head was spinning and her heart was pounding and her entire past was standing there looking at her like he could eat her up with a long-handled spoon and lick his lips when he was done.

She had no one to blame but herself. She started this when she kissed him in the restaurant. What had she been thinking?

Clearly, she had not been thinking. She sat on the edge of the mattress, suddenly realizing what a precarious situation she'd placed herself in.

"Let's take a look." Luke knelt on the floor in front of her.

It took a second for her to snap to what he was talking about. Her skinned knees, oh yeah.

He laid his hands on her kneecaps just above the abrasions. He was so warm, vital, virile. All male.

Her breath slipped over her parted teeth, hot and fast.

"Just needs a little cleaning." He reached for a suitcase lying on the floor beside the bed. He unzipped the side compartment and took out a first aid kit.

"You travel with a first aid kit?"

"Never go anywhere without it."

"What a Boy Scout," she mumbled, but she wasn't feeling as snarky as she sounded.

"I believe in being prepared." He opened up the kit. "You'll never know what you might need when you're on the road."

She spied a roll of condoms nestled beside the antiseptic and bandages. Quickly, she glanced away, but not before their eyes met. Yes indeedy. From the look of things the man was prepared for any eventuality.

She heard the tear of paper packaging, felt the cool sting of the alcohol swab against her skin, and she couldn't help peeking over at him again.

Luke was studiously cleaning her knee. His sleeves were rolled up, the crisp cotton bunched at the elbows. He'd deposited his jacket across the seat of the desk chair, his Stetson lying atop it. His hair was mussed, several sandy strands stuck straight up, and his eyes, heavy lids drooping, were indolent. He looked devastatingly handsome.

The room grew uncomfortably warm. Her skin was moist, her blouse plastered to her bosom. Was it the room? Or her?

The champagne. It had to be the champagne making her feel this way.

Her nerves were wiredrawn, taut and sensitive. She was alone with Luke Nielson in a hotel room. If her family knew, they would blow a major gasket.

But she was a grown woman and thousands of miles away from the pull of her kin. If she made love to Luke no one would ever have to know. It would be their little secret.

A buzzing sensation hummed through her and her pulse fluttered.

His warm, agile fingers quickly cleaned the wound and applied Band-Aids to her knees, leaving them tingling and leaving her feeling weak, disturbed.

He rocked back on his heels and looked up at her. "You do know that you're incred-

84

ibly beautiful."

Her cheeks flushed and she raised a palm to shield her face from his view. It was all packaging. If he only knew how much time and money it took to maintain the image. Keratin treatments and flat-ironing to control her unruly waves, ninety minutes a day at the gym, weekly manis and pedis and eyebrow threading, once-a-month microdermabrasion and body waxing. Not to mention she dropped a small fortune on her go-getter wardrobe.

Honestly, it was exhausting.

"Quaker," she blurted as an idea popped full-blown into her head.

His hazel eyes widened. "What?"

"Quaker is the answer," she said, her thoughts skipping like a schoolyard jump rope.

His brow furrowed. "What was the question?"

"How to bring tourists back to Cupid."

"And Quaker is the answer?"

She nodded. "Quaker."

"As in the peace-loving Society of Friends?"

"As in Quaker Oats."

"Hang on, let me process this. Oatmeal is the answer?"

"More specifically, Quaker cornmeal."

"Um. Okay."

Clearly, he was not accustomed to the quick-witted brainstorming of Madison Avenue, but then again, how many people were?

Luke got to his feet, but wavered a little.

From too much alcohol consumption? Or was he simply righting his balance after crouching for so long? Or was he bowled over by what was going on between them? She couldn't say which, maybe all three, but when he put out an arm to brace himself against the bed, his hand brushed lightly against her thigh.

Liquid heat scalded through her bloodstream, dove like a missile straight into her core, and the sultry expression in his eyes set her stomach quivering.

This was far too intimate. Goose bumps dotted her skin and his eyes darkened dangerously. He'd noticed her body's reaction to his nearness.

"Where is my purse?" she gasped, more to distract herself from this blistering hot man than anything else.

"There it is." He rushed away from her, an expression of disquiet on his face, bent, and scooped up her purse from by the door, where she didn't even remember dropping it.

She accepted the purse, but took extra care to ensure she did not touch him in the handoff. If he touched her again, she could not be held accountable for her actions.

Avoiding his gaze, she fished her cell phone from her purse and turned it on.

"Who are you calling?" he asked.

"Quaker."

"It's nine o'clock at night."

She waved a hand. "Perfect time for ad types."

"I'm not following you."

"I know," she said, feeling a bit sad for some strange reason. She rolled through her phone contacts, found what she was looking for, and punched in a number.

"Who are you calling at Quaker?"

"Someone who owes me a favor." She put a finger to her lips. "Shh."

He eased down on the bed beside her, the mattress sinking beneath his weight.

She immediately hopped up, turned her back to him, and concentrated on the ringing phone, but she couldn't resist glancing over her shoulder. Only to catch him staring at her ass, a big old cowboy smile spread across his face.

Her cheeks burned and she snapped her gaze toward the window that looked out over the city. New York, New York. If you could make it here, you could make it anywhere. Or so the song said. Except that she hadn't made it here, after all. Had she?

"Spencer," hollered a cheery male voice over the hum of people and piano music in the background. "You've been scarce lately."

She'd met Theodore Mercer when she first arrived in Manhattan. He was from Oklahoma and just as green and starry-eyed as she. They'd platonically shared an apartment for a year, then they'd awkwardly hooked up, but quickly decided it was a big mistake. He moved out, yet they stayed friends. The friendship had served them well as they'd both climbed the advertising corporate ladder, her in creative, him in accounts.

It struck her then that calling when she was on the wrong side of tipsy wasn't the brightest idea she'd ever had, but it wasn't as if she could hang up on him now, so she plunged ahead. "Teddy," she said, concentrating on not slurring her words. "Have I got the perfect account for you."

"Hustling business at this time of the night, Spencer? Don't you ever sleep or have a social life?"

"Am I interrupting something?"

"I wouldn't have answered the phone if you had."

"So where are you?"

"I'm out on the town with clients."

"And you accuse me of working too hard."

"Okay, so I'm a hypocrite."

"Do you need me to let you go?"

"No worries, they're busy slaughtering 'She Drives Me Crazy' at the piano."

"Sounds like you deserve hazard pay. Eardrum damage and all that. You sure you can talk?"

He heaved a good-natured sigh. "Pitch me. Who's the client?"

She tucked a lock of hair behind her ear and turned to pace. Luke was still sitting on the bed, still studying her with that hungry look in his eyes.

"You," she told Teddy, but her gaze was full of nothing but Luke.

He stretched out on his back, propping himself up on his elbows. The top button to his shirt had come unbuttoned, revealing a tuft of soft brown chest hair. Simply irresistible.

She gulped. Shook her head. *Focus.*

"Me?" Teddy asked.

"Well, Quaker."

"I'm listening."

Leaving out the part about the drought, she told her friend about Cupid, spinning the best pitch she could conjure under the current circumstances. That is, half-drunk and full-on horny for the cowboy on the bed.

"Cupid is quirky, one of a kind, and snuggled in the heart of the Davis Mountains. Off the beaten path, but definitely a tourist destination. They have caverns featuring a stalagmite in the shape of Cupid and there's a local legend that says if you write a letter to Cupid, he'll grant your love wishes. Volunteers gather to answer the letters. I've been on the committee in the past and it's a lot of fun."

"Sort of like *Letters to Juliet* concept, huh?"

"Exactly."

"Answering letters to the lovelorn even when you've never been in love yourself. That's ironic," Teddy observed.

Well, she wouldn't say *never.*

Luke got up off the bed and came toward her. The shirt shifted and stretched over his chest as he moved.

Her heart rate sped up. *Calm down.*

"Several movies have been made in and around Cupid," she said, talking faster. "*Giant* with Rock Hudson and Elizabeth Taylor and James Dean, *No Country for Old Men,* and *There Will Be Blood* to name a few. There are vineyards and mineral springs and the Marfa Lights. They're mysterious, unexplained illuminations in the night. There are artists and cowboys and the Mc-Donald Observatory, where you can view the darkest night skies in the entire United States."

"Wait a minute. Is this the same hometown you used to badmouth?" Teddy asked.

"That was youthful ignorance. I didn't realize what a gem of a place my hometown was until I looked at it from a New Yorker's perspective. It's a beautiful oasis, Teddy, nestled in the heart of the Chihuahuan Desert. It's a throwback to a gentler time. It's nostalgic and quaint. The kind of place you don't fully appreciate until you've lost that gentle quaintness from your life."

Luke loped closer, a smirk on his face. Melody backed up. What was he doing? What did he want?

"Okay, I'm intrigued," Teddy admitted.

Luke was just a few feet away from her now and her back was against the window; she felt the curtains brushing against her shoulders. Nowhere to go.

What was he intending?

"Spencer?" Teddy prodded. "You still there?"

"Huh?" she whispered into the phone, unable to look away from Luke.

"You sound distracted," Teddy said. "Should we have this conversation later?"

"Um, no, no."

Luke lowered his head to her ear. "See," he murmured, "you really do love your hometown."

She shivered, closed her eyes, his scent invading her nose, her mind, her entire body. She wanted him. Oh yes! But she was not. Going. To. Go. There.

"What do you have in mind for Quaker?" Teddy prodded.

She opened one eye. Luke was still there. *Still* staring.

Step off, she mouthed silently.

He half shrugged, gave a lopsided grin, and sprawled onto the chaise longue a few feet away.

There. She could finally breathe. "You've heard of the Terlingua Chili Cook-off?"

"Sure. It's iconic. Chili cook-off and a big music festival every November. So what?"

"Terlingua's not far from Cupid."

"And?"

"Cornbread."

"That's supposed to intrigue me?"

"Quaker makes cornmeal."

"I know."

"You're a country boy. You grew up eating cornbread."

"I've gone low carb. So has half the country."

Crap. She was losing him. *Quick. Think of something.* But that was a little hard to do when her head was champagne-woozy and her body was charged up from being around Luke.

"Don't you miss it?" she wheedled, her mind scrambling. "That sweet, crumbly yellow bread dipped into the juice of a bowl of black-eyed peas?"

"Sometimes," Teddy admitted.

"I remember my mother pulling a big pan of cornbread made from Quaker cornmeal out of the oven on a cold winter day and settling it on the kitchen table with a stick of creamy butter and bowls of hearty stew. My family would sit down to dinner together and we'd laugh and joke and tease and share our day with each other. Whenever I smell cornbread baking I think of my family. Their unconditional love and cornbread is forever knitted in my mind. Quaker cornmeal is the starch that binds families together. It's the symbol of home and hearth. And nothing says family louder than Quaker cornmeal."

"Wow," Teddy said. "Great pitch. Now I can't wait to visit the place."

Gotcha.

"Think about it. Pillsbury has cornered the market on yeast bread bake-offs. It's hard to compete in their arena, but cornbread is wide open. Imagine the Quaker Cornbread Bake-off held in Cupid. It could become an annual festival just like Terlingua and chili," she finished, amazing herself at what she'd been able to come up with in a crunch. "Then again," she said, for good measure. "I could call Pillsbury instead."

"Are we talking just cornbread bake-off?" he said. "Or will there be music like Terlingua?"

"Oh, definitely a music festival as well," she promised glibly.

"How soon are we talking?" Teddy asked.

"The sooner the better." Her tongue was running away from her. She didn't know what she was going to say next. "How about the Fourth of July?"

"That's a little soon, but maybe. Can you get the Food Network involved with celebrity judges? I know you're tight with the execs over there."

"If Quaker commits. You betcha." Adrenaline rushed; the high of closing a deal burned off the alcohol circulating through her system.

Teddy laughed. "You betcha? Your Texas roots are showing."

94

"So are you in?"

"I do owe you one. I haven't forgotten. I'll run it by management in the morning. You work on the Food Network judges and get a proposal to me."

"On it."

"Have a good night, Spencer." Teddy hung up.

She switched off the phone, and sank down on the end of the bed once more. From the chaise, Luke's booted feet were thrust out and crossed at the ankle. He looked as rebellious as James Dean.

"Your mother doesn't cook," he commented.

"So? I was creating an image."

"In other words, lying your pretty little ass off."

"It's not a lie. Not really. Cupid *is* about home and hearth and there *are* plenty of moms in town cooking cornbread."

"Just not yours."

"So what? It's advertising. Everyone knows advertising embroiders the truth. Put your best foot forward." This was what her boss had been trying to tell her. The picture you painted in the customers' minds was more important than reality.

He said nothing, but his eyelids lowered to half-mast. Was he judging her? Thinking she had compromised her principles? If he only knew, she had not compromised them nearly enough.

Feeling defensive, she sank her hands on her hips. "What?"

"You."

"What about me?"

"You're a force of nature."

"Like a hurricane?"

"Something along those lines. Maybe a tornado. Either one, you blow me away. One minute we're staggering into the room holding each other up after a significant amount of alcohol —"

"I wouldn't say significant," she protested, and then promptly hiccupped like Otis in Sheriff Taylor's cell at Mayberry.

"And the next minute," he continued, "you've got a brilliant idea and you're brokering a deal to prop up your hometown."

"Why are you so impressed? That's the reason why you came to see me, wasn't it?"

"Yeah." He nodded. "But I had no idea you were so good at what you do. What in the hell is wrong with those people at Tribalgate?"

"Don't count your chickens," she cautioned. "This thing with Quaker is not a done deal. Not by a long shot."

"But it's a solid start."

"It's a nibble. We're a long way from setting the hook."

He yawned. Stretched. "I don't know about you, but it's way past my bedtime. I can hardly hold my head up. Which side of the bed do you want?"

"You expect me to sleep here? I'm not sleeping here. We came here to talk and strategize about how to save Cupid. That's it."

"Sorry. I assumed that since you didn't have a place to stay and your shoe was busted that you were going to crash here tonight, save some money, and regroup in the morning, but suit yourself. Get your own room."

"I'll do that. Thanks." She picked up the phone and called the front desk, only to discover that there was a dentist convention in town and the Hilton was sold out of rooms.

Fine. She'd just find another hotel and grab a taxi.

And run around town in a broken shoe?

Great. She'd left her sneakers, which she always carried with her whenever she wore heels, back in the box with her things from the office.

"Look," Luke said. "I promise to keep my hands to myself. Let's just get some sleep."

He yawned again and started unbuttoning his shirt.

Startled by a glimpse of his muscular bare chest, Melody rushed to the bathroom and shut the door. Her heart pounded in her ears and she sank back against the door.

Okay, what now? She had no pajamas, no toothbrush or toothpaste, not even any makeup remover.

A knock sounded on the door.

Unnerved, she jumped. "Yes?"

"You might need these."

She opened up the door and peeked out. Luke was holding a bag of toiletries. Everything she needed, even cold cream.

"Where'd you get that?"

"Told you. I'm always prepared."

"With makeup remover?"

"I bought the overnight kit at the airport. The cold cream came with it."

"Thank you," she said, and took the toiletries, because what else was there to say? She shut the door.

He knocked again.

She opened it again. "What?"

He held out a burnt orange University of Texas T-shirt in his hand. "You'll need something to wear unless you sleep naked."

He'd actually said the word "naked." She could hardly speak. "Nope, I'm a nightshirt kind of gal. Your T-shirt will work just fine."

"I don't know whether to be relieved or disappointed." There was a faint smile at his lips, or maybe it was her imagination.

"If you have a pair of clean ladies' panties in your pocket I'm going to have to go to the *Cosmo* Web site and nominate you as sleepover companion of the year." Crap! Why had she mentioned panties?

"No ladies' panties," he said, "but if you give me a minute, I'll try to rustle some up. What size?"

"I'm kidding. Joke. Ha-ha." She snatched the T-shirt from his hand. Their knuckles brushed and her knees, well damn, they were just overcooked linguini. She slammed the door closed. Great. Now he was going to think he'd gotten to her.

Um, he did get to you.

She took an extra-long time in the bathroom. Showered. Shaved her legs. Flossed. Brushed. Took off her makeup.

Ulp.

Now he would see her barefaced in the morning because the only makeup she had in her purse was a tube of lip gloss.

Note to self. Always carry full makeup. You never know when you're going to have an unplanned sleepover.

She went back into the bedroom. All the

lights were off except for the nightlight on the far side of the bed.

Luke's side.

He lay on his back against the pillow, cradling his head in his upturned, interlaced palms.

She hesitated, unable to make herself cross the room. This was more than she bargained for.

"You look all of fifteen years old."

Melody ran a hand through her hair. "I'm a long way from fifteen. There's a lot of water under that bridge."

"You're more beautiful than ever." His voice was strangely husky. "Now come to bed."

"A Capulet in bed with a Montague," she quipped nervously. "It would be a scandal in Cupid."

"Good thing we're not in Cupid." He patted the spot beside him. "Besides, it's not the first time a Montague slept with a Capulet."

"Ah, but if you recall, things ended badly for Romeo and Juliet."

"We're just going to sleep, Melody. That's all."

The words were so innocent, his voice soft and gentle, but as she climbed into bed with him, she couldn't help feeling there was

nothing innocent about this.
Nothing innocent at all.

Chapter 6

Melody slid between the covers, her lithe body barely making a ripple against the soft cotton sheet. Instantly, the temperature in the bed shot up ten degrees.

Luke swallowed hard. Twice. He was acutely aware of every gorgeous inch of her.

Why did it have to be a queen-sized bed? Why couldn't it have been a king where he could have scooted far enough away from her so they wouldn't run the risk of touching accidentally during the night?

She turned over on her side.

Facing him.

He stared up at the ceiling, heard his heartbeat pounding in his ears. He was so turned on that he couldn't think straight. Hell, face facts. He was downright out of his mind for getting into bed with her in the first place. What sane man would do such a thing knowing he had to keep his hands to himself?

Sleep.

He needed to just close his eyes and sleep. He'd been yawning his head off ten minutes ago. Why was he now wide-awake?

Because he was in bed with the enemy, that was why.

Except in spite of their family history, he felt absolutely no animosity toward her. In fact, what he felt was the polar opposite of animosity. Goodwill. Benevolence. Concern. That's what he was feeling.

And, oh yeah, horny as all get-out.

The covers were making a tent. Or rather, his dick was making a tent of the covers. He rolled away, putting his back to her just in case she happened to look over and see Mr. Happy puffing out all proud of himself.

A few minutes ticked by. His dick did not deflate. In fact, if anything, he was harder than ever.

She sighed.

Luke held his breath.

She flopped over, punched her pillow, and finally stilled.

Air leaked from his lungs. Slowly, his muscles relaxed and he took a long, deep breath.

Inhaled her scent.

Gone was the exotic perfume. In its place she smelled fresh, clean, honest. Soap.

Damp skin. *Familiar.*

Normally, he slept buck-naked. In concession to the situation, he'd worn his boxer briefs to bed. She was in his T-shirt, and from the conversation they'd had earlier, probably wasn't wearing panties.

He bit down on his cheek to suppress the groan that rolled up from his throat. Shit, how hard could a man get and not explode?

"Is something wrong?" she whispered.

That was a loaded question. "I'm dumb as a fence post."

"I hear you. We should never have gotten into bed together. Or even gone out to dinner, for that matter."

"Hey, I wouldn't go that far. To tell you the truth I had a really good time tonight. Best I've had in a long while."

"Me too."

"It was good seeing you again." *Lame, Nielson. So lame. Sounds like you're shaking her hand after a church social.*

"Isn't it weird after getting fired and dumped, I still enjoyed myself this evening?"

"You did, huh?"

"Yes and it was all because of you."

Luke grinned. "Did you mean what you said to that friend of yours on the phone or was it just an advertising pitch?"

"Which part?"

104

"The part about Cupid being a gem."

"It *is* a unique place."

"Do you ever see yourself moving back home permanently?"

She didn't answer.

Silence was the answer. 'Nuff said. Big old *no.* But then he heard the soft sound of slow steady breathing. Had she fallen asleep? Probably so. He should try and do the same. He cleared his dry throat, closed his eyes, coughed.

From underneath the covers, he felt a hand on his shoulder blade and he almost jumped out of his skin.

"Cotton mouth?" she whispered. "Me too. I could drink a gallon of water."

Should he answer or pretend he was sound asleep?

"I'll get it," he offered, but then realized he'd have to stand up with a hard-on and she could plainly see what he was so desperate to hide.

"Thank you." Another touch of her hand, this time on his forearm.

He was sweating. "Ice. I'll go for ice."

Getting ice gave him an excuse to cool down and if he were smart, he'd put a dozen ice cubes in his shorts for good measure. He flung off the covers and stretched long to reach for the jeans that he'd left draped over his suitcase.

"It doesn't have to be ice water," she said. "No need for you to go running around the hotel in the middle of the night."

"No problem."

He stuck his feet into his jeans, yanked them up fast, making sure to keep his back to her as he wrangled with pulling up the zipper over his erection. Not bothering with socks, he jammed his feet into his boots and slipped on his shirt. Desperate to put some distance between them, he blew off buttoning up, grabbed the key card and the ice bucket from the top of the dresser, and got the hell out of there.

Melody wished she could twitch her nose and fall magically asleep and avoid this awkwardness. Then again, if she were going for *Bewitched* talents, why not twitch her nose and transport Luke all the way back to Cupid? Problem solved.

Maybe she should just pretend to be asleep when he got back. But that was childish and he'd gallantly gone after ice for her because she was thirsty.

Of course she could leave, but it was even later than it had been before and the heel of her shoe was still broken and her head had gone from fuzzy to achy, and although for the most part, the alcohol had worn off, inertia held her tethered to the mattress.

The door opened and Luke returned, backlit by the corridor lights. A recalcitrant cowlick stuck up from the back of his head and he held the ice bucket clutched to his bare chest framed by his unbuttoned shirt. The door snapped closed behind him, shuttering the room in darkness once again, except for the nightlight plugged into the socket on his side of the bed.

She heard more than saw him set the ice bucket on the dresser, scoop ice into glasses, and fill them with tap water from the bathroom sink. He brought her a glass, and held one for himself. She sat up, watching him in the dim light while he drank, head back, Adam's apple moving up and down.

How silly was it that she was turned on by the way he swallowed?

The water was cold against her feverishly hot lips.

He toed off his boots, positioned them at the foot of the bed, shrugged out of his shirt, and reached for the snap of his jeans. He looked so masculine, so utterly male. This situation was far too intimate. She was inviting trouble. She knew it. She didn't care.

The allure of the forbidden.

She finished the water, set her glass beside his. That seemed too intimate as well. She pushed at her tumbler with an index finger until it was on the other side of the bedside table from his.

He stripped off his jeans. He wore boxer briefs. Red ones from what she could tell in the dim light. Cotton. Probably Hanes. Jean-Claude had slept in silk trunks.

She was in a T-shirt and no underwear — she'd rinsed her panties out and hung them in the shower to dry — and he was nearly naked. Boldly, he stared at her, his gaze honing in on her eyes, her mouth, her chin. She grabbed her pillow, used it as a shield across her body.

"Want more water?"

"I'm good." She tried to keep her gaze trained on his face, determined not to look lower, but damn her treacherous eyes. They flicked over his chest, swept across his flat abs, took a stroll on down to his hips.

Egad! Was he getting a hard-on? Quickly, she jerked her gaze away and every muscle in her body tensed. Was she just going to ignore it?

Seriously? What was she supposed to do? Jump his bones?

It's a thought.

But not a smart one. Her brain froze as

her body melted, Popsicle-in-the-sun-gooey. Well, there were some tiles on the ceiling that needed counting. She could do that. Better than sheep, right? One. Two. Three.

He got back into bed beside her. God, he smelled good.

She pulled the covers up to her chin and squeezed her eyes tightly shut. *Go to sleep. Go to sleep. Go to sleep.*

A minute passed.

Then ten.

Twenty.

She lay on her back, stiff as a plank, listening to every sound. The soft hum of the digital clock, traffic noises on the street below, Luke's ragged breathing.

"This isn't working, is it?" she whispered.

"It's working just fine," he murmured, his voice drowsy. "Get some rest."

"I can't."

"I know. How does anyone in this city sleep with all the sirens, honking horns, and backup beepers going off?"

"You get used to it. Gets to where you miss it when you're not in the city."

"Thank God, I don't have to get used to it."

"You hate it here, huh?"

"I wouldn't say 'hate,' just not my cuppa coffee."

"I love New York."

"It is exciting."

"But you prefer wide open spaces."

"It's who I am. I'm not ashamed of where I'm from."

Meaning she was? Melody rolled over onto her side, put her back to him.

A few minutes later, Luke shifted, turned. His knee lightly touched her butt. Only the thin cotton of her T-shirt separated him from her bare ass.

And he let his knee just rest there.

Yipes!

Gooseflesh blanketed her body, but she neither protested nor moved. She closed her eyes against a bombardment of sexy images that lit up the thrill center of her brain.

He slipped an arm around her waist, heavy but reassuring.

She stopped breathing. "What are you doing?"

"I'm not trying anything funny. Honest. I normally spoon with my pillow. It's how I fall asleep. Do you mind if I spoon with you instead?"

Hell yes, she minded. Hanging by a thread here, buddy. "No," she croaked.

What are you saying? Get up. Get out. Slap his face. Slap your own face. Just stop this.

But the deal was, she liked it, and a warm

buzzy feeling, similar to how she felt after drinking the Dom Perignon, wove a drifty spell over her. The traffic noises crooned their sweet lullaby. Nice. Really, really nice. She floated on a river of languid sensation, felt surprisingly safe and steady. The tension drained from her body and she felt herself letting go.

Melody woke sometime later and for a groggy moment she thought that she was at Jean-Claude's apartment, but her back was pressed up against a man's hard chest, her butt curved against his pelvis, his arm wrapped around her waist.

Cuddling.

Jean-Claude wasn't a cuddler. He'd never once spooned with her and this guy was acting like they were tucked away in a silverware drawer together, stacked one against the other.

Memory tapped her on the temple. Not Jean-Claude, but Luke. She was in bed with Luke Nielson and he was snuggled up to her like . . . like . . . well, like she was *his* woman.

She should have been ready to run for the door, broken shoes or not, but instead, all she wanted to do was curl deeper into him.

So she did. Audacious, yes, but it felt so good lying here beside him, the ghost of her teenage fantasies stirring back to life. She remembered another time he'd held her, wrapped his arms around her as they sat on the picnic table looking at the moon over Lake Cupid. The way he'd kissed her hair and pronounced that she smelled like flowers.

In a matter of minutes it had all turned ugly.

She closed her eyes, blocking out the past.

His palm was pressed against her belly, his face buried in her hair. She could feel his breath on the nape of her neck, warm and lulling, and then she felt something else entirely. The head of his erect penis poking jauntily against her ass.

Panic seized her throat, squeezed hard. *Your fault. You got into bed with him. You knew better but you did it anyway.*

What should she do?

Although his penis stayed hard, he made no other move. Was he awake at all? Or was this just natural male biology? The glorious phenomenon of morning wood?

Bravely, she whispered, "Luke?"

He didn't answer.

Or move.

Yeah, okay. He was asleep. She would have been relieved, except for the man spear still poking into her.

She had to get out of here and fast.

Slowly, she eased out from underneath his arm, slipped off the bed, and padded to the bathroom. Exhaling heavily, she closed the door, sagged against it, her knees weak as boiled noodles, the rest of her body hot and moist and desperate. Blood charged through her veins, restless and thick.

Every feminine urge inside her was screaming to go back to bed and beg the man to make good use of his rock-hard erection.

After she used the facilities, she washed her hands and splashed water on her face. There, just what she needed to bring her back down to earth, a cold jolt.

She opened the door to find Luke standing right in front of her.

In his underwear. Although she did not dare look down to determine his state of arousal.

Ulp!

He stepped toward her.

She managed to hold her ground. "What is it?"

He didn't answer her question, just gathered her up into his arms and stared deeply into her eyes.

She should have pushed him away, told him to step off, acted offended. Except of course, she was not offended. Not in the least.

Instead of resisting, as a smart woman would have done, Melody closed her eyes.

Yes.

Stupidly, she let her eyelashes drift downward, and the minute her vision was cut off, the rest of her senses intensified. Robbed of sight, she could identify every note of his cologne — coriander, basil, bergamot, sandalwood, flannel, and cedar. Traditional, his scent. Straightforward. No bullshit. A throwback to a simpler, more uncomplicated time.

His kiss had changed since high school. Matured. Developed. Gone were the herky-jerky movements of an awkward kid trying hard to play it cool. Now, he was smooth as tumbled stone. Practiced. Accomplished. Everything flowed and melded with alarming ease.

He was different now.

So was she.

But the sparks were still there.

Sparks, eh?

Um, this was a full-blown forest fire.

His lips were perfect — firm, warm, just the right amount of moisture and heat. Gold medal quality. He slipped his tongue between her parted teeth, and, well, she didn't protest. In fact, she might have egged him on by moaning the tiniest little bit. He increased the pressure and everything turned urgent.

Gimme.

Gimme, gimme, gimme.

She ensnared his face with both hands, cupping her palms around his cheeks, egging him on with her tongue.

And then, damn him, he broke the kiss, swore under his breath, pulled back, and stared at her with heavily lidded eyes.

"What . . ." She gasped, splayed a hand to her chest, and fought to put starch into her knees. "Was that all about?"

He shook his head, long and slow. "That," he said, "was a very bad idea."

"Clearly."

Even as he said it, he did not let her go. In fact, he pulled her up tighter into his arms, pressing her against the rigidness of his body, letting her know exactly how much he wanted her.

A helpless sound seeped from her lips and she opened her mouth to say something — what, she wasn't sure — only to have him capture her lips again.

He reached up to cradle the back of her head in his big palm, his fingers sliding through her hair.

Her heart beat a rapid tattoo against her rib cage.

His tongue — the wicked thing — was plundering and tasting her with a long, lingering sip as if she was an exceptional vintage of a fine wine and he was a connoisseur.

Driven by raw animal need, she dissolved against his chest, opened her jaw wider, and tipped her head back.

Her arms acted of their own accord, slipping around his waist, spreading up the muscles of his back, his warm skin innervating her fingers, pulling his head down lower to deepen the kiss.

Blazing!

She hung suspended in that moment. Caught. A prisoner of desire. Feeling everything — the pressure, the heat, his scent so stimulating and masculine.

Abruptly, he wrenched his lips away, leaving her hauling in big gulps of air and longing, and feeling as if she'd just collapsed after sprinting to first place in the New York Marathon.

Melody blinked, and a sweet shiver shimmied from her spine all the way to her tingling toes. Lights inside her head danced like summer fireflies and she could hardly gather her thoughts. She widened her eyes, blinked, hardly able to believe where she was or what she was doing.

"Yep," he confirmed. "Definitely a bad idea."

"You just had to check to make sure?"

Luke looked so cool and unaffected, as if he did this kind of thing every day of the week. He cleared his throat. Twice. "I totally did not plan that."

"Which time? The first or the second."

"Both."

"You know third time's a charm," she said, shocking herself, and shrugged. "Just saying."

He stepped away from her, jammed a hand through his hair, ruffling the silky waves. "Or three strikes and you're out."

"Out of what?"

"Look," he said. "I pushed too far. I should have known better. I did know better, but I crossed the line anyway."

She peered at him. She could not read his expression. Was he teasing? "Known better about what?"

"I don't want to be the rebound guy."

"I'm not asking for anything but hot sex. Are you looking for happily-ever-after?"

"Maybe," he said.

Her heart quickened. "But not with me?"

"You're just out of a relationship, Melody,

117

and besides you're a Fant and I'm a Niel-son. Us being together simply wouldn't work."

"Not in Cupid, maybe," she agreed. "But this is New York."

"I'm a rancher, a country boy. This place isn't for me."

"I know," she said, her body aching all over. "But that doesn't mean we can't have one wild night."

"You mean it?" he croaked hoarsely.

"I've never wanted anything more."

He groaned. Tightened his grip on her. "Melly, are you absolutely sure?"

"No one ever has to know. One night and then we forget all about it."

"This is what you really want?"

"How many times do I have to say yes?"

"No regrets?"

"The only regret I have is that you're still standing here talking when we could be heating up the sheets."

"Hell, woman. I might be a lot of things, but I ain't stupid." Then he bent, scooped her into his arms, and carried her to bed.

CHAPTER 7

"Luke," Melody whispered his name soft and sexy, her thick golden hair falling in loose curls past her shoulders in the dim illumination of the nightlight. Her lids lowered seductively over big chocolate brown eyes, so worldly, and yet at the same time so disarmingly vulnerable.

Was this a smart thing to do?

She canted her head and studied him, the barest tinge of a smile plucking at the corners of her full pink lips.

Dammit.

The woman unraveled him in a way no other woman ever had. He wanted her . . . aw hell, who was he kidding . . . he *hungered* for her like a knuckle-dragging caveman, but his hyped-up libido wasn't what scared him.

Lust, he could handle, but this? Well, he'd never felt such a relentless pounding need and no matter how many times he'd looked for a substitute in other women, only Melody possessed the power to drive him to the brink of insanity.

And that was a damn scary thought.

Plus, he was alarmed to discover that over time his desire for her had not diminished but had only grown more intense. First youth and the bad blood between families, and then later the distance had kept them apart, but now those barriers were gone.

It was just the two of them alone in a hotel room. How often had he dreamed of this scenario? A thousand times at least.

He could smell her, the intoxicating scent of her womanly aroma. And the heat from her body! He could feel the sizzle radiating off her.

She touched him. Two fingertips. On the back of his hand. That was all it took for him to get harder than he'd ever been in his life.

A groan rolled from his throat, detonated in the darkened room. Did his growl sound as loud and desperate to her ears as it did to his?

Shit, he was in deep trouble.

He ached at the thought of her sly little mouth on him. He captured her face between his palms, saw her pupils widen, felt her breath on his skin. Warm. She flicked out her tongue. Wicked. Licked her lips. Wet.

"Mmm," he growled, and planted his mouth on hers. Was this a fantasy or was this really happening?

Ever since he'd decided to come to New York to plead for her help, he'd been dreaming of a moment like this, even as he'd tried to convince himself that acting on his impulses was a bad idea.

His head ticked off all the reasons why this relationship could never work. Chief among them was distance and their feuding families.

Yeah? So what? Take what you can get and be grateful for it. One night is plenty.

Ah, but that was a lie. One taste from her lips and he knew once would never be enough, but once was better than nothing.

He'd never been a man to deny his physical needs. And who knew? One blissful night with her just might do the trick. Clear his head. Snip away those old memories that he could never completely cut from his conscience.

Juggle fire.

That's what he'd done when he allowed himself to share a bed with her. He'd thought he was strong enough to resist temptation, but he hadn't counted on Melody's eager receptiveness.

He wanted to be tender with her, but he felt so needy, so desperate, so out of control. He ground his pelvis against hers and she writhed against him, arching her spine, raking her fingers down his bare back, letting loose with a fierce little growl.

Wildcat.

Her skin was mouthwateringly hot against his, and her teeth playfully nipped at his throat.

He couldn't get enough of tasting her. His mouth branded her lips, her cheeks, her eyelids, the tip of her nose, and the end of her chin.

At last. At long last.

It had taken him fifteen years to get here, but they were finally doing this. Consummating that long-ago lurking passion they'd just barely started to stir when they were horny, love-struck teens.

Her fingers were threaded through his hair, and she wrenched her mouth from his. "Gotta . . ." She gasped. ". . . have you *now*!"

He stared deeply into her eyes. "Say please."

"You want me to beg?"

"Tell me what you want," he commanded, cupping the back of her head in his palm.

"You," she said. "I want to feel you inside of me."

He pushed her back onto the mattress, loomed above her. She peered up at him, a wicked smile on her face. He shoved the T-shirt up around her neck, exposing her creamy white breasts and proving that yes, indeed she was not wearing panties.

God, she was the sexiest thing he'd ever seen.

He parted her legs with his, planting his knee deep into the mattress just below the tantalizing V where her thighs joined, and leaned farther over her.

She blinked up at him.

"You've got a beautiful mouth," he murmured. "I love that crooked front tooth."

She tucked her upper lip around her top teeth. "I hate it."

"Why?"

"It ruins my smile."

"The hell it does. It *makes* your smile."

"How?"

"Makes you look interesting. Not your run-of-the-mill perfect beauty."

"Mother is always nagging me to get it fixed."

"Don't you dare," he said. "I love it."

"Really?" Her insecurity touched him. Didn't she have any idea just how beautiful

123

she was?

"Really."

"Jean-Claude said the tooth ruined my smile."

"I thought we already established that your ex is a boring douchebag. Let's not talk about him ever again."

"I'm for that."

He kissed her again so long and hard that when he pulled back her lips were red and swollen. Probably so were his.

As she lay there panting, he went about his endeavor, kissing a path down her chest to first one breast and then the other, taking time to nibble and suck each hard-budded nipple.

She cried out, arched her back higher. God, he loved how responsive she was.

"Luke," she whispered his name so softly he could scarcely hear her.

"Tell me what you need, darlin'."

"You. Inside me. Now."

"Not yet." He shook his head.

She whimpered, pursed her bottom lip in a lust-fueled pout.

Ah man, he was getting in deep here.

Something at the back of his mind prodded caution. Urged him to back off, back out. Hell, get all the way out of New York before he did something irrevocable.

The cool air blowing against his back from the air-conditioner vents, her hot little body wriggling beneath him, her eager palms kneading his ass, jettisoned him into another realm. He spanned her hips with his hands, his palms sliding beneath her buttocks, tilting her spine upward, and giving him a heart-stopping view of that sweet spot between her legs.

His mouth watered. He couldn't wait to get to know every inch of her with his tongue, to explore every delicious nook and cranny. He wanted to shuck her open like an oyster, learn all her secrets, find that brilliant pearl inside her, taste all her delights.

He groaned, pressed his mouth to her abdomen and set off to mysterious territory, an intrepid explorer in the erotic land of Melody Spencer.

She sighed with pleasure. How he loved that sound! Walking away from her after this was not going to be easy. Why had he said he could do it?

His tongue found her most cherished region — warm, earthy, fully feminine. She rocked her hips against his face, urging him to go where she needed him most. Whimpering. Begging. Her taut thighs closed around his ears, locking him in place.

"Ooh, baby," she moaned.

"I know, darlin'," he murmured, deep in the thick of her. "I know."

Her fingernails combed restless through his hair, her hips rotating in rhythmic swirls. He picked up her pattern, mimicked it with a tempo of his own. Stroking her higher and higher, hotter and hotter. Her breathing came in short, high pants, moving air only in the upper part of her lungs.

He smiled against her moist skin. Her briny taste filled his mouth. Soon. She was so damn close. Soon. Very soon. She was almost there.

"Luke!" His name shot from her mouth on a sharp, guttural cry.

She pushed down, pressed against him, and he felt her come. Her body shuddering hard as she rode wave after wave of pleasure.

Grinning, he moved up onto the bed with her, pulled her into his arms. Kissed her face, smoothed her hair.

The woman was sexy as hell and he was so lucky to be here with her, to have caused that reaction in her. But she wasn't about to give him one minute's rest. Now that they'd started this, apparently she was in all the way.

"Get those condoms I saw in your first aid kit," she hissed through clenched teeth. "Get them now!"

He chuckled at her ferocity.

"I'm not kidding!"

"Yes, ma'am," he said, rolled off the bed, and groped around for the first aid kit.

"Hurry," she urged, leaning over the side of the bed.

"Doin' my best, angel," he drawled, but truth be told, he was just as anxious as she. His hands were trembling so hard from excitement that he fumbled the condom and dropped it twice before he made it back to the bed.

"C'mere." She was on her knees on the mattress. She reached over, hooked one finger inside the waistband of his under-shorts, and pulled him back onto the bed beside her.

He grabbed at the edges of the foil packet, desperately trying to get the thing open in the darkness.

"Let me," she said, yanking it from his hand and using her teeth to tear it open. This was a woman who knew exactly what she wanted and had no inhibitions about her sexuality.

He liked her boldness in bed.

Liked it a lot.

They were going to have all kinds of fun.

She spit out the foil, removed the condom from the wrapper, and before he knew what hit him, she had a firm hold on his Johnson and was rolling the condom over the throbbing head of his penis.

He was quivering so hard that he was terrified he was going to spoil it all by coming way too soon. He wanted this to last. He'd spent many a night dreaming over her. He didn't want it over in two hot strokes. *Think unsexy thoughts, think unsexy thoughts, think . . . God, what a supple body she had.*

"Here we go," she said, rocked back against the pillow, locked her legs around his thighs, and pulled him down on top of her.

It would have been so very easy to sink into her. Just slip right in and let Mother Nature take her course.

Melody arched her hips up, pushing against his pelvis. "I'm ready. Slide on in, cowboy."

He lowered his head. "Can't," he whispered against her hair. "I won't last eight seconds and this isn't a rodeo where eight seconds is a good thing."

She laughed, and the sound sent a saddlebag full of joy bucking down his spine. "Eight seconds is fine for me. We've got the rest of the night to play catch-up."

The woman was desperate for him. Luke grinned. Just as desperate for him as he was for her, but clearly, he was the one who had to put on the brakes because if she kept cupping his balls like that, he was going to explode in her hand.

He pulled his body back, but leaned down to press his forehead against hers and peer deeply into those sweetly wicked brown eyes. "No."

"Spoilsport." She pouted.

"You'll thank me later."

"Bragging, are you?"

"It's not bragging if you can back it up."

"You're running the risk of losing me," she threatened. "I cool off quickly."

"Not if I do this," he said, and bent his head to nibble at her earlobe as he remembered how she'd squirmed with delight when he'd done the same thing when they were teenagers.

"Oh!" she exclaimed. "You fight dirty."

"And don't you forget it," he growled playfully.

He teased her ear until she was writhing and begging him again. "Please, Luke. Please just get inside me."

He couldn't resist her, not one second longer, and he slid into her soft, welcoming wetness.

Bull's-eye. He was home.

All the air left her lungs in an audible

whoosh and her body clamped down on him and now he was the one who was having trouble breathing. She'd turned the tables on him again.

He clenched his jaw, tried hard to think of something that would keep a leash on the lust that was charging through him like a raging Brahman bull stampeding from the chute. Cupid. Drought. Family. Feud.

Whoa. Wait a minute. He wanted to rein things in, not stop the momentum entirely.

But he needn't have worried about getting sidetracked. Melody was massaging his ass with those amazing fingers of hers, kneading his muscles like he was a bread dough.

Yee-haw.

He slipped his hand around her waist, pulling her closer, diving in deeper.

She tightened her legs around his waist, her body encompassing his. He cupped his hands around her face, stared into her eyes. He felt as if he was falling, tumbling into a place he'd dreamed of but never fully believed existed.

Their bodies were locked. Their gazes cemented upon each other. Her hands were clamped around his upper arms, her fingernails biting into his biceps.

"Oh," she cried, and her eyes stared fixedly as if she were seeing through him, peer-

130

ing directly into his soul.

He felt something then, a movement deep inside his very center. Something shifted or melted or broke loose or hell, he didn't know what, but it happened. A change. An alteration. A revolution.

And then her inner muscles seized him and squeezed so tightly he knew there was no hanging on. He was gone and so was she. One last hard thrust and they burst together. Better than a bonfire, bigger than fireworks, brighter than a meteor shower — sizzling hot explosion, fire and heat and brilliant light.

Breathlessly, he collapsed against her. Not wanting to crush her underneath his weight, he moved to roll away, but she squeezed her legs around him, holding him down.

He had to admit it felt pretty damn good pressed so tightly against her sweaty, panting body. Anchored. Lord, but the woman was prime fine.

To keep from squashing her, he put his weight on his forearms and looked down into her laughing eyes.

"You . . ." she whispered, "were spectacular."

"Not so bad yourself." He kissed the end of her nose.

"We should have known it would be this

131

good. All those years of waiting. All that sexual buildup."

They lay like that for several minutes, limbs entangled, heart rate slowing in the afterglow of their lovemaking.

Not lovemaking, he corrected himself. Just sex. Just for now. Just for tonight. Her life was here. His was in Texas. She was a Fant descendant. He was a Nielson. Nothing more could happen between them.

But damn, he couldn't help thinking it was a crying shame, because he could get accustomed to spending time in her bed.

Very accustomed indeed.

Just before dawn, they used up the last condom in Luke's first aid kit.

What a wild and crazy night it had been.

Hooking up with Luke was a reaction to getting fired and dumped all in one day. Melody knew that. It was great sex because it was taboo and unexpected. She knew that too. It was nothing more than an off-the-chain, out-of-control, lose-your-mind impulse. She never wanted or expected anything more than this one beautiful, forbidden night, a sweet salve to soothe her wounds.

In theory anyway.

But as she lay beside him, staring up at

132

the ceiling, their hands linked, their legs knitted together like skeins of yarn, she couldn't quash an obnoxious little voice that whispered, *Too bad this can't be more.*

It could not, so no point in thinking about it.

But all she wanted to do was have sex with him again. Never mind that she was raw and achy and worn out. It was a good kind of exhausted.

"We're those people, you know," she said.

"What people?"

"The ones you hate to get a hotel room next to because they pound the bed against the wall all night long."

He grinned. "I guess we are at that."

"Should we feel guilty for being inconsiderate?"

"Nah. We're giving them something to aspire to."

"They're probably jealous."

"Oh yeah. I'd be jealous if I was in the next room, instead of in here with you."

She giggled.

"You wanna make them jealous all over again?"

"Tempting, but you're flying back to Cupid this afternoon and you haven't had a lick of sleep."

"I can sleep on the plane. What I can't do

is leave town until you have a place to stay."

"I'm a big girl, Luke. I can take care of myself. I'll just get a hotel room until I can make long-term arrangements."

"I know," he said. "But I'm a traditionalist. Let me at least take you back to get your things from the doorman."

"All right," she conceded, because she did not want to go back to Jean-Claude's apartment building by herself.

He pulled her into the curve of his body. "Close your eyes and try to sleep for an hour or two."

She snuggled against him. "This is the last time we'll ever do this."

"Well, never say never, darlin'. Now that I've seen New York, I might get a hankering to come up and visit every once in a while. Would that be okay with you?"

She nodded, wanting that too much to say so. She was treading on boggy ground here.

"And of course, you'll come home to Cupid to see your folks from time to time."

"We can't see each other when I come to Cupid. It's too risky."

He didn't answer, but he played with a lock of her hair. He knew as well as she did the kind of trouble the two of them pairing up would cause in their hometown.

"If I was a poetic guy, this is where I

would quote something pithy from Shakespeare," he said. "Something all Romeo and Juliet about star-crossed lovers."

"Good thing you're not poetic. It would sound cheesy."

He laughed and hugged her tighter. "You're one helluva woman, Melody Spencer, and don't ever let anyone tell you differently."

"I'll try to remember that the next time I'm getting fired and given the romantic brush-off."

"I believe everything happens for a reason. You're going to do great things with your life. Never doubt that. I don't," he said fiercely.

The guy sure knew how to get under a woman's skin. She had to give him that.

"I mean look at the way you thought of that cornbread bake-off thing to help bring tourists back to Cupid on the spur of the moment," he went on. "You've got a sharp mind."

"Not really. It's just my job. I'm always thinking of clever ways to sell things, the same way you think about cattle."

"Maybe, but this bake-off is going to be the shot in the arm that Cupid needs. I can just feel it." He shook his head. "And to think some people back home thought the trip up here to see you was going to be a waste."

She wanted to ask, *What people?* But she hated to spoil the short time they had left together by dipping into small-town politics and family grudges.

"Don't count your chickens," she cautioned. "This thing with Quaker is nowhere near a done deal. I just made the first overtures. The ball is in my court. I've got to find some celebrity judges or my proposal will never see the light of day."

"You'll do it." He sounded so positive that she was starting to believe it could happen. "One day Cupid will be as famous for its cornbread as Terlingua is for its chili."

"No pressure, huh?" She laughed.

"I have faith in you."

"Why?"

"Because you're a woman of your word. You do what you say you'll do."

"I wish I could be certain of that."

"You don't have to be. I'm certain enough for both of us." He kissed the nape of her neck and she turned in his arms to face him and they were kissing all over again.

"We're out of condoms," she panted after his kiss left her gasping for air.

"There's other ways of pleasuring each other," he said, and kissed his way down her body.

Within minutes she was tingling and quivering and calling out his name all over again, and in that exceptional moment, her mind detached from her body and she was nothing but pleasure.

The experience was so intense it was as if she were watching herself from a long distance away. Watched her arms draw him close. Observed her lips kiss his forehead, his eyelids, his cheek, his chin. He was so substantial, so powerful and solid.

"God, Melly." He breathed. "You are amazing."

Her mind, still objectively disconnected from her body, saw her arms twine around his neck and squeezed tightly, as if, it were up to them, they would never let him go.

In that moment, she knew she should not have done this. It was a terrible mistake. There would be no going back. No undoing what had been done.

She was forever marked.

CHAPTER 8

Melody woke sometime later. Sunlight seeped through the curtains, revealing that the spot beside her on the bed was empty. She squinted at the clock. Nine-thirty.

Oh crap, she was late for work.

It hit her all at once — the loss of her job, boyfriend, and living arrangement. And the fact that she'd had sex with Luke Nielson.

She sat upright in bed as the consequences of her actions fully set in. *Beware.* She had seriously screwed up. Midnight and Dom Perignon had a way of doing that to a person.

The door opened and Luke himself walked through the door, carrying a paper bag. Instantly, her body responded, nipples tightening, skin tingling, womb constricting. She was in some kind of trouble.

"Mornin', sleepyhead." He swept off his Stetson, and dropped it on the bureau.

She pulled the sheets up over her breasts,

suddenly feeling shy and exposed. It was a little late for modesty. Last night he'd seen every inch of her body. She had no secrets left from him.

He held up the white paper bag. "Bagels and cream cheese and coffee. Get it while it's hot."

She felt weird parading around naked. Where was that T-shirt? But she couldn't wrap the sheet around her either because he plopped down on the bed beside her and passed her a large cup of coffee.

"Got plain old joe. Didn't know if you like those fancy kinds or not."

"Regular coffee is fine."

"I snagged some cream and sugar packets too."

"Black's okay." She took a sip of the coffee, more to avoid looking at him than anything else. "Maybe I will have a packet of cream."

He passed it to her and she stirred it into the dark roast, studied the swirling cream instead of meeting his inscrutable gaze.

"You've got your choice of bagels," he said. "Cinnamon raisin, blueberry, or plain."

"Cinnamon raisin."

He smeared cream cheese on half the bagel before passing it to her. Then slathered the other half for himself. "And, oh yeah, I got you these."

From inside his jacket pocket he pulled out a pair of ballet flats. "So you don't have to go back to the Frenchman's place in broken heels."

For some stupid reason the ballet slippers really touched her. A lump formed in her throat that had nothing to do with the bite of bagel she'd just swallowed.

They were pretty flats. Green and blue brocade that matched the skirt she'd worn yesterday, and they were a size eight.

"How did you know my size?" she asked.

"I peeked inside your shoe."

"You've been busy."

"Hey, you're doing me a big favor. The least I can do is buy you breakfast and comfortable footwear."

"I'm doing this for Cupid," she said.

"You're doing it for me," he corrected. "Save Cupid and you save *my* ass. If I don't do something, I'll go down in history as the mayor who allowed the drought to kill the town."

"Things are really that serious?"

His ominous eyes, which were usually so teasing, met hers. "Melody, I've had to watch the grass burn past dry yellow to dusty gray and even that's dwindling as hungry cattle gobble up every dead patch

140

they can find. We feed them of course, but without grazing land it gets pretty expensive and it takes a real toll on pocketbooks. Most folks have stretched themselves thin with bank loans they won't be able to pay back if we don't get some relief soon."

A sick feeling sloshed in her stomach as it dawned on her just how desperate he must have been to come to her for help. "I'm not some messiah who can sweep in and fix everything."

"Maybe not," he said solemnly, "but you're our last real hope."

The next morning Luke took her to get her things from Jean-Claude's home. She packed up her most essential belongings in three suitcases and then rented a storage unit for the rest. They returned to the Hilton just long enough to switch the room from his name to hers and then he took off for the airport.

Leaving her feeling empty and restless.

Melody stayed holed up in the hotel room, working on the cornbread bake-off proposal for Quaker. She touched base with her contact at the Food Network and coerced an agreement from them that if Quaker supported the bake-off, they'd supply three celebrity judges. She told neither Quaker nor the Food Network about her change in employment status. It wasn't as if she actually lied about no longer working for Tribalgate, she just didn't volunteer the information. If they had come right out and asked, of course she would have told them the truth, but as it was, she saw no reason to stack the deck against herself.

In between working on getting the bake-off up and running, she also looked for a place to live that she could afford. Now that she was unemployed, Manhattan was no longer an option. She'd have to move back to Queens. Maybe Brooklyn or Jersey. She put out some feelers, but hadn't heard anything back from the real estate agent.

Late on Wednesday evening malaise took hold of her. She'd done what she could and now she was in wait mode. She hated wait mode. It was so . . . *static.* Besides, she had to find a place to stay and soon. She couldn't keep paying for a hotel or she'd drain her savings in no time. New York was a great city when you had money. But when you were down and out? Not so much.

As much as she hated it, she was going to have to impose on her friends and do some couch surfing until she could find a place to stay.

Loser.

She hadn't told any of her friends about her situation. She was too embarrassed, even though she knew they would understand. They would offer sympathy and wine, a shoulder to cry on and a place to crash, but she was used to being the one who offered the sympathy, not the other way around.

Even asking for help felt like major defeat.

On Thursday morning, still feeling disconcerted from her night with Luke, she packed up her three suitcases and checked out of the Hilton, and headed for her friend Bethany's house in Brooklyn. At least three-dozen people were backlogged for the hotel's taxi line and the arriving cabs were few and far between. At this rate, she wouldn't get a taxi for an hour. Feeling restless and edgy, she decided to try her chances hailing a cab on the street.

But the second she left the protective building, huge raindrops fell from the overcast sky. Talk about poor timing. She had an umbrella somewhere, but didn't know which suitcase she'd shoved it into.

Ah well, it was only a little drizzle. She wouldn't melt.

She struggled with the suitcases, juggling them through the crowd headed to work. The rain thickened, drumming on her head, and causing her hair to frizz instantly.

Determinedly, she trudged on, zigzagging her way through the crowd, scanning the street for an available cab.

Halfway up Sixth Avenue, the wheel of one of the suitcases caught on a deep crack in the sidewalk, jerking her backward. Chuffing out a breath, she yanked on the handle. "Come on."

Someone knocked into her and didn't even bother to mumble, "Sorry."

Her purse slid down her arm and she had to stop in order to hike it back up on her shoulder.

The sky opened up, dumping a torrent. Umbrellas bloomed like mushrooms. Shoulders hunched, people began sprinting to their destinations.

She was blocking foot traffic, getting in the way. She tried to move over to the side, but the pressing throng was too thick. She was stuck in the middle of the congestion and there were no empty taxis in sight.

Water froze up the wheels on her suitcases and none of the casters would turn. Gritting her teeth, she tightened her grip on the handles and dragged them behind.

Another person bumped into her. Then another. A woman jostled her elbow, and rushed around her with a disgusted snort.

"Watch where you're going, bitch," snarled a short, beet-face man with caterpillar eyebrows. "Keep up or get out."

Her chest tightened. Everywhere she looked people were glowering at her.

A homeless man sat on the ground underneath the awning of a bodega, seemingly immune to the rain as he peeled a banana. He looked up when she passed, made eye contact. Before she could look away, he yelled, "Who are you? You don't belong here!"

Knees shaking, she rushed past him. She needed to get somewhere she could think. Someplace quiet and serene. *Go back to the Hilton, idiot.*

That's when she spied an available cab. She stepped to the curb and stuck a hand up for it. One after another they passed her by. Finally, one did pull to a stop, but before she could muscle her suitcases to the curb, a man jumped into the backseat, commandeering the vehicle away from her without so much as an apologetic glance in her direction.

Life in the city. Survival of the fittest.

Normally, she sharpened her teeth on obstacles, a fearless tigress taking on the world. Today, she felt like a newborn kitten that'd been both defanged and declawed.

By the time another cab acknowledged her raised hand and pulled up, her hair was plastered to her face. The back tires splashed in a puddle, soaking her slacks up to her knees.

Perfect. That's the kind of morning she was having.

The driver did not get out to help with the luggage or pop the trunk, just jabbered at her in broken English and a scolding tone as she struggled to get the drenched suitcases loaded into the seat beside her. Exhausted, she sank back against the seat and pulled the door closed.

"Where you go?" demanded the cabbie, who frowned sternly at her in the rearview mirror.

Where indeed? Overwhelmed, she gave him Bethany's address and he took off.

She sat brooding, staring at the city gone gray and dour in the rain. Yes, she knew this pity party wasn't attractive, and she would snap out of it before she ended up on Bethany's doorstep. If she was going to be an uninvited guest, she had to at least be pleasant to be around.

Melody would allow herself to pout for the length of time it took the cabbie to thread his way through the midtown traffic and over the bridge into Brooklyn, but after that, she would be all smiles and a gung-ho attitude. She would come out of this entire mess stronger and more confident than ever.

Six minutes into the sulk, her cell phone rang.

Who was calling her instead of texting? Everyone she knew texted. Well, except her mother. Please, don't let it be Mother.

She pulled her phone from her purse, and took a peek at the screen.

Luke Nielson.

Her pulse quickened instantly and she had the sweetest flashback to saying good-bye to him in the lobby of the Hilton before he caught a taxi to LaGuardia. He'd pulled her up against his chest, his down-home scent wrapping around her like a blanket as his commanding mouth delivered an exclamation mark of a kiss.

After a long moment, he'd stepped back and murmured, "Just try and forget me."

She didn't know if it had been a challenge or a command.

Now, she touched her lips, smiled, and answered the phone. "Hello?"

"I got your text about Quaker going for the deal. That's exciting. I knew you'd make it happen."

"You could have just texted me back," she said, uneasy with his compliments. The deal could fall through at any moment until the ink was dry on the contract. "No need to phone."

"Call me old-fashioned, but I wanted to hear your voice."

Her stomach fluttered. "Where are you?"

"In my office. I just came from a board meeting with the Cupid Chamber of Commerce."

"And you told them about Quaker and the bake-off?"

"I have. Everyone is real excited, Melody. You should see them. They've finally got sparkle back in their eyes. This drought has been worrisome for everyone, but it's been particularly hard on the small business owners."

"We can't celebrate yet," she cautioned. "We still have a long way to go."

"I know, but it's a start. How are you?" he asked, his tone growing lower, more intimate.

"I'm fine."

"You don't have to put on an act with me," he soothed. "Feel free to spew. How are you really?"

She wasn't about to tell him that she was coming unraveled like one of Great-Aunt Delia's badly knitted afghans in a room full of kittens. Not on her life. She'd already shown him enough of her vulnerable under-belly, thank you very much. No matter how hot and sexy the man might be, ultimately she could never forget that he was a Nielson.

"It's raining here," she said, watching the droplets splatter on the cab's window. "I wish I could bottle it up and send it to you."

"I wish you could too."

An awkward silence stretched over the airwaves.

"Have you found another job yet?" he asked.

She stared out of the taxi at the water rushing underneath the Brooklyn Bridge. It was not fair that New York was deluged and Cupid was dried-up thirsty for rain. "No."

"Got a place to stay?"

Just tell him yes. You don't need him feeling sorry for you. "No."

"Are you stuck on staying in New York City?"

"Of course," she said. "Where else would I go?"

"You could always come home," he said.

"This is my home."

"No, it's not."

"You can't go home again," she quoted wistfully, cupping the cell phone against her chin and blowing her breath against the window, fogging it with condensation. On the misty glass she wrote with her index finger. *Luke Nielson.*

"Sure you can."

She crossed out his last name, leaving a streaky: Luke ~~Nielson~~ and she then drew a misty heart underneath it. "There's nothing for me in Cupid."

"I'd like to think otherwise," he murmured.

"Luke . . ." she whispered, caught her breath, and with the palm of her hand smeared away the sentimental artwork from the glass. "We talked about this. One night. One time. Our secret tryst —"

"This isn't about that," he interrupted. "I'm not talking about us."

"Oh," she said, embarrassment grabbing her by the scruff of the neck and giving her a hard shake. "What are we talking about?"

"We'd like to offer you a job."

Her throat tightened. "What? Who?"

"The Chamber of Commerce. The board members were really impressed by your idea for a cornbread bake-off and razzle-dazzled by the fact you've got so much pull with the Food Network."

"What kind of job?"

"It's not permanent." The tone of his voice changed again, but she couldn't decipher why or what the change meant. "It's a consulting job. Think of it as something to tide you over while you lick your wounds and plan your comeback."

"What kind of consulting job?" she asked warily.

"An image consultant, I guess. For the town."

"And that would entail . . . ?"

"Marketing, branding. Tell us what we can do to bring more money into the town."

"How long do you see this job lasting?"

There was a pause and then he said, "I guess until it rains."

"That could be months away," she pointed out. "Even years."

"God, I hope not. The rainy season starts in July. Maybe we'll get some relief then."

The rainy season in the Chihuahuan Desert was a bit of a misnomer, considering the average annual rainfall in a nondrought situation was twelve to fourteen inches. "Except you didn't have a rainy season last year."

"That's correct, we didn't. Which is why we're in the mess we're in."

"To be clear, you want me to take a temporary job with no official end date?"

"You could quit any time you wanted," he said. "I don't want you to feel boxed in or beholden if something better comes along, but this would be a lifeline for both of us."

She inhaled deeply. What should she do? On the one hand, returning to Cupid felt like a huge step backward. Not only career wise, but also because she'd be under her family's watchful — and extremely nosy — eyes.

And where would she live? Certainly she could not move back in with her parents. She'd been out on her own too long for that, and the thought of knuckling under her mother's rigid rules made her want to set her hair on fire.

"Those vacation condos on the mountain above town are renting out dirt-cheap because of the drought," Luke said, reading her mind. "I'm leasing one myself so I don't have to drive the twenty miles to the ranch every time a city council meeting runs late. They're pretty nice."

Of course, she should turn down the job offer flat. This was not a smart career move anyway you sliced it, but instead of saying no, she asked, "How much does the position pay?"

"Five thousand dollars a month. I know it's nothing like what you're accustomed to making, but it's good money for out here."

Actually, she was quite surprised the town

was able to pay that much for a temporary consultant. "Honestly, Luke, I appreciate the offer, but I'm not sure —"

"Are you going to make me beg, Melly?" he asked. "Because I'll do it. Cupid is in serious trouble and from where I'm sitting, you're the only one who's got a prayer of pulling us out of this nosedive."

The taxi stopped outside Bethany's house. From an upstairs window, the curtain flipped back and two small faces pushed against the panes — her friend's three-year-old twin sons. She was going to have to walk up those steps, knock on the door, and ask for help. She swallowed hard. Pride did not go down easy.

She could stay in New York City with no job, forced to sleep on friends' couches for God knew how long, or she could return home to both a job and an affordable place to stay. She could either be a loser in the Big Apple or be a hero in Cupid.

"I understand you need time to think this over. It is a big decision," he said. "I won't pressure you. I just wanted you to know that you do have options. We need and appreciate you."

And then he hung up, leaving her listening to a dial tone.

Well, what was she supposed to make of that?

From Bethany's upstairs window, the boys stuck out their tongues, making faces against the glass. Much as she adored Bethany and her family, the thought of imposing on them lay like an iron weight in the pit of her stomach. She didn't like owing anyone anything.

She pocketed the cell. "Driver, I've changed my mind. Take me to LaGuardia instead."

"Are you going to tell that Spencer girl that you're footing the bill for her consulting job?" From the doorway of his office, Luke's assistant, Eloise Harbinger — all four feet, eleven inches of her — eyed him as he tossed his cell phone on the desk after his call to Melody.

Eloise sank her hands on her hips and gave him her patented mother hen tsk-tsk-you're-screwing-up expression. Eloise had raised eleven children, some born to her, some adopted, some fostered, and she figured that gave her the right and privilege to tell everyone younger than she what to do, and how to do it.

Even though she could be a royal pain in the ass sometimes, Luke had to admit, she

kept him on track with his mayoral duties.
"I am not."

"That's not honest."

"If I told her I was the one paying her salary, there is no way she'd agree to come home. She'd see it as charity and she's got too much pride for that."

"Then maybe she shouldn't be coming home."

"She doesn't realize it yet," Luke said, "but this is *exactly* where she belongs."

Eloise arched a skeptical eyebrow. "Because you know her so well?"

"Believe it or not, I do."

"Sometimes I think your ego is bigger than the state of Texas."

"Sometimes it is." He grinned. "But not this time."

Eloise sniffed. "Uh-huh. What's Melody going to feel like when she learns you lured her here on false pretenses?"

"The pretenses aren't false. We do need help because of the drought and that's no joke. And what better way to stop this stupid family feud forever than by having a Fant and Nielson work hand in hand to save the town they both love?"

"You're playing with matches. Manipulated is how she's going to feel," Eloise went on, completely ignoring his argument. "And probably a little pissy to boot. If you're thinking about romancing Melody this isn't the way to go about it."

Luke pressed his lips together to keep the warmth that was creeping up the back of his neck from reaching his cheeks. He was a grown man. He shouldn't be embarrassed over what had happened between him and Melody in New York.

But he was and there was the rub.

His embarrassment didn't stem from their hot one-night stand. He'd enjoyed being with her more than he'd enjoyed anything in a very long time.

But he wished he could erase all of it.

Well, not the making-love-to-her part. He'd keep that. Just change the circumstances leading up to the lovemaking. Then again, change the circumstances and she would never have gone to bed with him. He knew that. It was another reason for the flush burning his ears.

"Strong romantic relationships are based on honesty and trust." His assistant scuttled across the room to straighten a pile of papers on his desk.

"Good Lord, Eloise," he blustered. "What on earth are you talking about? I have no romantic designs on Melody Spencer."

"There's no love like your first love,

especially when your particular young love ended so tragically."

"We weren't in love," he growled. "We were just kids fooling around."

"And yet you think you know exactly what she needs. Why is that, Mayor?" She tilted her head like a curious sparrow and gave him the hard edge of her stare.

Luke pushed back from the desk, got to his feet and grabbed his Stetson from the deer antler hat rack mounted on the wall.

"She's going to resent you trying to control her, you know." Eloise tracked after him as he stalked toward the door. "Why do you think she moved all the way to New York? She was desperate to get away from that mother of hers and the bad blood bubbling between your families."

Luke stopped short.

Eloise smacked into his back. "Good gravy, Nielson. Warn a woman when you're going to jam on the brakes."

He spun around, lowered his head until he was eye to eye with Eloise, and growled, "Don't follow on a man's heels nipping at him like a Jack Russell terrier if you can't accept the consequences."

Eloise notched up her chin. "You don't scare me, cowboy. I wiped your snotty nose right along with my own kids."

"Which is why I'm saying this politely. Butt out of my personal business."

"Now see, you're speaking from both sides of your mouth," Eloise yammered and it was all Luke could do to keep from rolling his eyes. "On the one hand, you claim you're luring Melody back to Cupid for the town's sake. Then you say it's because she belongs here. On top of all that you declare you have no romantic intentions toward her and yet you tell me to butt out of your personal life. Which is it?"

He decided not to answer, pulled his Stetson down over his eyes, and walked right out the door.

"Run away all you want, Mayor," Eloise called after him. "It's not going to change the fact that your feelings for Melody run deep and if you bring her back here, it's going to cause more problems than it will solve."

CHAPTER 9

Unable to catch a flight out of LaGuardia until late afternoon, Melody spent Thursday night in a layover at DFW before catching another flight to El Paso. In El Paso, she picked up the Corvette she kept in storage for the drive home. Her father had bought her the 1971 white convertible muscle car for high school graduation. She smiled and stroked the dashboard, remembering. She named the car Courtney and they'd had a helluva summer, playing chase with the boys up and down the back roads of Jeff Davis County, until she got accepted at NYU and everything changed. Courtney was the only vehicle she'd ever owned and they were going home.

Home.

She was going home.

For the last twelve years, home had been New York City. But had it really been home or just the place she lived and worked? The

Trans-Pecos was the place of her heart. It was also the place she'd been desperate to escape, in no small part because of Luke and the Fant-Nielson feud. She had wanted to get as far away from all that craziness as she could get.

And then there was her lofty dream to be *somebody*. That's what she told her high school guidance counselor when the woman asked Melody what she wanted to be. Somebody.

Look at you now, big shot, Little Miss Nobody, running home with her tail between her legs.

"It's going to be okay," she told Courtney, even as an instant headache bloomed the minute she drove the Corvette out of the car storage parking garage and into the baking sun. "We'll be back on top. This is just a hiccup in the grand scheme of things. We have to look at it as an opportunity to redeem ourselves. Think how good this will look on our résumé. Facilitated the town of Cupid's turnaround after a record-breaking drought. How many people can say that?"

She stopped for gas, bottled water, ibuprofen, and a pair of cheap sunglasses. Her three-hundred-dollar Oakleys were MIA in the midst of her life's upheaval. Just one more thing lost.

No matter how she sliced it, coming home was a culture shock. Trading fast pace for slow moving. Tight confines for wide open spaces. Cement for sand. Humid for arid. Shopping for . . . well, nothing. Whenever she came for visits, she didn't feel the same impact because she knew she'd be leaving again, but now, there were no guarantees.

She commiserated with Eva Gabor in *Green Acres,* her grandmother Rose's favorite show. Even as a kid, whenever she watched the reruns with her grandmother, she wondered why in the hell Eva hadn't packed her bags, served Eddie Albert with divorce papers, and beat a hasty retreat back to the Big Apple.

Yeah, and why don't you?

No means, baby. No means.

Eva's character Lisa Douglas had been rich. Melody was not.

The farther southeast she drove from El Paso, the more arid the terrain became. Cupid dangled on the edge of Chihuahuan Desert, in the Davis Mountain Range, so while the area was dry and warm, the elevation kept it from being insufferable and the mountains added an austere beauty found nowhere else in Texas. It was a climate of rugged contrasts and fascinating vistas; the interplay of shifting shadow and light drew

161

the eye to the mountains jutting above the flat rocks, desert sand, and outcroppings. The extreme landscape drew artists from all over the world, eager to capture the isolated extremes of earth and sky with a brush and canvas.

She hadn't been home in almost a year, since her cousin Lace's wedding the previous summer. Her parents had come to New York for the Christmas holidays to see her because she'd simply been too busy at work to get away.

Whenever she took the drive from El Paso to Cupid, Melody couldn't help feeling awed, humbled, inspired, and insignificant in the face of such vastness, but this time she felt something more.

This time, she was scared.

There was the normal desert, full of interest and charm, and then there was this . . . this . . . blight, burning malignant and long-armed, scalding the earth from El Paso southeastward across the Trans-Pecos. The dragon's-breath of a west wind scorching every last bit of green to the color of dried bones. Familiar water holes were nothing but dry gulches. Sand billowed across the asphalt, covering long stretches of lonely road in serpentine ropes that shifted with the wind, in haunting, mesmerizing undulations.

She gnawed on her bottom lip, dried out already from the lack of moisture in the air. Steering one-handed, she drank from her water bottle, dug a tube of Carmex from her purse and dabbed it on her lips.

The drive took her from one small town after another. "For Sale" signs peppered yards. Businesses were boarded up. Lean cattle with hipbones showing wandered barren fields, trying to graze dirt.

Her throat tightened and her eyes were dry and itchy.

Why hadn't anyone told her it was this bad? Of course, her mother had spoken of how dry it was, but she hadn't really paid much attention. Dry spells were nothing new in the Trans-Pecos. It always rained. Eventually.

Except clearly it had not.

The baling-wire sensation came over her and the closer she got to Cupid, the tighter the band around her lungs grew. Relentless sun had baked the once bright blue awning over the roadside farmers' market stall west of town to a dingy gray. The stalls were empty. No cars in the parking lot. No produce to sell.

She drove past the True Love Performance

Hall, where local theater troupes, musicians, dancers, and stand-up comedians brought their art to life every weekend during tourist season. A big white banner, declaring, "All Performances Canceled Until Further Notice Due to Extreme Drought," stretched across the entrance.

Melody stopped at one of three stoplights in Cupid. No cars were coming in either direction. Idly, she waited for the light to turn green and glanced over at the Perfect Buddies Animal Shelter that boasted an ironclad "no kill" policy. A "No Vacancy" sign was posted in the window, with an added plea penciled in underneath. "Please don't abandon your pets, but if you're absolutely desperate, Angi Morgan can take one or two more. Call 432–555–5555."

Her heart wrenched. People were in such dire straits they were having to surrender their beloved pets? By the time she pulled up in front of her parents' house on the affluent Stone Street, the muscle in her left eyelid was jumping so hard and fast she could barely see.

It struck her then exactly what she was up against in this laughable attempt to bring tourism back to Cupid.

Mother Nature was a vicious bitch of a villain and Melody was armed with nothing but the ridiculous belief that she could possibly make a difference.

"Can you believe my darling daughter gave up her career on Madison Avenue to come home and save our town?" Melody's mother, Carol Ann, pressed a hand against her heart like she was about to say the Pledge of Allegiance and glanced around the table at the women who gathered at the Cupid Community Center every Monday, Wednesday, and Friday at noon to answer the letters from the lovelorn who wrote to Cupid.

"Mother," Melody protested, "that's not —"

"Don't be modest, darling." Her mother draped a hand over Melody's shoulder, a subtle warning to go along with her version of events. "Everyone knows what a sacrifice it was for you to leave Manhattan and give up everything you've built in order to aid in our town's struggle for survival."

Her mother sure knew how to spin things. As much as Melody hated to admit that she was anything like her mother, it was probably where she'd gotten her talent for casting things in a creative light.

She had no more walked into her parents' home than her mother had grabbed her arm and said, "Come on. Now that you're back home, you're permanently on the volunteer committee. We're shorthanded this week because Mignon and Sandra decided to go on a cruise together and we lost Zoey to love when she got engaged to Jericho and they took off for some dig site in Belize."

Zoey was Melody's youngest first cousin, and the latest of Millie Greenwood's four great-granddaughters to find love. Of the four women, Melody was the lone holdout. She never really bought into the romantic notion that if you wrote a letter to Cupid, begging for his help with your love life, you'd find your soul mate. Great-Grandmother Millie, a pretty housemaid, had been the genesis of the legend in 1924, when she wrote a letter to Cupid begging divine intervention in her seemingly hopeless love for the wealthiest man in town, John Fant. On his wedding day, John had left his betrothed, Elizabeth Nielson, standing at the altar and declared his undying love for Millie, sparking the infamous family feud.

Then again, Melody's three cousins had believed the legend and look, they all found enduring relationships.

Pah!

That soul mate stuff was wish fulfillment,

nothing more. They expected to find love and so they had. Honestly, how on earth could writing a letter to a mythical god cause a person to find her soul mate?

And what the hell was a soul mate anyway?

"So why did you *really* leave New York?" Great-Aunt Delia asked from her place at the head of the table. The old gal was closing in on eighty and believed she'd earned the right to freely speak her mind.

Melody took the empty seat to Great-Aunt Delia's right. "Well —"

"It was a broken romance," her mother interjected. "Melody's former boyfriend, the renowned photographer Jean-Claude Laurent, was always off on a photo shoot. You know it's so hard maintaining a long-distance relationship. They decided it just wasn't working."

Great-Aunt Delia slid a look at Carol Ann, who was standing between her and Melody. "So your lover dumped ya, huh?"

The veins in her mother's neck bulged. "Must we say the word 'lover'?"

"It is a more accurate term than boyfriend," logical Lace Bettingfield Hollister pointed out. Lace was a botanist and married to former Dallas Cowboys quarterback Pierce Hollister. "Since Jean-Claude is neither a boy, nor much of a friend. That is unless he *wasn't* your lover, Mel."

"I was living with him," Melody confirmed sheepishly. "But only for two weeks."

"That's not how I raised you." Her mother sniffed. "To live in sin."

"Chill out, Carol Ann." Great-Aunt Delia smacked her cane against the floor. "The girl is almost thirty. She's entitled to have sex. What did you expect her to do? Hang on to her virginity forever?"

"Natalie did," her mother replied. "*She* waited for Mr. Right."

"Natalie's different. Can't compare apples to oranges." Great-Aunt Delia leaned forward, her gaze locked on Melody's. "So what happened with the French fella?"

"He left my things with the doorman of our building and locked me out of the apartment."

"What an ass," declared Natalie McCleary Vega as she bounced her five-month-old son, Nathan, on her knee. Natalie was the oldest of Millie Greenwood's great-granddaughters and the cousin closest in age to Melody. "You're better off without him."

Melody concurred. In retrospect, she wasn't proud of her choices.

"You poor thing. Locked out of your own apartment. How humiliating that must have

168

been for you," Junie Mae Prufrock soothed, and reached over to pat Melody's hand. Junie Mae was a dead ringer for Dolly Parton, bouffant hair, Southern twang, and all. She owned the LaDeDa Day Spa and Hair Salon right next door to Natalie's B&B, Cupid's Rest. Junie Mae was also on the board of directors of the Cupid Chamber of Commerce. Slapping a palm over her heart, Junie Mae exclaimed, "I would have been devastated."

"Oh," Melody said. "The breakup with Jean-Claude was a nonentity compared to —"

"Ahem." Mouth twitching, her mother scowled at Melody, shook her head sharply. She smoothed nonexistent wrinkles out of her crisply ironed size-four skirt and then waved a hand at the stack of letters in the middle of the table that everyone was gathered around. "We should be getting down to business. These letters won't answer themselves."

"What is your mother trying to prevent us from finding out?" Natalie asked, gently pulling her car keys away from her son, who was using them as a teething ring. "Shoo, honey, those are nasty."

"I got fired from Tribalgate," Melody confessed.

Defeated, her mother sank down in the vacant chair catty-cornered from where Melody was sitting and flapped a hand. "Fine, go ahead. Spill all your secrets. I was just trying to save you some shame and embarrassment."

"I appreciate that. But you and Daddy taught me that honesty was the best policy."

"Unless it's something you should keep your mouth shut about," her mother muttered, and reached for a letter. "Let's see here —"

"Why did you get fired?" Lace asked.

"Coincidentally enough, for being too honest."

"See there." Her mother sliced open the envelope with a letter opener. "Sometimes it *is* better to play your cards close to the vest."

"Keeping secrets leads to trouble. As long as you are on the up-and-up, you don't have anything to worry about, but when you start slipping around doing things you're not supposed to do . . ." Great-Aunt Delia was staring right at her.

A moment of stark panic flashed through her. *She knows I slept with Luke!*

But that was ridiculous. How could Great-Aunt Delia know about that? Unless Luke blabbed. But why would he?

"To continue with Mother's card-playing analogy, that's why I'm laying my cards on the table even when she wants me to pretend I quit New York and not the other way around. I'm not doing anything clandestine."

"You sure? 'Cause the guilty dog usually barks first."

Oh Lord, she'd forgotten what a handful Great-Aunt Delia could be. "Nothing to bark about, Auntie."

"You don't want to tell us how Luke Nielson managed to coax you back here?" Great-Aunt Delia's eyes were sharp as a whetted blade.

Melody lifted one shoulder, did her best to look nonchalant. "He offered me a job when I had none."

"That's it?" Great-Aunt Delia sounded disappointed.

"What were you expecting? That I came back to Cupid because of Luke?"

"You're young, he's hot, things happen."

"Aunt Delia!" her mother exclaimed. "He's a Nielson. Melody would never be involved with him."

"I wouldn't say never," Great-Aunt Delia muttered. "She made out with him once."

"Long ago," her mother rushed to say, but she threw Melody a worried frown. "When

she was fifteen, and an impulsive child acting out. She's a grown woman now and she
knows better. "She's not stupid enough to
sleep with a Nielson. Not after what happened."

Just call me Stupid.

"Would it be the worst thing in the world
if she did?" Great-Aunt Delia raised her
chin. "Might mend a few fences."

Her mother gasped. "Do you want a
repeat of fifteen years ago?"

"I'm not sleeping with Luke," Melody
said. Not currently anyway. That was truth-
ful enough. No one need know about their
indiscretion. It was never going to happen
again.

"Well, I for one don't care what brought
you back." Peacemaking Natalie came to
her rescue. "I'm just happy that you're
home. We've missed you something fierce."

"Amen." Junie Mae nodded. "We heard
about the cornbread contest. You are a
creative genius."

"And she managed to get three top-tier
Food Network judges to put in an appearance," her mother bragged. "Don't forget
that. Melody has important connections."

"We shouldn't be countin' those chickens." Great-Aunt Delia rapped her knuckles
on the table. "I've raised chickens all my life

and ninety-nine percent of the time, there's a few that don't hatch. And even of the ones that do, usually a chick or two will die right off the bat."

"Shh, Auntie." Natalie covered Nathan's ears. "He'll learn about the harsh side of life soon enough."

"He's five months old," Great-Aunt Delia said. "He has no idea what we're saying."

"One day he will understand. It's good to get into the habit of monitoring our tongues now." Natalie kissed the top of her son's head.

Great-Aunt Delia rolled her eyes and muttered, "First-time mothers."

"Melody *is* going to save Cupid." Her mother wore the same resolute expression she used all those years ago when she pushed Melody to win those beauty pageants.

"No pressure, right?" Melody gave a shaky laugh. "Just make it rain."

"No one expects you to do that." Junie Mae smiled. "You've made a wonderful start with the bake-off. We know you'll keep coming up with inventive ways to bring tourists back to town even if this is the worst drought in the history of Jeff Davis County."

"We believe in you," Natalie reiterated. "You won a Clio, after all."

They were hoisting her upon a pedestal. She glanced around the table and saw in their faces — well, except for Delia, who had been around long enough to grow skeptical of everything — that they all truly believed she was going to wave some kind of magic marketing wand and make a silk purse from a sow's ear.

Oh crap, what had she gotten herself into?

"Cupid has been through tough times before and survived." Junie Mae took knitting needles from her handbag and started in on a basket weave scarf. She knitted when she was worried. "With your help, Melody, we'll come out of this with our heads held high."

"What were some of those hard times?" Melody asked, desperate for anything that might light her creative spark.

"When tourism lagged in the forties because of the war, your grandmother Rose was the one who came up with the notion of using the letters that people were leaving in the cave at the foot of the Cupid stalagmite, and making a big mess by the way, to generate additional income for the town," Junie Mae went on.

Melody leaned forward. "How did that come about?"

"Rose set up the mailbox in the botanical

gardens and printed the Cupid letters in the greensheet, and asked local merchants to hand them out for free. You've got to remember that before that happened, the volunteers were posting the answers to the letters on a bulletin board outside the caverns. If you didn't know about the legend and the letters, there was no way for you to find out beyond word of mouth. Once the letters went into the greensheet, they became entertainment and it brought additional customers into the stores looking for the greensheet."

"So Grandma Rose was a forward thinker."

"Once that happened, everything changed. Answering the letters went from a disorganized mess that no one was overseeing to actually bringing in money. Tourism doubled the first year. Tripled the year after that," Junie Mae said. "Your family's romantic legend about Cupid granting your love wish has mythological power."

"Melody knows all this," her mother said impatiently, took the letter from the envelope she'd been toying with, and slipped on her reading glasses. "I've told her the story a hundred times. Let's get down to business."

Yes, she'd heard the story before, but

she'd never really thought about how her grandmother Rose had impacted the town. Now that she was attuned to anything and everything that could help her resurrect tourism, her ears pricked up.

Her mother cleared her throat and started reading the letter. "Dear Cupid . . ."

They went around the table, dividing up the letters to be answered by subject matter. Each woman had a preference for the types of letters they liked to answer. Natalie favored love at first sight and soul mate stories. Great-Aunt Delia offered advice to the widowed dipping into the dating pool again or those with long-term marriage problems, looking to recapture the spark. Because she was a CPA, Carol Ann answered the love letters with a financial twist. Lace took the unrequited love and stories of teenage first love, while Junie Mae responded on issues regarding divorce and blending stepfamilies. Normally, Zoey's domain was friends-to-lovers relationships and forbidden liaisons, so it looked like Melody would be inheriting those topics.

Once they switched their attention from the drought to the letters, everyone relaxed. As she watched the women interact and tease one another, sharing inside jokes she missed out on because she was not a regular part of their community, she felt as if she was standing on top of one of the mountains that overlooked the town, spying on the group through a telescope — far away and out of touch.

She was from them, not of them. She'd changed too much. She was too different. They knew it and she knew it.

And it was a damn long, hard fall off that pedestal.

CHAPTER 10

On Saturday morning, Luke was coming down the steps of the second-floor condo that he rented halfway up the mountain overlooking Cupid, when a white Corvette pulled into the parking lot. He stopped mid-stride, one foot on the top step, the other foot two steps below.

Only one person in town owned a white vintage Corvette.

The driver's door opened and blond hair glinted like gold in the blistering afternoon sunlight. Long tanned legs swung out of the car and a pair of white kitten heels hit the sand-dusted asphalt. Graceful as a ballerina, she stood and shook that fall of gorgeous hair. She wore an ocean blue sundress with skinny little straps that revealed creamy shoulders and arms. The material of her dress rippled in the wind, blowing around shapely legs. She sported oversized dark sunglasses and looked like water — cool, fresh, and thirst quenching. A balmy oasis in the midst of a drought.

He sucked in a bamboozled breath and in a flash he was back in that New York City hotel room with her. It didn't matter what she was wearing because in his mind's eye that cool blue dress was pooling around her ankles and she was as naked as the day she was born.

Yes, he promised her that night in the city was a one-time thing, a red-hot fling not to be repeated, and he liked to think he was a man of his word, but in that moment, he knew it was not a promise he was going to be able to keep.

She raised her eyes and their gazes locked. The smile on her face froze, then wobbled and finally disappeared.

"Hey," he said, doing his damnedest to appear casual, even though his stomach was pitching and rolling. "You looking for me?"

"No, I was not. I did not even know you were here. I came to see about renting a unit."

"The rental office closes at noon on Saturday."

"Oh. Well. I guess I'll have to wait until Monday to get a look at the condo." She turned back toward the car.

"Wait." Luke sprinted down the remainder

of the stairs.

She paused, fingers on the door handle, but she quickly released it. "Ow, hot."

"You *are* in the desert."

"I'd forgotten how quickly things heat up around here." She licked her lips.

He remembered now why he'd purposefully avoided her every time she came back to Cupid for a visit and it was not just because she was a Fant. For over a decade he'd managed to keep a strong padlock on his "Melody" footlocker. He'd dated. A lot. A whole helluva lot, to be factual. He even had a reputation as something of a ladies' man.

But it was all a sham.

He courted a whirlwind of women to keep from thinking about the one he really wanted, the one that got away, and he'd been damn successful at it. So successful he'd begun to believe he was Melody-proof. But that night at the Hilton had shown him how delusional he really was.

And now?

Seeing her looking juicy and succulently ripe in the dry, blistering dearth of their hometown torched any lingering illusion that he possessed self-control.

Memories assaulted him. She was fifteen, he was seventeen. The two of them, riding across the high plains on Maverick, the sorrel mustang he captured and tamed himself, Melody behind him in the saddle, her arms latched around his waist, her legs flapping against his outer thighs, her breasts bouncing into his back as they galloped in the early morning light. A handful of times they'd ridden like that together — before that terrible Fourth of July — Melody slipping away from home to meet him in the mountains at dawn. They disobeyed their families, threw caution to the wind for the sheer joy of being with each other. Riding Maverick turned him on, but with Melody behind him, he never failed to get a rock-hard boner as that long blond hair of hers streamed behind them, a fetching flag of their teenage rebellion.

When the ride was over, she would pull a comb from her back pocket and he'd brush out the tangles for her, eradicating the evidence of their wild adventure, his fingers tingling as he unsnarled the silky strands, her breathing warm and quick. Hot lust always licked through him, seared low and painful in his belly while he ticked off the reasons why he could not do what he wanted so badly to do.

One: She was only fifteen.

Two: This teen beauty queen was destined

for bigger things than Cupid, and his roots ran so deep in Trans-Pecos soil he knew there'd be no transplanting him.

Three: She was from Greenwood-Fant stock and he was a Nielson. Loving her was forbidden. Taboo. In his family it was the worst sin you could commit.

So why had he kept pushing? Kept sneaking off to meet her?

"I'll see you at the Chamber of Commerce meeting on Tuesday," Melody said, snapping him back to the present.

"I could show you my unit," he blurted, and then realized how that sounded and cringed. The woman had the uncanny ability to turn him into a lust-addled idiot.

She lowered her lashes, gave him a half smile. "While I appreciate the generous offer, I think I'll pass. I've already seen your impressive *unit.*"

His neck burned and it wasn't just from the sun beating down, but he couldn't let that comment pass unchallenged. "Too much for you, huh?" he quipped.

She snorted. "Are we really going there?"

"I'm sorry," he backtracked, instantly contrite. "I didn't mean to spin things in that direction and I'm desperately trying to reel it back in."

"I think the fish already got away on that

182

analogy, cowboy," she said, her tone as parched as the desert stretching out around them. "In case you haven't noticed, the water is all dried up."

"I didn't intend to sound like a major jackass. It's just that you . . . I . . . um. What I mean is that whenever I'm around you, my brain goes into reverse and I can't think straight."

"So you're blaming the Beavis and Butt-head antics on me?"

"Yep. You're so gorgeous you reduce me to a tongue-tied imbecile."

"Sounds like a personal problem to me," she said, but her eyes twinkled. She wasn't mad.

"Can we start over?" he asked.

Slowly, she shook her head.

"C'mon, let me show you my condo. If you like it, I'll put you in touch with the person who can get you squared away in a rental this afternoon and you won't have to spend the weekend under your parents' roof."

She hesitated.

"I'm not trying any monkey business to lure you into my lair, if that's what you're thinking."

"It wasn't. You're not *that* obvious."

"What is it then?"

She sized him up for a long moment. "If I move in here do you promise you'll keep your distance?"

"If that's what you really want," he said smoothly. *Don't make more promises you can't keep.*

"It is."

"All right. You have my word."

"Okay then." She waved a hand. "Lead on."

He hurried up the steps ahead of her, fishing in his pocket for the keys. Halfway up, he stopped to make sure she was following him and caught her pushing her sunglasses up on her head so she could get a better look at his ass.

Gotcha. Ha! Her mouth said one thing, but her eyes said another.

Quickly, she glanced away, pretended to be studying the withered cactus planted along the walkway. "You know a drought is bad when prickly pears are dying."

He reached the landing and waited for her to catch up. He could smell her scent, and his nose tingled. Ah, memories. He opened the door, pushed it wide, and stepped aside for her to enter.

The cleaning lady had been there that morning so the place sparkled and the aroma of pine lingered in the air. The small foyer melded into the living area. A brown leather couch and matching loveseat dominated the room and faced the big plate-glass window that looked out over the town below. Nondescript, floor-length beige curtains flanked the window. A Craig Johnson Longmire mystery lay open on the glass coffee table, page side down, and there was a small oak bookcase that ran along the back wall.

Melody moved about the room, inspecting everything, but Luke couldn't take his eyes off her.

"The units — er, condos — come furnished," he said.

"Even the books?"

"No, those are mine."

"You read?"

"Don't act so surprised."

"In high school, you were more interested in chasing girls than in your studies."

Yeah, he might have done his share of chasing, but he'd never caught the one he'd really wanted. "The kitchen is through here," he said, showing her the way.

"What's the total square footage?"

"Thirteen hundred."

"A palace by New York standards."

"Fridge," he said, stating the obvious and draping his arm over the top of the appliance. "Oven. Dishwasher."

"All the essentials." She ran her hand over the backsplash behind the oven. "Love the subway tiles."

His gut tightened. Damn. He was jealous of subway tiles.

"Two bedrooms," he said, leading her from the kitchen to the first bedroom, which he used as a workout room. He'd taken down the bed, but left the dresser for storage and put in a treadmill and weights.

"Two en suite bathrooms. Granite countertops just like in the kitchen." He shut the door and moved down the hall. "And here's the master."

She didn't come into the room, just poked her head around the door frame.

"You can come on in," he said. "I promise your virtue is safe with me."

"Yeah, you said something along those lines in New York and look what happened."

"Um, as I recall, you were the one who kissed me first."

Her face flushed. "You're right. My bad."

"On the contrary, it was very good." He lowered his voice. "I wanted more."

"Luke." She said his name in a way that sent the wrong kind of quiver through his body. "Don't go there."

"What do you mean?" He stalked toward

her. "Why can't we go there?"

"You know. My family. Your family —"

He stopped right in front of her. "Anything between us would set off a powder keg?"

She shrugged. "It has before."

"We're adults now."

"It doesn't erase the past."

"Maybe if we were together it would heal the past. Ever thought about that?"

"Luke, it's more than just our families. My stay here is temporary. I don't belong in Cupid anymore. You do."

"So you're saying —"

"Having sex with you was a huge mistake and under no circumstances are we to repeat it."

"I don't consider it a mistake."

"Well, I guess we'll just have to agree to disagree."

He stepped closer. Toe to toe. She stood her ground. Brave. Stubborn. He liked that about her. "Are you issuing me a challenge?"

She sucked in a deep breath. "On the contrary, I'm stating a fact."

"You're not just playing hard to get?"

"No. I *am* hard to get. In fact, for you, I'm impossible to get."

"That's not how I remember it," he murmured. "Although we did have a lot to drink that night, my mind is pretty clear when it comes to you, Melly. I remember things being real nice and easy."

Her earlobes turned bright pink and she tugged at the left one. "You caught me at a bad time. I had my guard down."

"And now the ramparts have been raised."

"Exactly."

He lowered his head. Their noses were almost touching. "There's no scaling those castle walls?"

"None whatsoever," she declared staunchly, but her hands were trembling.

"Not even if I asked you to let your hair down, Rapunzel?" he whispered.

They stared at each other, the tension in the air between them as thick as a cheese wheel.

"Not even," she whispered back.

"Okay then." He nodded, readjusted his cowboy hat. "If that's the way you want it."

Her chin went down but her lips tipped up, and she nodded. "It's what I want."

"That's all you had to say." He held up both palms, took two steps backward, even though what he wanted most in the world was to scoop her into his arms and persuade those soft pink lips with a hard, demanding kiss.

She raised her arms, her palms above her

shoulders as if she were being held hostage at gunpoint. "Strict hands-off policy."

"The only way I'll touch you again," he drawled, and lowered his eyelids as he gave her his best woman-stunning stare, "is when you beg me to do so, and even then, I might be tempted to let you suffer, just to prove a point."

"Oh, you're full of bravado now, aren't you, big man," she countered in a saucy tone, and she waggled an index finger under his nose. "But I bet if I begged you to take me to bed right now, you wouldn't be able to hold out for five minutes."

"There's an egg timer in the kitchen," he said. "Wanna test me?"

He saw a flash of a grin before she tamped it down and immediately he wondered what he'd done wrong. Maybe he should stop beating around the bush and tell her that, hell no, he didn't agree to her one-time-only fling. He wanted more and he was determined to have her.

Before he could decide if the straight-forward approach was the way to go or not, Melody crossed her arms over her chest and said, "Thank you for showing me your condo, but I don't think this location is going to work for me after all."

Desperate to get to the cute little Holstein pastured across the road from the Rocking N Ranch, a horny Angus bull — unimaginatively named Ferdinand — knocked down the barbwire fence that kept him from the object of his affection and proceeded to have his way with her.

"I know exactly how you feel, old boy," Luke told the bull, who was docile as a lamb now that he'd gotten what he wanted and was back on his side of the property line. "Those fetching women can drive a fella right out of his gourd, but she's a dairy cow and you're from beef cattle stock. Not the best match-up. Next time consider a pretty Hereford."

The bull ran a conciliatory tongue over the block saltlick next to the dried-up stock tank. The cattle version of a cigarette after sex?

It had been hours since his encounter with Melody at the condo, but he couldn't stop thinking about her. Luke ratcheted the pull bar on the wire stretcher, tugging the fence up tight, his biceps bunching with effort. Sweat trickled down his brow and the afternoon sun burned through the top of his straw Stetson. Sand dusted his everyday cowboy boots, turning them from faded black to washed-out gray.

Heat of the day. Granted, not the best time for the chore, but Ferdinand had left him with little choice. Fix the fence pronto or put the dairy herd in a different pasture. Repairing the fence was quicker than a roundup. Although he supposed he could have just moved Ferd to the barn, but the fence would still need fixing and Ferd's placid mood wouldn't last long. Soon enough, that old testosterone itch would come over him again and he'd go back to cantankerous. The bull had busted through more than one barn stall.

Yep. Luke understood. He was feeling a bit grumpy himself. Having Melody withdrawals.

In the distance, a cloud of dirt swirled around a pickup barreling down the one-lane road.

Luke put down the wire stretcher, tugged a red bandana from the back pocket of his Wranglers, and mopped his face. From this distance, he couldn't yet make out whose truck it was. His ranch hands were back at the house, working on the well pump. He prayed the compressor had simply gone out instead of the well running dry, but he suspected the latter.

Damn this drought.

He shaded his eyes with his hand, blocking the sun that managed to filter through the Stetson, and watched the pickup spin closer. White Ford. Blasting Hank Williams through the rolled-down windows. Luke shook his head. Why didn't the old man just get the air conditioner fixed?

The truck skidded to a stop, covering him in a plume of grit.

Luke spat sand, wiped his mouth with the back of his hand.

"Is it true?" his father bellowed, piling out of the pickup without bothering to shut off the engine. Hank was wailing, "Lovesick Blues."

The pickup kept on driving by itself.

"Shit, Dad." Luke leaped to the truck, grabbed the door his father had left standing open, slapped a hand on the steering wheel, and got a foot inside to slam on the brake.

He put the truck in park and killed the engine, cutting Hank off in mid-whine, and turned around to find his father toeing off with him.

"Is it true?" Gil Nielson demanded, blue veins popping out on his temples. He was unshaven and his blue chambray work shirt was rumpled and stained. Was he off his meds?

Luke lowered his voice. Keep calm. If Dad was having a manic episode, slow and quiet was the best way to handle him. "Is what true?"

"You hired Melody Spencer to take over the town?"

"Dad," he said. "She's simply a consultant, trying to help us bring tourist revenue back to Cupid."

"So it is true." His father smacked his forehead with his palm. "You've sold us out!"

"Calm down. I don't know what you've heard, but you're blowing it all out of proportion."

"Are you purposely trying to hurt me, son?"

"No. As mayor, I'm doing what I think is best for Cupid. Melody Spencer is —"

"I don't care what her last name is, she's Greenwood-Fant through and through."

Normally, Luke would drop this thread of conversation like a hot biscuit, but a bullet of anger shot through him. Enough was enough.

"Seriously, Dad, isn't it time we let go of this stupid family feud?"

"Stupid! Stupid!" his father sputtered, his

eyes rolling wild. "If it wasn't for those god-damn Fants your brother would still be alive."

Bomb. There it was. The word bomb.

Luke winced. Fifteen years later and the pain was still sharp as ever. "Holding on to hate isn't going to bring Jesse back. Besides, Jesse is the one who —"

"Don't you dare say a word against him." Dad knotted his hands into beefy fists and shook them in the air. "Jesse was protecting *you.*"

"It wasn't Jesse's battle to fight," Luke said grimly. "We've got to let this thing go before it poisons future generations. It's already wreaked enough havoc. That's part of the reason I hired Melody. To help put an end to this nonsense."

His father's lips flattened and his eyes narrowed stubbornly. "I swear to God sometimes I don't think you're my son. Nielson blood runs through your veins, boy, and don't you ever forget it. You can't go around trusting Fants. Ever. They'll just screw you over in the end."

"Do you realize how ridiculous that sounds? Painting every single member of a family for the last ninety years with the same brush." Why was he even trying? If his father had stopped taking his lithium, there

194

was no talking sense to him.

"Beyond what happened to Jesse, do I need to remind you all the things that the Fants and Greenwoods have done to us over the generations —"

Luke held up his palm. "As if the Nielsons haven't done anything in retaliation? And if we're telling it like it is, why don't we admit that Nielsons were actually the ones who shot the first salvo."

Dad shook his head so hard his jowls quivered. "Of course we retaliated after John Fant made a fool of your great-aunt Elizabeth. We're not cowards. We don't take insults lying down."

"I've hired Melody Spencer," he said stonily. He'd been listening to this kind of stuff his entire life and enough was enough. "Cupid needs her. I suggest you get used to the idea."

His father curled his upper lip in a snarl. "There's nothing that bitch —"

"Don't!" A furious heat blasted Luke in the stomach, spread out through his body like a virus. Yes, his father suffered from a mental illness, but those words had lit Luke's own fuse. There was only so much crap a man could take. He took a step forward, knotted his own hands into dangerous fists. "Don't dare say one word against her."

His father's mouth dropped and his eyes widened. "You're carrying a torch for her!"

"Just because I won't stand for you bad-mouthing her doesn't mean I'm carrying a torch," Luke declared, but he was shaking all over as adrenaline lit up his bloodstream.

"You can't be in love with a Fant!" His father slammed a fist in the palm of his other hand. If they'd been inside, Luke had no doubt he would have put it through a wall. The old man was big on wall punching. The sheetrock in the original family farmhouse had been replaced so many times he'd lost count. But hey, at least Dad punched walls and not people. For the most part.

"There's nothing you could do about it if I were," Luke said.

"I won't stand for you marrying that woman and bringing her to live on the ranch where I raised you kids."

"How did we get from me hiring her to do a job to me marrying her?"

"It's your fault." His father shook his finger under Luke's nose. "You knew better than to take up with a Fant and you did it anyway and your brother is dead because of it. I always suspected you carried a torch

196

for her, but I thought you were smart enough to let it die out and here I find out you're courting her!"

"I'm not courting her, but it's got nothing to do with your disapproval. If I wanted to marry her, I would."

"But you don't?" His father's shoulders slumped and a look of relief passed over his face. "Want to marry her?"

"No. Melody would never be happy in Cupid. Her dreams are too big for that. She's not the kind of woman you can tie down. I don't want to tie her down. It would be like clipping the wings off a butterfly."

Dad splayed his hand over his chest. "Well, thank the Lord for that, you just about gave me a heart attack."

"It's time to stop this hatred," Luke said. "I'm not going to be party to it anymore. I don't want to hear another bad word against a Greenwood or a Fant ever again. Even if they assassinated the governor of Texas."

"You're dishonoring your brother's memory. He's rolling over in his grave."

This fight had been a long time coming and he couldn't help wondering how things would have gone differently between him and Melody if he had the guts to speak his mind to his father back in high school.

"I prefer to think Jesse wouldn't hold a

grudge. He had a short fuse, but he was a reasonable guy once the anger burned off. We don't have to keep perpetuating this feud. It can stop. Peace is possible."

"Jesse's dead because of you," his father declared, decades of suffering dulling the light in his eyes.

Luke understood where his father was coming from, but the accusation hurt as much now as it had the night his father first slung them at him. He sucked up the pain, held it in like a sponge, stood strong. He was tired of trying to please his family. Tired of hating the Greenwoods and Fants because that's what he'd been taught since childhood.

"No," he said. "Jesse is dead because we Nielsons stubbornly cling to this ridiculous feud and unless we learn how to forgive and forget, the past is going to eat us alive."

CHAPTER 11

In the wake of her sexually charged encounter with Luke, the unrealistically high expectation from the community, and the daunting effects of the drought on the land, Melody battled the urge to flee.

Fought it hard.

She didn't have to be here. She left Cupid twelve years ago precisely to escape the fishbowl of small-town life. Realizing she was back in a place where her every move was observed, cataloged, and discussed made her twitchy and claustrophobic. She thought leaving Manhattan would get rid of the baling-wire lungs and eye tics?

Ha! If anything it was worse.

People were counting on her and she'd made a commitment. Leaving wasn't an option. Not until she'd done everything she could to bring tourist revenue back to her hometown. Besides, she didn't have any other job opportunities, and her savings wouldn't last a month in New York.

Jumpstarting the tourist trade was a tall order considering the gaunt condition of the TransPecos. She was in for an uphill battle. Good thing she was a fighter.

In the long run she ended up renting the condo in Luke's complex. Never mind that all two hundred and six bones in her body were screaming, *This is a stupid idea.*

There simply weren't any other rental properties in Cupid that were affordable, available on a month-to-month lease, and came fully furnished. Since Luke only used the condo on those occasions when he didn't want to drive back to his ranch after late-night meetings, maybe she wouldn't run across him much outside of business hours.

Justifications, she knew, but it was all she had to hang on to.

She moved in on Monday. She had only the three suitcases she brought from New York, so it hadn't taken her long to unpack, particularly when Lace and Natalie came over to help and brought a bottle of chardonnay as a housewarming gift. They gossiped and drank wine, ate takeout pizza, and painted the living room a crisp celery color that made her think of salads. Reconnecting with her cousins was one of the best things about coming home. She'd forgotten how much fun they had together.

Tuesday morning was her first meeting with the Cupid Chamber of Commerce board of directors to introduce herself and tell them in person about the cornbread bake-off and her other plans for turning the town's economy around. She was feeling pretty confident about her pitch until she pulled into the parking lot of the restored old train depot that now housed the Chamber of Commerce and she got a call from Teddy.

"Perfect timing," she told him. "I was about to go into a meeting with the mayor and board of directors and I'd love to have more dets on the project to share with them."

Teddy cleared his throat. "Ah, bad news, lamb chop. I'm afraid it's a no go."

Melody cupped a palm around her ear. "Excuse me. The reception out here is horrible. What did you say?"

"The cornbread thing. It's dead in the water. Or in this case, dead in the desert."

Melody sucked in a breath and sweat beaded on her brow in spite of the fact she still had the engine running and the air conditioning blasting. "Why? What happened? You were so enthusiastic about it last week."

"For one thing," Teddy said, "you didn't tell us that the Trans-Pecos was in the grips of a record-breaking drought."

"It's not as dire as it sounds," Melody tried to persuade him even as she surveyed the brittle, desiccated landscape stretching out beyond the train depot. "It is a desert after all. People expect things to be dry."

"Secondly." Teddy made a chiding noise. "You didn't tell us that you were no longer with Tribalgate. I'm disappointed in you, Mel. You're usually so honest."

Honesty was what had gotten her fired. Now not being forthcoming had put her in a jam. "My leave-taking from Tribalgate is very recent." She couldn't bring herself to say the word "fired." Not to him. "Teddy, I —"

"It's fine that you left, but seriously, you should have told us. You've made the executives nervous and you know how that goes. It leaves a bad taste in their mouths, and once they get nervous they run like jackrabbits. Sorry, but there's nothing I can do to change minds."

She let her forehead fall forward against the steering wheel. *Damned if you do and damned if you don't.* "Thanks anyway, Teddy."

202

"Chin up. You'll pull through this. You're the scrappiest woman I know."

"That and five bucks won't even get me a venti frap at Starbucks. Not that there are any Starbucks within two hundred miles of here."

"Don't underestimate yourself," he said. "You'll be back. Just keep your head down and keep working."

"You're sounding dangerously like a fortune cookie."

"Listen, I gotta go."

"Thanks for trying," she said, but he'd already hung up.

Oh joy. Now instead of bringing the board members a basketful of hope, she'd be handing them empty pipe dreams.

For a brief moment, she contemplated putting the Corvette on the highway and simply driving away as far as a tank of gas would get her, but she'd never been the type to run from her problems. She'd made promises, she would have to find a way to make good on them.

Reluctantly, she got out of the car, picked her way over the abandoned train tracks, gravel crunching beneath her heels. Crisis management was one of her strengths. She'd always been able to think fast on her feet, but right now, her mind was a big fat question mark.

When she walked into the building, the receptionist, a round-faced redhead who looked like she was still in high school, hopped up from the front desk.

The girl grabbed hold of Melody's hand — she had a tattoo of a blue dolphin on her wrist — and started pumping it as if she could extract water from her if she kept at it long enough.

"Oh my goodness, Cousin Melody. I am so excited you've come home. I *loved* that commercial where those families were feuding over the last box of Frosty Bites cereal. We all know where you got the inspiration from." She gave an exaggerated wink. "You surely deserved that Clio."

"Remind me again how we're related?"

"I'm the great-granddaughter of Millie Greenwood's youngest sister, Jenny. I was raised in North Carolina, but my folks moved back home to Cupid a few years ago. You were already living in New York by then."

Melody cocked her head. "You're Emma Lee Gossett."

"Did my hair give me away?" She fluffed her curly locks. "I'm the only redheaded Greenwood in five generations. The carrot top comes from my daddy's side."

"Last time I saw you —"

"I was small enough to jump rope with a grasshopper." Emma Lee's grin showed a wide gap between her two front teeth.

"If you don't mind my asking, how old are you now?"

"I'm sixteen. This is my first job 'sides babysittin' and I jest love it."

"Aren't you still in school?"

"Oh yeah, I'm in the work-study program. I work here eight to ten, Monday through Friday mornings, and then take classes the rest of the day."

"Clever girl."

Emma Lee beamed. "I am so in awe of you. I want to be jest like you someday. Livin' in New York City. Makin' a livin' doin' somethin' glamorous like thinkin' up commercials."

"Advertising sounds glamorous, but in all honesty, it's a lot of hard work."

The girl thrust out her chest. "I'm not scared of hard work. You'll learn that 'bout me. If you need anythin', anythin' at all, just whistle and I'll fetch it for you." She let loose with a long, loud whistle to demonstrate.

"Thank you. I appreciate that."

"The board of directors are waitin' for you. Jest go in." Emma Lee fluttered a hand.

Melody glanced at the clock, five minutes to nine. "I thought the meeting didn't start until nine."

"Oh, they were so excited to hear about this Cornbread bake-off thingamabob that they showed up early. Well, except for the mayor." She leaned in to whisper behind her hand. "That man is gorgeous, but he does have a tendency to run late. Then again, he is a Nielson after all and they're the tardiest people on God's green earth. At least that's what my mama says, but I don't get the big deal 'bout why we're supposed to hate Nielsons."

Why would the girl understand the family feud? She had been an infant when the last big incident had occurred and she'd been brought up in North Carolina.

Melody marched in the meeting room armed with a smile and nothing else. Immediately the five board members, whom she'd known her entire life, surrounded her.

They shook her hand and hugged her and told her how proud and excited they were to have her back home and working for them. They plied her with coffee and doughnuts and settled her at the end of the table.

And for a silly minute there she had herself convinced that everything was going to be all right.

Mustachioed, silver-haired Ricardo Gomez, who owned La Hacienda Grill on Main Street, plunked down to her right. The restaurant had been in his family for over seventy-five years. On the walls of his Tex-Mex joint hung pictures of the movie stars who'd dined there — Rock Hudson, Elizabeth Taylor, James Dean, Sal Mineo, and Dennis Hopper while filming *Giant;* Daniel Day-Lewis and the cast of *There Will Be Blood;* Tommy Lee Jones, Javier Bardem, Josh Brolin, and Woody Harrelson from the Coen brothers' version of Cormac McCarthy's *No Country for Old Men.*

Next to Ricardo loomed paunchy Guy Grover, a distant cousin of Melody's who owned the Chevy dealership. Guy was one of those big, colorful men who tended to dominate conversation, made the best backyard barbecue this side of the Pecos River, and bled Dallas Cowboys silver and navy blue.

Across from Guy sat Pat Yamaguchi, the tough-as-dragon-talons female proprietor of Pat's Automotive Repair. She was the youngest of eight, all the rest brothers, and even in her late fifties, she could outshoot, hunt, and fish most any man in Jeff Davis County.

Junie Mae perched beside Pat and she gave Melody a three-fingered wave.

207

The remaining board member, Walker McCleary, a well-to-do pharmacist recently turned *New York Times* best-selling author, bore an uncanny resemblance to Teddy Roosevelt. He was Natalie and Zoey's distant cousin on their father's side. Kids loved him because he gave out bite-sized candies whenever parents had their prescriptions filled at his pharmacy.

They sat there looking at her like she held the keys to a treasure trove.

How was she going to tell them all that the plan she'd come up with to boost tourism had withered and died on the vine? Just like everything else in the godforsaken valley. She hadn't even started her new job and already she was a failure.

The door opened and Luke stalked in, the diminutive mayoral executive assistant, Eloise Harbinger, trotting behind him.

"Got hung up at the hay barn. Sorry I'm late." Luke flashed a charming, I-know-you-all-forgive-me smile around the room.

Her pulse galloped. Seriously? She was going there? Oh, come on.

He wore starched Levi's with a razor-sharp crease and handmade cowboy boots. As he moved, he rolled down the sleeves of his white business shirt and buttoned the cuffs over thick manly wrists, and then he

208

paused to shrug into the suit jacket that Eloise held out for him.

Melody tried not to stare, but she couldn't seem to wrench her gaze away. He doffed his straw Stetson, dropped it onto the table, and ran a tanned hand through mussed hair, dislodging bits of hay in the process.

Eloise busied herself running a lint roller down his back, picking up bits of straw on the sticky paper.

He caught Melody watching him and his eyes darkened as he swiveled his head to take her in. An impish grin plucked at the corners of his mouth and deepened the dimple in his chin.

Was that a smudge of blush-pink lipstick on his neck?

He'd been kissing someone.

She put a hand to her stomach, sank deeper into the chair cushion. Gut punched. She felt gut punched.

That was fast. Just a week ago he'd been having sex with her, and now he was already kissing — or worse — some other woman.

She curled her fingers, jabbing her nails into her palms, and swallowed back the burn of bile. She was not jealous. There was nothing to be jealous about. Their time together had been brief, no strings attached, and that's the way she wanted it. The man could kiss anyone in a hayloft that he chose to kiss. It was none of her concern.

She could not care less about Luke Nielson's sex life. But good grief, he'd already been for a roll in the hay so early in the morning? What? Did he drink Viagra in his morning coffee?

No, not jealous at all.

Eloise plucked a Kleenex from her pocket, passed it to Luke, and motioned to a spot on her own neck that corresponded to the lipstick spot on his. Without even looking sheepish, he wiped away the lipstick, crumbled up the Kleenex, and tucked it into his pocket.

Melody pulled her bottom lip up between her teeth and bit down lightly, felt the hot vein at her temple throb.

He sank down into his seat at the head of the table, directly opposite from where she was sitting. Eloise landed on the edge of the chair beside him, a small tablet computer in her lap. She appeared prepared to leap to his next beck and call.

"Are we ready to get started?" Melody asked.

"You're the consultant." He swept a hand. "Take the bull by the horns."

"All right." She got to her feet and glanced around the table at the five business owners. Everyone looked at her expectantly.

Except for Luke, he was looking at her as if . . . well . . . as if he wanted *her* lipstick stains on his neck. Greedy man.

Realizing she'd gotten trapped in his gaze again, she broke eye contact and addressed the group at large. "I'm afraid I've got unfortunate news."

That sent a murmur of alarm around the room.

"Because of the drought Quaker is rescinding their sponsorship of the cornbread bake-off and music festival I proposed to them." She left out the part about Quaker being unhappy with her for not telling them she'd left Tribalgate. Was that dishonest? She ran a hand down the column of her throat.

Guy grunted. "Another one bites the dust. We should have known it was too good to be true."

"What do you mean?" Melody asked. "Is there something I need to know?"

"Two weeks ago, Universal Pictures backed out of discussions to turn my biography of my uncle August McCleary into a movie," Walker said glumly. "It was a big blow."

"We were anticipating an economic boon because of that movie," Ricardo lamented, his eyebrows dipped in a woeful expression. "Most of the area merchants have already put a small fortune into sprucing up their businesses. Myself included."

"Plus with the water level in Lake Cupid disappearing, we've had to cancel all the water-related, income-generating summer activities." Junie Mae sighed. "It's a disaster."

"I'm sorry," Melody apologized, feeling responsible even though it was not her fault. The drought was beyond her control, but she'd let them down by losing the Quaker deal.

"Son-of-a-hog-tying-bitch," Guy exclaimed, and pounded a hammy fist on the table.

"Can't we hold them to their sponsorship?" Pat asked. "Threaten legal action? Hit them in the wallet, I always say."

"The agreement was verbal. They hadn't yet signed the contract," Melody explained.

"But the Food Network celebrities are still coming, right?" A hopeful smile wavered at the corner of Junie Mae's mouth. "I do so love Bobby Flay."

Slowly, Melody shook her head. No Quaker, no music festival, and no trio of Food Network celebrity judges. No music, no celebrities, no spectators. No spectators, no additional tourists coming into town, and ultimately no tourists, no Cupid. It was the town's only real source of revenue.

"But . . . but . . . I have already spent over ten thousand dollars on improving the restaurant." Ricardo tapped his fingers rapidly against his palms. "I have *niños* in college."

"I know it's a blow, but we'll think of a way out of this." She had no idea what that solution was, but she had to trust her creative process. It rarely failed her. A solution would come to her if she just gave it time.

Except the sands of the hourglass were draining out quickly for Cupid.

"This drought is going to ruin us all." Junie Mae patted her severely hair-sprayed coif. "You know it's bad when people are going three months or longer between haircuts and skipping massages all together."

"Everybody take a deep breath," Luke said.

"Easy for you to say," Ricardo bemoaned. "Your income doesn't hinge on tourism."

"I brought Melody here, didn't I? Just calm down. We'll make it through this if we all pull together. Unity is the key."

Melody scowled. "Platitudes don't solve

problems."

"Neither does panic. We can't let ourselves get caught up in a negativity spiral." Luke cocked back casually in his chair, interlaced his fingers, and cupped the back of his head in his palms, looking far too nonchalant for the occasion.

"So what do you suggest we do?" She sank her hands on her hips.

"Try to relax. We've been through worse times."

"Name one," Guy Grover snapped.

"The Depression."

"That was before our time and besides, the whole country was in the same boat." Guy planted his elbows on the table.

"What about when Olive Cooksey embezzled half a million dollars from the town coffers. That was a pretty big deal," Luke pointed out.

"Pierce Hollister saved us there," Walker said.

"Damn straight." Guy waggled a finger at Melody. "There's your answer. Put together another fund-raiser with Pierce as the headliner."

"I was already planning to ask Pierce to be the master of ceremonies for the bakeoff. Now we need a new venue for him to star in. I can't just put Pierce on an auction

214

block and raffle him off to the highest bidder. Lace wouldn't like that very much," Melody said.

"Too bad." Pat shook her head so fiercely the ends of her blue-black pageboy slapped the side of her wrinkled chin. "I'd bid on him."

"You know," Luke drawled. "That's not a bad idea."

"What?" Melody raised her eyebrows.

"A bachelor auction. Pierce couldn't be in it obviously, since he's not a bachelor but —"

"Are you offering your services?" she asked, purposely putting him on the spot.

"Would you bid on me if I did?" His voice turned silky and his eyelids lowered to half-mast.

Seriously? After he'd just kissed some other woman in a hayloft, he had the audacity to flirt with her? The turkey.

And yet her damn womb undulated as a sweltering heat slid underneath her skin. She was not falling for his smooth moves. No way. She refused to be seduced. "A Fant bid on a Nielson? That's like asking a Hatfield to bid on a McCoy. Pure blasphemy."

"Ah, c'mon now." He flashed her a dazzling smile. "You're not going to let something as silly as a century-old family feud get in the way of the town making a little money, are you? Because it's past time to put that mess to bed."

Bed.

The word hung suspended as his gaze latched on to hers again, and for some unfathomable reason she could not force herself to glance away. That single word conjured dozens of erotic images from their night together, the pictures coming so hard and fast it was like flash-flipping through the pages of the *Kama Sutra* — the Rocking Horse, the Glowing Triangle, the Padlock, the Bridge, the Reverse Cowgirl, the Nirvana.

"No," she said firmly, a seedling of an idea planting roots in the back of her mind. "Not at all, in fact if we want to bring tourists to the town, I think the opposite is what we need. It's time to stir the feud up again."

"What!"

Ah, no longer Mr. Cool. "You heard me."

Luke jumped to his feet and stalked around the table to where she stood, his warm masculine scent, all hay and leather and sun and sand, wrapping around her like a force to be reckoned with.

Well, that had certainly pushed his buttons. She'd never seen him move so fast or look so powerful. An electric thrill flipped along every nerve ending in her body, lighting her up like Christmas.

The board members glanced from Luke to Melody and back again, obviously awaiting fireworks. Eloise pushed her glasses up on her nose, and clutched her tablet computer with both hands.

He stepped closer, crowding her personal space, coming within inches of touching her, but she wasn't about to back up or appear intimidated.

Goose bumps blanketed Melody's arms and her throat tightened.

The impulse to reach out and touch him, to bridge the gap that time and distance had created between them, took hold of her. But she could not. She wouldn't be here for very long and he would never leave. Besides, he was a Nielson and she was a Greenwood-Fant, and it was the original obstacle to a relationship that had never progressed beyond the tender bud stage. They could not change who they were. No amount of wishing could alter their DNA.

Ah, but if they were not in the fishbowl of Cupid, would it even matter that their families had hated each other for generations?

His face had gone stony as the Davis Mountains rising outside the window, all hard lines and angles, impossible to read. A faint half-moon scar curved out of his right eyebrow.

She knew how he'd gotten that scar because she'd been the one to give it to him. Fourth grade. Fencing match with cheap metal curtain rods with the rubber tips missing. Cloakroom of the First Baptist Church of Cupid when they played hooky from Sunday school.

"I must have misheard you all the way across the room. Did you say you wanted to resurrect our family feud?"

"I did."

"You want to cause more trouble, light a match to that stale old gasoline?"

Melody squared her shoulders, notched her chin up. "I do."

His nostrils flared. "Why in God's name would you want to do something so divisive?"

"There's a reason why *Romeo and Juliet* is the most poignant love story ever told."

"Yeah? What's that?" he growled.

All right, he looked pissed, but at least he'd asked the question. She'd intrigued him, which was more than she expected. "It's also the same reason why John Fant and Millie Greenwood's romance spawned not only a legend, but a tradition that has brought money into Cupid for almost a century. You can't ignore that kind of mass appeal."

"I've taken the bait," he said. "Time for you to set the hook if you want to reel me in. What are you talking about?"

She held his stare. "Forbidden love."

"What about it?"

"That's the emotional appeal."

"Forbidden, huh?" His sexy gaze drifted to her lips.

"Yes. You know how it goes, the more forbidden something is, the more you want it." She was spinning this on the spur of the moment. Had no idea where she was going with it, but it was the right path, she felt it in her gut.

"Is that so?"

"Uh-huh," she murmured, momentarily forgetting about everyone else in the room.

"Which is why I can't ever lose weight on a diet," Walker interjected. He took off his glasses and rubbed the lenses on the tail of his cotton shirt. "Cupcakes kept calling my name. Tell me that I can't have something and I'll move heaven and earth to get it."

"Proving my point," she said, unable to drop Luke's stare.

"What does forbidden love have to do with the town's financial difficulties?" Luke

219

drilled her with his hot gaze.

"It's the solution." Or at least she hoped it was.

"How's that?"

"It takes advantage of both the legend and the family feud. Play it up. We stage a reenactment of the major events that formed the town, including the love triangle between John Fant and Millie Greenwood and Elizabeth Nielson. We could even put on a *Family Feud*–inspired game show."

"Sounds kind of limited," skeptical Guy said.

"Not if we have it as a running stage play at the True Love Performance Hall. Do you realize how many movies have been made about the Hatfields and McCoys legend? Why is that?"

"Controversy?" Junie Mae asked hopefully.

Melody pointed a finger at her. "Exactly. Conflict creates emotion and emotion is the reason anyone partakes of entertainment. It makes them feel something."

"I'm feeling something right now," Luke said, "and it's not congeniality."

"It's a good idea," she said staunchly.

"It's a disaster is what it is. We are not poking the embers of that seething fire." Luke's eyes narrowed to angry slits.

"Why not?" Walker asked, putting his polished glasses back on. "Sounds entertaining to me. There's a Hatfields and McCoys dinner theater in Pigeon Forge, Tennessee. We could have something like that here."

"You're not a Nielson who has been wronged by Fants for generations," Luke said. "That's why not."

"So it's all the Fants' fault?" Melody challenged. "Who was it that burned down Zeke Fant's —"

"This is exactly why we're not using the family feud to spur tourism. It would divide the town all over again. It's dangerous. People could get hurt. I'm the mayor and we're keeping things nice and peaceful. End of discussion." Luke made a motion like a football referee declaring the play was no good.

"But you brought me here to turn things around and now you don't even want to consider my recommendation?" Melody asked.

"Not on something this inflammatory, no." His eyes darkened and he didn't say it out loud, but she knew he was thinking about that horrible night that ruined everything that might have once been possible between them.

"You're afraid to take chances, afraid to

rock the boat," she challenged, knowing full well they weren't just talking about the matter at hand. They'd had a very similar discussion back in high school, when she'd wanted to make their relationship public.

"And you'll do anything to make a buck," he declared.

She hissed in a breath through clenched teeth.

"Oh now, Luke," Junie Mae said. "That's just mean. Melody is only trying to help."

"That's okay, Junie Mae. He's right. Making money is important to me. I've never made a secret of my desire to make something of myself," she said.

"Meaning I didn't make something of myself?" Luke's voice was flint.

She shrugged, but her heart was slamming against her rib cage. "I didn't say that."

"There's more to life than money," he grumbled.

"Um." Ricardo raised a hand. "I have five kids to feed and send to college. I'm all for making money."

"I'm just spitballing here," Melody said, backing down. She hadn't meant to upset him, but the drought had everyone on edge. They had the same goal. She had to remember they were on the same side. They just had different ideas on how to achieve that goal. "I'm not married to the idea."

Luke swung his head toward Ricardo. "There's other ways to make money without digging up old hurts that are better off staying buried."

"Like what?" Junie Mae ventured.

"A bachelor auction for one thing."

Melody fake yawned and covered her mouth. "Why not throw in a Sadie Hawkins dance along with it? Yee haw."

"Why, that sounds like a splendid idea," Luke retorted, obviously still irritated with her. "A bachelor auction followed by a Sadie Hawkins dance."

"It was a good idea in 1937 maybe," Melody said.

"That's the whole allure of our little hamlet," Luke argued. "Cupid takes people back to a kinder, gentler time."

"Well," Junie Mae said. "Except for the feud. Nothing kind and gentle about that."

"Precisely." Luke nodded. "You should know this, Melody. You're in marketing. When you're trying to persuade someone to buy something you don't list the product's negative qualities."

"Why don't we take a vote on it?" she asked. "All for reenacting the —"

"We're not reenacting the day your great-grandfather stood my great-grandmother up at the altar and slashed the first cut in a wound that's lasted ninety years. That's not up for negotiation."

"Who died and made you king?" She narrowed her eyes. "Last time I read the town charter, the position of mayor wasn't a dictatorship."

"No, but I'm the one who'll have to stay here and pick up the pieces from the fallout, while you flit back to New York once you get finished licking your wounds."

He had her there. She would not be here long-term. If he was going to be this touchy about her suggestions, why had he asked her here in the first place? "Okay, that's great, but we'll need something more than a bachelor auction. Something that has appeal beyond our own small borders."

"And it can't be water-related," Junie Mae reminded.

"You're right." Melody tapped an index finger against her chin. "We'll have to play to our strengths. What do we have an abundance of that others might be interested in?"

"Sand," Guy said. "We've got a ton of that, but who'd be interested in it, I have no idea."

"The starriest night sky in the United States," Walker added.

"All right. That's something to work with. It's not as Cupid specific as the legend and the family feud, but okay. Let's brainstorm," she encouraged. "What activities can we center around sand and stars?"

"VIP stargazing party at McDonald Observatory," Ricardo suggested. "With celebrity guests. There is where Pierce could help. I could cater the event."

Junie Mae waved. "I know, I know, what if it's a masquerade stargazing event? People love dressing up. A night of mystery under the stars."

"I like the way you think." Melody noted the suggestions on her tablet.

"Now that the stars are taken care of, what could we do with the sand?" Pat asked.

"Ooh." Melody snapped her fingers. "We could hold an all-terrain vehicle rally. Start with qualifying heats to bring in serious racers, but also have fun runs for the casual enthusiast."

"We could have several categories. Dune buggies. Utility ATVs. Sport models. Side by sides." Walker shifted in his seat.

"Yes." Ricardo clapped. "We could have a youth division. One for seniors. A ladies-only ride."

"What about various other competitions along with the races like load hauling or winch tug of war?" Pat proposed.

Melody grinned, loving how everyone had taken her idea and run with it. She looked to Luke. "What do you think?"

"I like it." He nodded, a smile creeping back to his face. "We could also have team races in the side-by-side category. But there's a kicker. The teams are selected by random lottery."

Junie Mae cringed. "I smell trouble. What if a Fant or Greenwood gets picked to be on a team with a Nielson? That could be a disaster."

"That's the point of the random draw. To promote harmony in the community. We'll make it a stipulation of entry. If anyone kicks a fuss up about it, they'll be disqualified."

"That's aggressive," Walker said.

"Yeah, well I'm aggressive about stamping out this stupid feud. Enough is enough." He flicked his gaze to Melody. "Peace or else."

"All right." She shrugged. "If you're willing to draw the line in the sand, let's go for it. Random draw it is."

"Get to it then." Luke picked up his cowboy hat. "I've got another appointment. I'll see you folks later."

He sauntered past Melody, boots scraping

against the wooden floors, his scent wafting over her in seductive waves. How did he manage to smell so darn good? Did he bathe in eau de manhood?

"Oh, and by the way." He stopped at the door, turned back to address the room. "All board members are required to participate in the events in one capacity or another and that means you too, Melody. In any case, I'm going to be racing my new side by side."

"Mayoral edict?" Melody arched an eyebrow.

"If that's the way you want to put it, sure. Go ahead." He settled his Stetson on his head. "We lead by example and it's time we presented a unified front."

CHAPTER 12

"Mayoral edict, my fanny," Melody huffed as she paced the small kitchen of her condo. Luke had hired her for her expert opinion and then blatantly ignored her marketing advice. What the hell was that all about? She was right about using the feud to boost tourism, and every bit of the marrow in her bones knew it.

On the counter sat a Lean Cuisine frozen entrée that she'd nuked for dinner, but hadn't been able to eat because she was so irritated. Why had he hired her if he was going to tie her hands behind her back? The drought was a brutal enough enemy without Luke aligning himself against her.

Maybe he was miffed because she refused to continue their affair. Was he really that petty? The boy she'd once known was not, but this man? Never mind that she'd seen him naked and licked his body, she didn't really know him all that well.

She pushed her hair off her forehead with her palm, picked up the plastic container, and took a bite of butternut squash ravioli. Mmm, pretty good.

Her cell phone rang. Tossing the dinner aside, she grabbed for it. Maybe it was Luke calling to apologize for being a giant horse's ass.

But it was Teddy on the other end, not Luke. That was a surprise.

"Hello?" she answered.

"Lamb chop, how are you doing?"

"Still scraping my spirits up off the floor after our conversation this morning, but I'll bounce back."

"I know you will."

"Thanks for the vote of confidence. I'm a little shaky on that myself. I figure if I keep telling myself I'll bounce back, then I will."

"The old fake it till you make it."

"Works pretty good, by and large. What's up?"

"Listen, I felt so badly about having to pull the trapdoor on you, just wanted to call and make sure you were okay."

"I appreciate it."

"Did you need to talk about what happened at Tribalgate? It had to be pretty traumatic for you to pull up stakes and leave the city for the hinterlands of Southwest Texas."

She took a deep breath and told him why she'd gotten fired.

"That was harsh."

"You're telling me."

"I bet there's more to the story than you were told. Probably office politics. You know you could have fought it. Gotten a lawyer. Those grounds for your dismissal sound flimsy to me."

"I don't want to work at a place that's forced to keep me. They'd find ways to make my life miserable."

"True that, but now you're all the way and gone to Texas."

"I know." She paused. "Teddy?"

"Uh-huh?"

"Could I ask you a question?"

"Shoot."

She told him about her idea for using the family feud to bring tourism back to Cupid. "What do you think about that idea? And please be honest."

"I like it. Great marketing hook."

"So do I. Not only because it has pathos, but because I think sweeping the feud under the rug is what's kept it simmering beneath the surface all these years, ugly, dark, and ready to explode at a moment's notice."

"This is that lovely little town you were trying to get us to invest in?" He laughed. "Lamb chop, you are audacious."

"It's a good town. Full of good folks. Which is why this drought is breaking my heart. I've got to do something. They're valiant people but they're struggling. The problem is the mayor. The very guy who hired me to come down here and help them put together some kind of marketing plan to lure tourists back to the Davis Mountains. He's standing in the way." Briefly, she told him about Luke and the opposition he had to her plan.

"Is there a way to go behind his back and call attention to this feud in an indirect manner?" Teddy asked.

"Not really," she mused.

"Didn't you tell me something about letters to Cupid? Is there something you can use to —"

"Oh, Teddy!" she exclaimed. "You're a genius."

"I am?"

"Yes! Why didn't I think of this before? I'll write a letter to Cupid pretending to be a young girl whose love life is affected by the feud. The letters get printed in the local greensheet. If I can generate a little interest from that, I'll have proof to back me up."

"Get that stuff on social media if you can. Remember you have twenty-five thousand followers on Twitter. That shit's gold."

He was right.

"Is it too underhanded, do you think?" she worried.

"Maybe a little, but that's the business. It's a move that would make Tribalgate proud."

"You've got a point."

"Go for it. You know what they say."

"What's that?"

"It's easier to get forgiveness than permission."

After her conversation with Teddy, Melody was fired up, and convinced her plan — along with her strong following on social media — would generate the kind of buzz that would get noticed. First, she needed a special envelope, one that would be easy to spot at the committee meetings.

She left the condo and drove down the mountain into town. She parked at the Chamber of Commerce and strolled over to a small gift shop on Main Street that mostly sold cards, souvenirs, and knickknacks. The owner, Christy Hanson, was just closing up the shop when Melody arrived.

"Sure, come on in," the woman said,

ushering her inside. "I need every penny I can scrape together. Another month like this one and I'm not sure how much longer I can keep the doors open."

"But you've been in this location since I was a little kid," Melody protested.

"Drought's eating me alive." Christy clucked her tongue. "I'm thinking of selling everything and moving up to Fort Worth to live with my daughter, but who in the heck would buy me out?"

"Maybe it will rain soon," Melody said because she had no idea what else to say. People like Christy were the reason why she'd decided to go behind Luke's back. Maybe it was underhanded. Yes, okay, it *was* underhanded and he might be upset with her when he learned what she'd done, but the rewards outweighed the risks, and as Teddy pointed out, getting Luke's forgiveness would be easier than getting him to approve of her plot.

She bought two boxes of red silk envelopes and matching stationery so the letter would stand out at the Cupid letter committee and she could easily snatch it out of the stack. Not because she needed two boxes, but because it was one small thing she could do for Christy. She thanked her and went to her cubbyhole office at the Chamber of

Commerce and got down to work.

It took her numerous drafts to come up with a letter she thought struck the right note and when she looked up, she was surprised to see it was nine o'clock at night. She rubbed her eyes and read through the letter one last time.

Dear Cupid,

I'm in love! He's my soul mate, my one true love. This should be a happy time, right? But here's the deal. Our families hate each other. We're talking bone-deep, Hatfields and McCoys hatred. My guy and I know we belong together, but there's no way our kin will stand for it. We can't quit each other, but neither can we fan the flames of a long-standing family feud. We feel as if we're sitting on a powder keg with a lit fuse. One false move and we'll be blown to bits. What should we do? Break up or destroy our families?

— Modern Day Juliet

Okay. She took a deep breath, and sealed the letter in the red silk envelope. She tucked the boxes of stationery in her desk drawer, left the Chamber of Commerce, and walked the half mile to the botanical gardens.

Once inside the gardens, Melody dropped the fictional letter into the white wooden box stenciled with "Letters to Cupid" in bold block font. The letterbox glowed like a congenial ghost in the pale moonlight. Beside the box was a posted sign detailing the letter-writing rules.

1. All letters should be submitted using a pseudonym.
2. Letters will be answered within one week.
3. Letters of a sexually graphic nature will not be published.
4. The letters are for entertainment purposes only.
5. The town of Cupid is not to be held responsible for what the letter writers do with the advice.

A spider of doubt crawled up the back of her neck. Her plan had better succeed.

If it didn't, the Fant-Nielson feud might never end, although it might not matter anyway because the drought could destroy them all.

She cast a nervous glance back at the box, too late for second-guessing. It was done.

Except she saw that a corner of the red envelope protruded from the slit in the letterbox. Not too late. She could still grab hold of it, pull it out, rethink her plan, and see if she could find some other course of action that did not involve dishonesty.

Not too late, the corner of the envelope tempted. *There's still time to change your mind.*

She rubbed her fingers together. What to do? Flick the letter deeper into the box or pluck it out, quit her job, and just walk away from Cupid? But see, here was the thing, even though she'd slid all the way down the rainbow back to where she started, she was not a quitter. Surrender simply was not in her DNA.

Was she really dithering?

The corner of the red envelope taunted, accusing her. She'd learned her lesson well from Michael Helmsly. Showmanship was the only thing that mattered. Put truth on the shelf behind a box of sodium bicarbonate and forget about it.

Doggedly, she thumped the corner of the envelope, sending it sinking out of sight into the depths of the letterbox.

There. Decision made.

Ready to trek back to her car, she dusted her palms, and pivoted on her heel, only to be stopped in mid-step by a rustling noise. Her stomach flew up into her throat and the baling-wire sensation squeezed her chest. What was that?

The bushes shook.

Javelina?

Even though she'd grown up in this arid terrain, she'd never really felt part of it, nor had she, like the majority of Cupid's citizens, grown shoulder-shruggingly accustomed to the wild javelina hogs that roamed the area. At heart, she was a city girl through and through. Give her smoggy traffic, bustling crowds, and even the occasional mugger, over desert drought, meddlesome family members, and unpredictable wildlife.

"Problems with your love life?" A throaty male voice cut through the night, wrapped around her like a hug.

Slowly, Melody swiveled her head in the direction of the rich baritone. Fear sped along her nerve endings to imbed deeply into her brain. Who was he? How much had he seen?

Stupid!

She was laying everything on the line and yet she hadn't been sharp enough to scope out the gardens to see if anyone was lurking among the plants before posting her letter. Was she secretly self-destructive? Her former boss would say yes.

From behind a thicket of Spanish broom shrubbery, which were alive in this drought solely due to Lace's innovated water conservation measures, Luke stepped from the shadows.

His Stetson was tipped back on his head, revealing the adorable cowlick that insisted on flopping across his forehead. Tempting as sin, and twice as handsome. Honestly, running an ultra-marathon while going braless beneath a burlap shirt would chafe less than his smug, knowing smile. One hand went to his hip, casual, nonthreatening.

She felt threatened anyway, tossed her head, sniffed. Haughty. Whenever she felt threatened, she defaulted to haughty. She knew it, wasn't proud of it, but there it was.

"Well?" he prodded.

"I have no idea what you're talking about."

"You just mailed a letter to Cupid." He stepped closer, his straight white teeth flashing seductively in the dark. He knew how to get to her. Just flashed that charming grin and expected her to liquefy.

"I didn't," she denied, and thought about deception and sticky webs woven.

"I could have sworn I saw you slip one into the slot."

"Not me." She shrugged, tried to ignore

her racing heart.

"You sure? 'Cause I'm pretty sure I saw a letter in your hand."

"You might want to get your eyes checked. I have zero interest in writing letters to Cupid."

"So there's no old lost love you want to reclaim?" he teased.

"Nope."

"If you didn't just mail a letter then why are you standing beside the letterbox looking guilty?"

"I do not look guilty." Her stomach contracted. Forget that. She went on the offensive, answering a question with a question. "What are *you* doing here?"

He stared at her for a long moment, before his hot gaze flicked low to take her in with a leisurely eye stroll. She suppressed a shudder, wishing she wore a down ski suit instead of white capri pants, sandals, and a lavender paisley-patterned handkerchief halter top. Melody concentrated on not breathing so he couldn't watch her breasts sliding up and down, but she couldn't hold out for long. Finally, she breathed in a gulp of air.

His eyes darkened. "Maybe I'm here to ask Cupid's help with my love life."

She snorted. "Praying that you don't catch

herpes?"

"Ouch." Playfully, he clutched the left side of his chest. "Stab me through the heart, why don't you?"

"You have to have a heart to get stabbed in it."

"You're saying I'm heartless?"

"I'm saying you wouldn't know real love if it bit you in the butt."

He raised an eyebrow, one side of his mouth quirking up in a sardonic expression. "And you would?"

Honestly? No. Her workaholic tendencies saved her from that fate. "More so than you."

"Because you volunteer for the committee that answers the letters to Cupid?"

"Yes."

He laughed.

"Are you making fun of me?"

He gave a one-shoulder shrug. "Why so sensitive?"

"Who says I'm sensitive?"

"Okay, insecure. Like that better?"

She bristled. "I'm neither sensitive nor insecure."

"And yet you're calling *me* out on love." He canted his head.

Damn, why did he have to be so gorgeous? "Why are we talking about this?"

"Because we're in a garden in moonlight. Sounds almost biblical. Can you imagine Adam and Eve's conversations?"

"I see no point in doing that."

"Really?" He gave her The Look, and doffed his Stetson.

That patented expression had made her weak-kneed in ninth grade. The one he'd no doubt perfected in the crib and was at least partially responsible for the hordes of women who threw themselves at his feet on a daily basis. The Look was part come-hither, part I've-got-eyes-only-for-you, and most potently of all, I'm-such-a-bad-boy-in-bed-when-I-make-love-to-you-you'll-know-you've-been-well-and-truly-fu—

It wasn't an idle promise. She'd been to bed with him. He could back up that smile. *Stop thinking like this!*

"No secret Garden of Eden fantasies?"

"Nope," she fibbed.

He leaned in and set a tripwire of goose bumps detonating over her skin. "I've come a lot closer to love than you have."

"Uh-huh." She backed up a step, shook her head. "Sure you have."

"Well, maybe I haven't so far, but I want to."

A short bark of laughter shot from her lips. "That's rich."

"What?" he said. "You sound skeptical. I'm serious."

"Since when have you ever been hard up for love? You can have any woman you want."

He closed the gap she'd created between them, narrowed his eyes. The moon shone down, bathing his blond hair in a gossamer glimmer.

Her pulse revved. Involuntarily, she placed a palm over her chest. *Seriously? You're letting him affect you that much?*

"Not any woman," he murmured.

She hardened her chin. "What would your girlfriend say about that?"

He looked puzzled. "What girlfriend?"

"You had lipstick on your neck at the board meeting this morning and hay all over your clothes. I just assumed she was your girlfriend."

"Oh that." His eyes twinkled. "You've been going around thinking I had a girlfriend? No wonder you've been standoffish. It's not what you think."

"You don't owe me any explanation. We're not dating."

"The lipstick smear came from Carly's daughter, Haley. That little girl is a pistol. She's three going on thirty. Carly and her family were in town, visiting from Marfa.

Haley got into her mother's makeup, realized she was going to get a scolding, and hid out in the hayloft. Uncle Luke volunteered to coax her down."

She could see him crawling into a hayloft, convincing a little girl she wasn't in trouble and to come on out. Her insides went all gooey at the image. The lipstick had come from his niece. She couldn't help smiling. "Really?"

"What?" He pretended to be offended. "You thought I was bedding you one week and a week later going at it with someone new?"

"I've heard the talk around town. You do have a reputation as a ladies' man. It was not an illogical assumption."

He leveled her a hot look. "I've enjoyed being a bachelor, no doubt about it, but when I'm with a woman, I'm with her. Got it?"

"Why should I care?" Dammit, why did her voice have to sound so reedy, needy? "We're not together."

"We could be."

"A lot of things could be. For instance the government could do away with the IRS."

"Creative way of saying it's never going to happen?"

"We've had this discussion already."

"Hey." He spread his palms wide. "Can't blame a guy for trying."

"Well, I could, but it's not going to stop you, is it?"

"Probably not."

What did he mean by that? Melody straightened, put starch in her spine. "Good luck with your love quest."

She turned to go. He moved quickly, blocking her path. In spite of his blondness, he looked dark and edgy.

"What do you want, Mayor?" Her heart skipped a beat — or three.

"You know."

She moistened her lips. "Not gonna happen."

"Why not?" he asked cheerfully. "Do you remember the time —"

"Nope," she cut him off. If her old boss could see her now, he'd be impressed at how easily she dispensed with the truth.

"Under the bleachers —"

"Wasn't me."

"I could have sworn it was you."

"You've had so many girlfriends, it's no wonder you can't keep them all straight."

"Is that why you pulled the plug on us? You were worried about all the women I've been with? I always use a condom, I swear, and I get a medical checkup once a year."

A faraway look came into his eyes. What was he thinking? She gulped and drew in air but couldn't seem to fill up her lungs. "You never did answer my question. What are you doing here?"

"Taking a walk, just like you."

"Have you been stalking me again?" she teased.

"I saw your car was still parked in the Chamber of Commerce parking lot. I wanted to apologize about this morning. I acted like a jerk, plus there was something else I wanted to discuss with you. So I walked over from the courthouse, but you weren't there. I was headed back to my car when I saw you going into the gardens."

"Luke," she whispered, turned away. "Please."

He took her elbow, turned her back to face him, dropped his Stetson to the ground, rested his forehead on hers. "Please what?"

"Please don't. I —" She closed her eyes. She couldn't keep staring at him. It hurt too much, wanting him, knowing it was better to resist than give in to the hot desire pushing relentlessly at her.

"Melly." He pressed his lips to the smooth spot between her eyebrows.

She wrenched away from him, rushed for the exit. "I have to go."

"Wait," he said, coming after her. "I'll walk you back to your car."

She didn't wait. In fact, it was all she could do not to run. He took two long-legged strides, caught up with her, fell into step beside her.

"Really," she said. "I have no need for an escort. As you've pointed out to me before, this is Cupid, not New York City. Safe as can be."

"That's not entirely true. There's javelinas and mountain lions and —"

"Lions and tigers and bears, oh my. I'm a big girl, Luke. I can take care of myself." But even as she said it, she couldn't help feeling safer just having him beside her. She was afraid of those little javelina suckers.

"Uh-huh," he said.

Terrific. What now? She couldn't think of a thing to say. Only the sound of their footsteps on the soft asphalt punctuated the quiet. Finally, she couldn't stand the silence any longer.

"What was it you wanted to discuss with me?"

He stopped in front of La Hacienda Grill; the restaurant lay empty, but the air was still thick with the smell of enchilada sauce. She stopped too, caught sight of their twin reflections in the window. He towered a good five inches over her five-foot-seven stature.

"This."

"Wha—" Before she realized what he intended, Luke pulled her into his arms, tipped her backward, and kissed her.

CHAPTER 13

After the kiss, Luke had been the one to walk away.

How rude was that?

She'd been resisting him and resisting him, but then after he'd taken her lips by force, he stopped abruptly, readjusted his Stetson, and left her standing there on Main Street without another word.

Okay. Fine. He'd gotten his point across. She knew exactly what she was missing. Her life would be thinner for it, but oh well, such was the way of the world.

"Melody?" Her mother's voice broke through her reverie.

It was noon on Wednesday. She had walked into the community center and plunked down in her customary seat without even greeting anyone. That's how befuddled he'd left her. "Yes, Mother?"

"Are you all right?"

"Fine." She smiled perkily.

Her mother eyed her suspiciously, but didn't say anything else as she reached for the bag of letters and upended it in the middle of the table.

Melody straightened. Her letter was easy to spot in the red silk envelope, which was why she used it, of course. She reached for the letter. "I'll get us started."

Her mother gave her a strange look because Carol Ann was always the one who got things under way and kept everyone on task.

Melody bit down on the inside of her cheek. By taking the lead, was she giving herself away? Quickly, she put the letter back. "Just trying to help."

"No, go ahead," her mother said. "It's nice to have someone else get us started for once."

"Before we start, there's something I wanted to speak to you guys about." Melody toyed with the envelope, tapping first one edge and then another against the table.

"What's that?"

Melody paused, looked around at the group, and prayed she wasn't going to sound as obvious as she feared. "I'm planning on starting several social media sites for the town of Cupid."

"You mean MyFace or SpaceBook or

whatever it's called?" Great-Aunt Delia asked.

Lace chuckled. "It's MySpace and Facebook."

Great-Aunt Delia waved a hand. "You know what I mean."

"Yes, Auntie, like that. Anyway, I was thinking about what you said about Grandma Rose coming up with the idea of putting the letterbox in the garden during tough economic times and how it really increased tourist revenue. What do you all think about doing the modern-day version of that by putting the letters on Facebook or a Web site blog about Cupid?" Melody proposed.

"We talked about using the Internet before to answer the letters," her mother said, "but remember we decided against it because of the manpower that would require, and it would reduce tourism if people didn't have to come to Cupid to post their letters here in order to have them answered."

"Oh, I'm not suggesting we change that policy." Melody ran a fingernail under the flap of the red envelope. "Just that we pick a few select letters to feature every week. The ones we think have the most universal appeal and post the answers. Just to get a wider audience."

"It sounds all right to me," Great-Aunt Delia said. "What do you girls think?"

"I say let's get behind anything that can boost tourism." Lace bobbed her head.

The rest of the group nodded. Everyone seemed to be of the same opinion, including her mother, who added, "Who's going to be in charge of that?"

"I vote Melody," Great-Aunt Delia said. "It was her idea and she's the one who's going to set up the Face thingy."

"What about when she leaves?" her mother asked. "Who's going to handle it then?"

Melody cocked her head. "You know, I can still handle that from afar. You guys pick the letters you want to feature and e-mail them to me. I'll put them up on the Web site. It wouldn't take much time at all."

"Perfect," Great-Aunt Delia exclaimed. "All in favor of Melody picking and posting the letters online raise their hands."

It was unanimous.

Melody suppressed a smile. Her plan was working out perfectly. She took the letter from the envelope, unfolded it, and read the letter she'd dropped in the letterbox the night before.

"Gosh," Lace said. "That letter could have

been written by you, Melody, fifteen years ago, before —"

"We all know what happened." Her mother pursed her lips. "No sense in dragging up the past."

"But the letter has universal appeal," Melody said. "It's just the kind of letter I'd be interested in featuring. Lovers torn asunder by a family feud."

"Well," Lace said. "You're the expert. What is your response to Modern Day Juliet going to be?"

"I'd like to hear that." Great-Aunt Delia took a sip of her iced tea and gave Melody an appraising stare. "Are you going to tell her that love is worth any cost? Even the risk of losing your family over it?"

Melody met her great-aunt's eyes. "I'm going to think it over carefully, but I'm probably going to tell her that if your family truly loves you, they will accept the man you choose, no matter what his bloodline."

"Have you seen this bullshit?" His father carried his laptop computer into the barn where Luke was shoeing his hardest-working quarter horses.

Luke raised his head from where he was bent over the horse's back hoof. "What is it, Dad?"

252

"Your little girlfriend's got a Web site set up about the town of Cupid."

"She's not my girlfriend, Dad, and I think a Web site is a great idea. Don't know why someone around here didn't think of that sooner." Luke tossed aside his tools, stretched out his back.

"Yeah? Well, she looks to be airing your dirty laundry."

"What are you talking about?"

"Here." His father thrust the laptop at him. "See for yourself."

Blowing out his breath and hanging on to his patience, Luke accepted the laptop, squinted against the sunlight's glare off the screen. He didn't see what his father was talking about at first. The Web site was pretty. There was a snapshot of Cupid in more prosperous days, before the drought. It looked lively, inviting. The way Luke thought of his hometown.

"I think she did a good job with it," Luke said. "I don't see what you're complaining about."

"That letter." His father leaned over his shoulder to tap the screen. "On the blog."

Luke clicked the tab for the blog. Read Melody's announcement about the Cupid legend and how each week they would be featuring one of the letters to Cupid on the town blog. Okay. No biggie. Might be a good idea.

And then he read the letter from Modern Day Juliet.

"See now?" His dad elbowed him in the ribs. "See what I'm talking about. This letter is about you and Melody."

"No it's not. This was written recently, by some local young woman," Luke said, but an uneasy feeling nagged at him. Melody wouldn't write a fake letter, would she? Not after she promised to stay away from the family feud. But by publishing the letter, she was stirring things up anyway. She could have picked any of the hundreds of letters written to Cupid every week, and yet she'd chosen this one. She was pushing her agenda, no doubt about it.

"That's worse," his father said. "That means the feud is gearing up again with a whole new generation."

His father was right. That's exactly what it meant.

Luke pulled a palm down his face. Part of him wanted to storm into Melody's office and demand to know what in the hell she was thinking. Another part of him wanted to call a town hall meeting and put everyone on notice. He was not going to put up with any kind of feud-related crap. But his gut told him to stay his course. Keep quiet for now. Making a big deal out of the letter was only bound to feed the flames of hostility. He would watch things closely, but stand back and to see if it burned itself out.

And it probably would.

Just as long as Melody didn't keep kindling the embers.

Over the course of the next three weeks, Melody worked overtime to set up a series of events that would hopefully bring tourists back to Cupid, and for the most part, she managed to do it all while avoiding being alone with Luke. Since he rarely went to the Chamber of Commerce except for the weekly board meetings and she worked out of the condo a lot, they ran into each other only a couple of times. And she almost convinced herself they really could work together without sexual attraction tripping them up.

Besides the Web site and blog she set up for the town, she also created a Facebook page for Cupid, a Twitter account, and a YouTube channel. Then she recruited students from Sul Ross to film the upcoming events and run the social media sites.

To get the ATV rally in before it simply got too hot for such activities, Melody scheduled it first, attaching the races to the Cinco de Mayo weekend. Cinco de Mayo was a big holiday in South Texas and Ricardo's restaurant was sure to be packed with visitors. The board members had brainstormed a name and voted to call the rally the Cupid Sand Fest.

For the weekend after Cinco de Mayo, she slated the masquerade stargazing party, reserving the McDonald Observatory for the private gathering and convincing Pierce Hollister to recruit the VIP celebrities as a draw for the event.

Finally, she scheduled the bachelor auction and the Sadie Hawkins dance for Memorial Day weekend. That Saturday also coincided with the annual Founder's Day parade. The money raised by the auction was going to fund the expansion of Perfect Buddies Animal Shelter.

The night before the ATV rally, she was so keyed up that she woke at five a.m. Whenever she worked on ad campaigns, the closer the deadline loomed, the more problems she had with insomnia. Here, the stakes were even higher than with her career. The future of an entire town hung in the balance and they were counting on her to work miracles.

She was a bit worried about Luke's team

racing idea. The thought of using a random drawing to pair people up seemed risky. He was the one who was adamant about keeping the peace between Fants and Nielsons at all costs, rather than using the longstanding quarrel as an opportunity to both make money and open a dialogue in the community.

Wasn't Luke concerned that the competitive streak inherent in any sport would only make things worse between the two camps? Then again, maybe the random drawing would end up being a good thing. A rousing fight could be the start to mending fences. Beefs were better resolved dragged out into the light, than continually swept under the rug. Just as long as no one got hurt.

And that was the kicker, wasn't it? The Fant-Nielson feud already had too many casualties. It felt safer to ignore the hurt bubbling under the surface than to tackle it head-on. Which was why Luke's idea of a random drawing was out of step with his stated mission of peacekeeping. Maybe this was his way of testing her theory.

Maybe the townsfolk were ready to let go of the Fant-Nielson feud and this could be a new beginning. The response she'd gotten from publishing Juliet's letter on the town's blog seemed to suggest that. Within twenty-four hours, two hundred and twenty-three readers had left comments, much more than she expected for her fledgling effort, and ninety percent of the comments agreed with Cupid's reply to Modern Day Juliet. Letting her know that she was on track with her response that love and forgiveness were what mattered most.

It was a lovely sentiment, and even though she wanted to believe it was possible to mend the feud, she wasn't counting on it. To that end, she'd hired muscle for Sand Fest in the form of Natalie's husband, Dade, and his best friend, Red Daggett, both former Navy SEALs who'd started their own security firm.

Hmm, it was going to be an interesting day.

To burn off excess energy and calm down, she decided to take a quick jog. She donned white running shorts, put on a brand-new green T-shirt and her cross-trainers, and left the apartment.

As she jogged down the stairs, she couldn't help glancing at the parking lot, illuminated by security lamps, in search of Luke's vehicle. Had he spent the night at his condo since he had to be at Sand Fest so early in the morning?

Sure enough, there was his pickup truck.

Her pulse quickened.

The first tendrils of sunlight were nothing more than vague wisps of orange brushing the edge of the sleepy navy blue night as she took off toward town. She'd forgotten how utterly peaceful it was at this hour, so quiet, cool, and serene. The complete opposite of New York City.

Surprisingly, that no longer seemed like such a bad thing. Over the past few weeks, she'd started remembering what she liked about small-town life. The quiet serenity offered respite to a world-weary New Yorker. The awe-inspiring landscape, a compelling mix of blue mountains and desert terrain. An interesting climate that could toast you hot in the day and send you shivering for a sweater in the night air. The town of Marfa, just a thirty-minute drive away, had a whole colony of Manhattan ex-pats. The way people truly relied on each other out here. They had to. They were so isolated. A strong community was their only option. In spite of the almost century-old grudge, the one way to get Fants and Nielsons to work in harmony was to have a natural disaster where they had to pull together.

As evidenced by Luke asking her to help save Cupid from the drought.

Maybe she and he could be the cornerstone of a new beginning for the town. It was a lovely thought.

She jogged the mile into town, ran past the botanical gardens. She had no sooner rounded the corner of the Bettingfield Livery Stables than a figure appeared from the shadows of the alley between the stables and the gardens.

"Eep!" she let out a terrified squeak and spurred into a sprint.

"Melody," a familiar voice called out. "Don't be afraid. It's me."

She put a hand to her throat, stopped, and whirled in the street to face him.

There was Luke. Wearing nothing but a pair of jogging shorts and Nikes.

Damn him. Couldn't the man put on a shirt?

Her treacherous eyes zeroed in on the hard planes of his body, traced the honed ridges and lines. He did not carry one ounce of fat on his lean, muscular frame. Perspiration drenched his skin.

And she remembered, boy did she remember, exactly what it felt like to be underneath that man. And on top of him and in front of him and . . . and . . . Her mouth watered and she tasted salt as surely as if she'd licked his bare pecs.

"Mornin'," he said, the dry heat instantly

evaporating the moisture from his body.

"It's not nice to pop out of an alley at someone. You just about gave me a heart attack."

"This is Cupid, not Manhattan. You've got nothing to be afraid of."

You. You're the one who scares the crap out of me. Not wanting to lose momentum, she jogged in place. "I'm surprised you're not getting ready for the rally. It starts at eight."

"I could say the same thing about you."

"I was feeling restless. Jogging calms me."

"Same here." He walked closer.

The sun was up enough now for her to make out the sprinkling of hairs on his chest. Her finger itched with the memory of what it felt like to skim through those wiry strands.

Luke lowered his eyelids, took her in with a long, lingering gaze. A fine bristling of beard stubbled his hard chin. "You look sensational."

Her pulse fluttered at the hollow of her neck. Stupid pulse. She hoped he didn't notice. "Thank you. Now if you'll excuse me, I need to get back to the condo and get ready for the rally."

He didn't move, just stood grinning as if she was a prize in his box of Cracker Jack.

That's when a terrier mixed-breed trotted from the alley and veered over to plop down at his feet.

"You've got a dog?" She slowed from jogging in place to shifting her weight from foot to foot.

"Nah, he's just a running buddy. Lives over on First Street."

The terrier licked Luke's bare leg.

"Can I pet him?"

"I dunno. Can you?"

She reached down to scratch the dog behind the ears. The pup democratically transferred the love, licking the back of Melody's hand. "Good boy," she cooed.

She raised her head to find Luke studying her with lust on his face, and a sweet shiver went down her spine. Goose bumps. She pointed her feet toward the mountains. "Well, it's been nice chatting with you —"

"Wait."

Against her better judgment, she lingered.

"Let's jog back together," he proposed.

"What are you going to do about him?" She indicated the terrier.

"Digger, go home," Luke commanded.

Digger trotted off.

"Now, where were we?"

"Going our separate ways."

"How are we going to do that? You're jogging back to the condo. I'm jogging back to the condo. We're headed in the same direction."

She glanced around. "You could give me a ten-minute head start."

"Why would I do that?"

"People might see us together."

"So?"

"We don't want to set tongues wagging."

He took a step closer. "We don't?"

"No. You're the one who's adamant about not stirring up the Fant-Nielson feud. Although if you don't want to stir things up, why are you for planning a random lottery drawing for teams in the side-by-side race? Fants or Greenwoods could be teamed with Nielsons. It's a recipe for disaster."

"Call it an olive branch. It's my way of dipping my toe into the turbulent waters to see if maybe your way will work."

She canted her head. "Seems more than a toe-dip."

"It's not as bold a move as it sounds. Think about it. Only the Fants and Nielsons who are open to the possibility of team racing with each other will even enter the contest in the first place. And on the whole, Greenwoods are not as invested in the feud. They take the Fant side because they feel obligated. If we end up with a few Fants or

Greenwoods paired with Nielsons and all goes well, it's a starting place."

"And it if doesn't go well?"

"Then my point of view will have been vindicated and you'll have to stop doing things like publishing that divisive letter you put up on the Web site."

"You saw that, huh?"

"I'm the mayor. I know everything that goes on in this town."

"So you know who Modern Day Juliet is?" She dared to hold his gaze.

"I have an inkling." He didn't blink.

"No kidding?" she challenged, juggling fire. Did he suspect what she was up to? Was he going to call her out on it?

"About the jogging," he said. "Most people are still in bed. If we hurry we'll miss the bulk of the busybodies."

"Ha. In this town all it takes is one big-mouth busybody and everyone knows your business."

"That would be the end of the world?" He leaned in closer and his masculine musk surrounded her.

"Yes, everyone would assume we were see-ing each other."

"And?"

"We're not seeing each other."

"I'm looking at you right now. And it

seems you're looking right back. I'm enjoying the view." His rakish gaze slid down her body, lingered on her breasts before strolling back to her face. "How about you?"

"Which is why we can't jog together."

"You've got a ruthless streak, you know that, Ms. Spencer?"

"I prefer to think of it as coolly detached." If he only knew how her hot and sticky body was singing, *Merge, merge, merge.*

"Detached, huh?"

Her stomach flopped over. "As a Zen monk."

He took another step toward her. He was close enough to touch. "I don't believe that for a second."

"Believe what you want." *Jog away. Go.* She stayed.

"C'mere." He crooked a finger at her.

"What?"

"Lean in a minute."

"Why?" She leaned away from him.

"Stubborn as ever. Always gotta do things your way."

Yes. "Listen, I need to go." She started to trot off, but he snagged her elbow, stopping her in mid-stride. Instant heat fled through her body and she wrenched her arm from his grasp.

"Easy," he said in that smooth voice of

his. "I'm not trying to manhandle you. There's a price tag sticking out of your T-shirt. That's all."

"Oh." Her cheeks burned. She ducked her head and reached around to feel for the tag.

"I'll get it for you, Melly." His fingers were on her neck, his touch sending provocative signals straight to her groin.

Closing her eyes, she willed herself not to tremble. She could not afford to let him know how much he affected her. It was hot enough around here without adding an accelerant to the bonfire.

She felt a tug on her T-shirt, heard the faint snap of the bit of plastic that held the tag in place.

"Got it." He exhaled.

She turned to face him. He tucked the tag into the waistband of his shorts like he was a Chippendale dancer and it was a dollar bill, and the way he was looking at her made her want to strip those running shorts off him and press her body against the length of his hard ridges.

Stop drooling.

A gray Chevy Volt cruised up, Eloise sitting behind the wheel. She stopped, rolled down the window. "Morning, Melody."

"Eloise." Melody nodded, smiled.

"Luke," Eloise said. "Might I have a word

with you?"

Yay, an escape route. She took it. "See you at the Sand Fest, Mayor," she said, and ran away as fast as she could.

Luke watched Melody's sweet little rump jog away and with a sigh, turned to Eloise. "What is it?"

"Get in." She nodded at the passenger seat. "I'll give you a ride."

"The conversation is going to be that long?"

"It is."

"Do we really have to have it?"

"You need to know what I think."

"You know, Eloise, you're not my mother."

"No, she's off living in Florida with her third husband, but I'm here. Get in."

"Were you this bossy to Mayor Thornton?"

"I didn't catch Mayor Thornton smoking cigarettes behind the barn with my son Kenny."

"That was twenty years ago."

Eloise waggled a finger. "And you're still just as naughty."

Luke got in and she drove off. They passed Melody on her way up the mountain. Eloise tooted the horn. She waved.

He turned to watch Melody toil up the

hill, wished he was toiling with her.

"We could give her a ride."

"She can't be privy to our conversation. We're going to be talking about her. Stop watching her boobs bounce."

"How do you know I'm doing that?"

"You're a healthy heterosexual male, aren't you?"

"Last time I checked."

"It was a rhetorical question."

"So what's up?"

"You apparently."

Luke's cheeks burned. "Eloise!"

"I finished setting up your *random* lottery." She said the word "random" like it tasted bad.

"Thank you."

"I'm not proud."

"No, but you're loyal. I appreciate you putting your ethics aside to do this for me."

"Did I have a choice?"

"Sure. You could have told me to go butt a stump."

"And then you would have just done it yourself."

"I would have."

"That would be usurping my job. I'm your assistant. That's what I do. Assist."

"If I killed someone, would you help me hide the body?" he teased.

"Don't push your luck."

"This is going to work."

"I'm glad you're so optimistic."

"I'm also confident it's eventually going to rain and when it does, if I don't have her locked in, Melody is going to leave."

"Are you sure you really want to go through with this?" Eloise asked.

"Is that why you're here? To try to talk me out of it?"

"She's just going to break your heart."

"Probably."

"It's my duty as your surrogate mother to point that out."

"Duly noted. Consider me sufficiently warned, *Mom,* and feel free to say 'I told you so' when it blows up in my face."

"I'm not that gloaty, am I?"

He held out his palm, tilted it back and forth in a balancing gesture that said it could go either way. Eloise was right on all accounts. Manipulating the lottery was an underhanded move and Melody was, most likely, going to break his heart.

"As long as you're sure the potential reward is worth the risks," she said.

"When a guy's dream woman is within reach, he's gotta try."

Eloise pulled to a stop in front of his condo.

"But would hooking up with Melody ultimately be a dream or a nightmare considering your families' animosities for each other?"

That was the question.

Luke scouted around for any sight of Melody jogging up the mountain. No sign of her yet. He had to have her and that's all there was to it. But with the dark past of the long-standing family feud, they had a long, rocky road ahead of them unless he could ease the relatives into the notion of union between the Nielsons and the Fants.

The rigged drawing was his first foray onto that particular battlefield. If that went well, he would take another tentative step and then another. Yeah, it'd take a while, but he was a patient man. He'd waited fifteen years for her, what were a few more weeks?

Because he had to convince her that happily-ever-after was a real possibility and the first step on that journey was to get her into his bed again.

After that, he'd worry about how to prove to her that she belonged here in Cupid right by his side.

CHAPTER 14

Sand Fest was held fifteen miles north of town. They'd had to go that far to find sand dunes land large enough to accommodate the event that neither a Fant nor a Nielson descendant, nor someone with allegiance to one party or the other, owned. Neutral ground. The only safe bet.

Melody stood at the registration tent, surveying the crowd and sizing things up.

Riders signed in at the registration table, while pickup trucks, pulling trailers loaded with all-terrain vehicles, drove through the entrance gates in a continuous stream. Some had arrived the night before, sleeping in motor homes and travel trailers parked to the side of the rally grounds.

Dads revved engines. Moms smeared sunscreens on their children. Teens were already zipping four-wheelers around the dunes, chasing each other and having a blast. Senior citizens found strategic spots to set out camp chairs and sheltering umbrellas.

Vendors pushed food carts or set up kiosks, selling everything from burritos to barbecue to hot dogs to funnel cakes, peppering the air with a cacophony of scents — roasting meats, garlic, onions, molasses, mustard, lard. Beverages were everywhere; water stations to prevent dehydration, beer kiosks for those so inclined, ice chests loaded with soft drinks, five-gallon jug dispensers of tea and lemonade.

Long picnic tables, covered with red and white checkered tablecloths, had been set up under a large canvas canopy. Cases of motor oil and gas cans were stored in a protective wooden hut. Brightly colored advertising banners fluttered in the breeze. In the wake of passing vehicles, sand swirled in gritty eddies.

The Sul Ross students she'd hired were moving through the throng with cameras and a boom mike, filming everything.

Yes, an impressive turnout, so far so good. Everything was running smoothly.

Satisfied, she unclipped her cell phone from her belt and texted Luke. *Let's get this party started.*

Several hundred yards away, Luke stood on a small stage that had been erected the night before. He checked his phone, grinned at her, and picked up the bullhorn beside him. After welcoming the competitors, and thanking the event volunteers, he explained how the races were going to work and then he kicked off the first event.

The morning passed in a flurry of activities as buggies jumped dunes, quads sped over the basin of desert flats, utility ATVs had winch tug-of-war challenges, and riders tried to see who could shoot up the highest rooster tails of sand. There were trophies for every event and prizes donated by local merchants.

Melody spent her time troubleshooting and making sure everything stayed on schedule. They took an hour break at noon for Ricardo's catered lunch that the entry fees had paid for. At one, they were ready to start the drawing for the side-by-side team races.

She was anxious about this event. Would the Fant-Nielson feud erupt as she feared, or would it, as Luke seemed confident, go off without a hitch?

Luke went up onto the stage and used the bullhorn to urge everyone involved in the side-by-side races to gather around for the drawing.

A circular lottery cage on a spindle filled

with Ping-Pong balls, and used to call bingo at the senior citizens center every Friday night, had been brought up onstage. There was also an oversized whiteboard on a stand with the names of the contestants written on it. Drivers were listed on one side, passengers on the other. Luke himself was entered in this event.

"To make things interesting," Luke said, "for this race, the two-person teams in the side-by-side races will be selected by random lottery. You have no say in who your team member will be and you're stuck with whomever the Ping-Pong ball pairs you with."

A murmur ran through the crowd. Although the rules had been printed on the entry forms, some people had not bothered to read them.

"Hey cuz," Pete Nielson, one of Luke's first cousins, hollered. "What if you can't stand the person you're paired with, like a Fant?"

Melody's muscles tensed and she knotted her hands into fists. How was he going to handle this?

"Glad you asked that," Luke said. "If you don't like your partner, you can always disqualify yourself from the race."

"After I just souped up my new side by

side? Not on your life." Pete widened his stance.

"Then if you draw a Fant as a teammate, I suggest you get along with him or her if you care about showing off that beaut of a machine."

"In hell." Pete scowled and crossed his arms over his chest.

"Any other questions?" Luke asked.

There were a few minor questions about the rules, but no other Fant or Nielson protested the drawing.

Melody blew out her breath. If that was the only ripple of dissent they had all day it would be a miracle.

"Let the drawing begin." Luke beckoned to Eloise, who climbed up onstage with him to man the lottery cage.

She spun the cage, withdrew a ball, passed it to Luke.

He announced the pairing, neither was a Nielson, Fant, or Greenwood.

Melody pressed the back of her hand to her forehead. There were twelve drivers in total and Pete Nielson was one of them. Eleven more chances for disaster. How many potential brawls were in the offing? She ran her gaze over the passenger list, and that's when she saw it for the first time.

There. On the bottom. Number twenty-four.

Melody Spencer.

Luke glanced down at the Ping-Pong ball in his hand. There was no number on it indicating which people were to be paired up as he'd led the audience to believe. Instead, written in black Sharpie, just as there had been on all of the other balls plucked from the cage so far, Eloise had penned: "Foolhardy."

He'd managed to avoid pairing any of the feuding families together because he'd spent the better part of yesterday morning working out that strategy. There were two names remaining to pair with the final driver, other than himself. One of those names was Melody's.

He glanced out at the crowd, searching for her, and found her standing near the stage, arms akimbo, a stern expression on her face. Okay, he knew she was going to be ticked off that he'd entered her in the side-by-side rally without telling her, but it was all part of his plan.

She caught his eye and slowly shook her head.

He looked at the ball in his hand, glanced back to her.

Don't you dare, she mouthed silently.

Luke grinned. "Deputy Calvin Greenwood, you're paired with Eli Parker. Leaving me with Melody Spencer."

"Hard luck, cuz," Pete called out. "Looks like you're the one who got stuck with a Fant. Payback's a bitch."

"You got me there, Pete." He made a face like teaming with Melody was the worst thing ever. "Team race starts in fifteen minutes after the single rider heat." He clambered down the steps of the stage.

"Oh no, you didn't pair us together," Melody hissed, the minute his boots hit the earth in front of her.

"Oh yes, I did."

"Luke." She glowered.

"Melody." He beamed.

"I did not enter this race."

He pulled an entry form from his back pocket. He always came prepared. "Oops, and yet here it is, all filled out. Remember, mayoral edict. Everyone on the board has to participate."

"I'm here. Running the show. That's participation enough."

"Aww, come on. It'll be fun."

A tendril of silky blond hair had fallen from her ponytail and he stared at it, mesmerized.

"I'm not doing this."

"Um, you sure about that?" He nodded at the filmmaking students he'd asked to show up at this moment.

"What?" She whirled around to face the camera.

One of the students extended the boom mike toward them.

Luke slung his arm around her shoulder, ignored the fact she went stiff as a broomstick. "This is the incomparable Melody Spencer, who set up this kickass event. And to show what a great sport she is, she's even agreed to ride with me in the side-by-side races. Now that's what I call teamwork."

The student cameraman gave him a thumbs-up. "Got it."

"Come on." Luke steered her toward his travel trailer. "Let's get you geared up."

"You rigged the drawing," she accused.

"Of course I did."

"There was never any danger of Fants being paired with Nielsons."

"Except for you and me."

"That's what all this was about? Getting me in an ATV with you?"

"Consider it a covert operation. It's a way for us to spend some time together without ruffling family feathers. The luck of the draw. Who can argue with that?"

"The rigged draw."

"You should be proud I want to be with you."

"On the sly? Sounds like you think I'm something to be ashamed off."

"Never," he said. "It's the family and the way they behave that I'm ashamed of. You heard my cousin Pete. Besides, sneaking around can be pretty thrilling."

"I'm doing this under protest," she grumbled.

"Duly noted."

"Just as long as you understand that I fully intend to make you pay," she said, "and you're going to suffer big-time."

"Darlin'," he drawled, "I wouldn't expect anything less from you. Everything you do is with grand style or you don't do it at all."

Melody wasn't nearly as put out with him as she was letting on and that worried her. She should be livid. Instead, she was excited.

And turned on.

He rigged the lottery in order to spend time with her without either Fants or Nielsons getting their noses out of joint about it.

Luke guided her up the steps of his travel trailer that he'd parked there that morning.

He closed the door after them and when he turned around, some naughty demon inside her slipped her arms around his neck.

"What are you doing?" he croaked.

"I told you I was going to make you pay," she said, and planted her lips on his.

His arms went around her waist. "Punish me, baby, punish me."

Needfully, she trailed her fingertips over the nape of his neck and leaned in to kiss the throbbing pulse at the hollow of his throat. His taut muscles softened beneath her mouth and a tight groan escaped his clenched teeth.

Her hand crept from his neck down to his chest, which was heaving like a freight engine with each breath. A simple but lingering touch, running her fingers over his cotton shirt to feel the ripped abs beneath.

Outside, engines revved, people called to each other. Inside, the small air conditioner hummed, cooling their heated skin.

She wriggled into him, grinding her pelvis against his. His quick intake of air, rough and ragged in the tight confines, shot her desire into the stratosphere.

The air smelled electrically of testosterone and estrogen. The trailer wobbled on its jacks. She did not completely understand the spell he had woven over her, but she could think of nothing else except melding with him again.

He tugged the back of her ponytail, pulling her head up and nibbling at her chin. The rasp of his teeth against her skin rocketed a searing blast through her nerve endings and she moaned loudly.

Rascal!

"Torture me, will you?" he growled, and his lips found hers. As they kissed, he raised a hand to touch her breast.

Her nipple hardened underneath his palm.

His thumb brushed against the hard nub. She leaped into his arms, snaking her legs around his waist and deepening the kiss.

Luke's arms cradled her buttocks and he dipped his head to gently suckle at her nipple through the material of her T-shirt. She gasped and clutched him tighter.

"We've got to stop." He wrenched his mouth from her nipple. "The race is about to start and we're not geared up."

"I don't know about you," she teased. "But I'm plenty geared up."

"Me too," he said huskily, "but we've got a race to run."

"I don't care."

"Yes, you do."

He was right. She did. Making a success of this event was important to her.

"Later," he murmured. "We can talk about this. Right now, we have five minutes to get dressed and get out to the starting line."

Sighing, Melody let go of him and he eased her to the floor. "All right, tell me what to do."

"Put those things on." He pointed to a helmet, boots, and other ATV riding equipment.

"Do I really need all this gear?" she asked.

"Yep. You do. Safety first." He handed her a blue jersey made of thermoplastic rubber and Lycra, and then reached for a matching one of his own.

She wrestled into the jersey, happy to have it hide the indiscreet wet spot on her T-shirt right at nipple level. Just remembering the feel of his mouth had her nipple hardening again.

"Quadrant protector." He handed her a plastic guard that went over her head, rested on her shoulders, and covered her chest. "Gotta protect the girls."

He donned his chest protector while she slipped hers on.

"Pants next." He tossed her a pair of pants that was the same matching blue color as the jersey. "You can put them on over your shorts."

Simultaneously, they tugged up their pants.

"Now for the protective goggles," he said. "Here, I'll help you put them on."

Before she could tell him that she was perfectly capable of putting on her own goggles, thank you very much, Luke was slipping them down over her face and adjusting the strap around her ears.

Immediately, her body grew soft and moist, receptive. Damn her. Damn him. Why did he have such a devastating effect on her? *Your fault. You're the one who kissed him. You had him staying at arm's length and you're the one who broke the barrier.*

"How's that?" he asked, his fingers lingering on her head.

She squirmed away. "Too tight."

"It's supposed to fit tightly," he said. "To keep out the sand."

"I feel like a scuba diver."

"We finish with the boots. They're hard to get into, so have a seat and I'll slip them on for you."

"If they're so hard, how do you get into yours?"

"Years of practice." He patted the sofa where their equipment had been laid out.

"I feel so helpless."

"You don't always have to be in charge.

Let go and let someone else do something for you for once. Sit."

Not knowing what else to do, she plopped down.

He knelt beside her, patted the front of his left thigh. "Put your foot up here."

Feeling like a perverse Cinderella, she rested her foot on his thigh.

He slipped off her sandal and dropped it to the floor, then produced a clean, thick sock from inside one of the boots and rolled it onto her foot. His calloused fingers felt so good against her skin, manly and strong. She closed her eyes, struggling to fight off the desire mounting inside her.

"Other foot."

She opened her eyes and switched feet, savoring the feel of denim and rock-hard muscular thigh against her bare foot.

He covered that foot with a sock too.

Next, he reached around behind him and came up with a pair of white motorcycle boots.

"Where did you get this equipment? Don't tell me you bought it all for me?"

"The gear belonged to Carly, but she gave up riding ATVs after she had Haley."

"Smart woman."

"Luckily, she wears a size eight too." He eased her foot into the stiff material that reminded her of ski boots and snapped down the buckles. "How does that feel?"

She wriggled her toes. "Fine. I won't be walking in them anyway, right? It's just to protect my feet while we're riding."

"That's right."

"You seem pretty adept at dressing women in motocross gear. How many women have you taken out in your side by side?"

"You're the first."

"I find that hard to believe. If you don't take people riding with you, why the two-seater? Most of the other riders are driving single ATVs."

"Because my machine is the bomb. You'll see. We'll smoke those other riders. Besides, I never said that I didn't take people with me, just no dates." He gave her a meaning-ful look. "Guess I was waiting for someone special to share my hobby with."

Oh crap. What was that look about? They were going to have to have a long talk after this.

"I'm scared. I've never ridden in one of those contraptions before," she admitted.

"You'll do fine." He put on his own boots, then stood and offered her a hand. "Just the helmet is all you have left and we're ready to get after it."

"Okay."

He settled a white helmet on her head and did up the chinstrap. "There you go. You look badass, woman."

"Mmm, if you say so. Since I'm not sure what badass looks like, I'll have to take your word for it."

They left the trailer, got into the side by side parked outside the trailer, and made it over to the starting line just in the nick of time.

The flagman (who was actually Pat Yamaguchi) held the black and white checked flag aloft.

"You buckled in tight?" he asked.

"Bug-in-the-rug snug," she said.

Pat dropped the flag.

The twelve side-by-side ATVs leaped into action.

"Hang on tight." Luke goosed the engine.

Melody squealed and clutched the grab bar in a death grip. They sped over the hard-pack, cactus-strewn desert ground of the sand flats, barreling for the dunes rising straight ahead.

She shot a glance at Luke. His hands were on the wheel and he had a huge grin on his face. He looked like a kid ripping the ribbons off his birthday present.

He hit the first dune doing a good thirty miles an hour, the ATV's paddle tires churning up the sand. Vehicles raced around them, weaving in and out of the dunes. It was dizzying the way the side by side whipped and shimmed.

They scaled the top of the dune, and Melody's cousin Calvin and his passenger came out of nowhere, their red and black ATV jumping in front of them, quick and lithe as a long-legged spider.

"Take that, Nielson," Calvin hollered, and sped off.

Luke floored the accelerator and took off after him. "I'm not about to let a Greenwood or a Fant win this race."

"How in the hell did I let you talk me into this?" Melody groaned as he spun the ATV in a wide circle. "Oh wait, I didn't. I was drafted."

"Fun, huh?" Luke yelled over the roar of the engine.

Actually, it *was* fun. Once she got past the terrified part and let herself enjoy the thrill of a fast, bumpy ride in the middle of the desert.

The wind whipped her hair into her face, but the goggles protected her eyes from the sting of sand blowing over them. Luke was an expert driver, delivering excitement, but without doing anything too foolhardy. The man had control. She had to give him that.

She licked her lips, tasted salt and sand.

"Here we go," he said. "A big one."

A massive dune loomed ahead of them and he took it at a startling clip. They crested the top and . . .

The bottom loomed yards below them.

"Oh my God, oh my God, oh my God," Melody shrieked at the top of her lungs.

The ATV jumped and was airborne.

They hit the soft sand with a thudding impact. Her teeth rattled. Adrenaline flooded her system. It felt like great sex. She understood now why he liked this sport. It was a kick.

"You okay?" Luke shouted, his face knitted with concern.

She gave him a thumbs-up. Grinned.

He grinned in return.

After that jump, they were ahead of Calvin now. Zipping at a dead run for the finish line, Calvin in crazed pursuit.

"Eat my dust, Greenwood," Luke yelled over his shoulder.

Melody sank down in the seat, fingers hanging on to the grab bar so tightly that her knuckles had gone numb. "Beat him, beat him," she urged, surprised and delighted by her bloodthirsty chant.

A second later, they flew over the finish line, Calvin right behind them. The ten other side by sides arrived shortly thereafter.

Luke grappled with his seat belt, tumbled out of the ATV, and came around to her as she fumbled to get her seat belt undone. Her hands were shaking, her body tingling from head to toe, and she couldn't ever remember feeling so alive.

"We won!" he said, pulling her from the ATV and spinning her around. "We won! You're my good luck charm."

"We did at that." His enthusiasm infected her, sent a restless fever surging through her belly.

"If we weren't out here in view of everyone," he said, "I'd kiss you."

"But we are."

"Later then. After the rally is over. Meet me at midnight. Our spot. We need to talk."

CHAPTER 15

The lake was basically gone, but the cement picnic tables were still there, circled around the dried-up basin like mourners around a gravesite. A scythe moon cut a slender chunk from the night sky, a glitter of stars glowing around it.

Luke paced, stopping repeatedly to check his watch and run his hand through his hair. It was five minutes after midnight. Would she come?

Maybe she'd fallen asleep. She'd put in a full day at Sand Fest. Why had he suggested midnight? What was wrong with him? She had to be exhausted.

He started toward his pickup when headlights appeared on the horizon. In the desert, you could see for miles, and he watched the car grow closer. Was it she?

The sound of the Corvette engine reached him and within a matter of minutes, she was pulling up to the picnic table, shaded by a couple of desert willow trees. She parked and got out of the convertible, the top was down, and she came toward him with an enigmatic expression on her face, unreadable, as if she was trying to be nonchalant but didn't really know what to expect.

Neither did he, for that matter.

Her tousled hair fell to her shoulders, tangled and wild. It reminded him of how her hair had looked after that handful of early morning horseback rides they'd taken together through the mountains. Her complexion was smooth and cool in the moon glow and she'd changed from the casual shorts and top she wore at the rally to a filmy white sleeveless dress. She looked like some kind of storybook sprite.

This was how he remembered her. That spirited girl.

Before the night that changed everything. Before she'd gone to New York, become someone else. She still had the spunk and the grit, but she'd lost that sense of wonder and awe. He supposed he had too.

He tried to be cool, to let her come to him, but damn, he couldn't stand waiting. He covered the space between them in long, determined strides, almost running, but she was rushing too. He held out his arms. She flew into them.

They clasped each other in a simultaneous embrace. It had been only a few hours since he'd seen her. How was it possible to miss someone so much in such a short amount of time?

He kissed her the way he'd wanted to kiss her in the trailer that afternoon, with hot, unchecked abandon. She responded in kind, her mouth driving him past insanity.

"I didn't think you were coming."

"Got held up tallying the profits and losses for Sand Fest."

"And?"

She made a face. "We lost money on the event."

"But maybe the local businesses saw an uptick in business."

She bit her bottom lip. "Maybe, but let's not talk about that now. Let's kiss."

Who could resist an invitation like that? He claimed her mouth again. She moaned, melted against him.

"Woman," he growled, wrenching his mouth from her. "I can't stop thinking about you. You're on my mind all the time. Everywhere I go, I smell you. Everything I eat tastes like you. I cannot get enough of you."

"Ditto," she said, and attacked his mouth again.

Minutes later, they broke apart, laughing and gasping.

"Thank you," she said.

"For what? The kisses?"

"Well, that too, but I'm thanking you for forcing me to go with you on the ATV ride and rigging the drawing so I'd be on your team. That was a stroke of genius. I had fun. You showed me . . ." She trailed off.

"What?" he prodded when she did not go on.

She slanted her head downward, cut a shy glance upward at him. Melody? Shy? In what universe?

"That I could do something different and not be in control and still enjoy myself," she said.

"I could show you more." He stretched out his hand. "If you wanted."

She chuckled and danced away from him. "Oh, I just bet you could."

"You're going to make me work for this, aren't you?"

The shy smile was back. God, it was like they'd stepped into a time machine and jettisoned the last fifteen years.

She sashayed over to the picnic table, climbed to sit on top of it. "Are you going to tell me why you told me to meet you here?"

"It's our place," he said.

"Forever tainted."

The mood shifted, just like that. But what had he expected? Asking her to come here of all places.

"Not forever," he explained. "That's why we're here. To make a new memory on top of this picnic table."

She shook her head. "We can't trivialize what happened that night, Luke."

Were they finally going to talk about it? Was that really why he'd asked her here? Closure?

He moved to join her on the table, reached out to take her hand. This time she did not resist him. "I should never have kissed you that night."

"But you did."

"And it's made all the difference."

"I know. If we'd never kissed your brother wouldn't have died. You wouldn't be a rancher, since the Rocking N was Jesse's legacy as the oldest son. You'd be off riding the rodeo circuit."

"I gave up that dream a long time ago. And you know what? I love being a rancher. I just wish Jesse was here to work the ranch with me."

"We can't change the past, Luke. Contrary to *Back to the Future* movies, there is no DeLorean that can whisk us back to high school so we can fix everything."

"I know." He traced his thumb over her knuckles.

"So we have to let it go. We've moved on."

"Yeah." He moistened his lip. "I know it in my head, but I guess there's a part of me that still hasn't accepted it in my heart."

She leaned her head against his shoulder. "It was a terrible, terrible thing."

"I remember what you were wearing that night," he said. "Short, tight cutoff blue jeans and a red blouse that you'd taken the hem and knotted under your breasts to make a midriff top out of it and red cowgirl boots. I wanted you so badly I could have chewed those shorts right off your body."

"I was scandalous." She sighed. "I thought I was Miss Thing."

"You certainly got my attention." He wrapped his arm around her, drew her closer to him.

She draped her right leg over his left thigh. She was so warm and soft. "I remember what you were wearing too." She paused. "Wranglers and a black T-shirt. That ended up torn and covered in blood by the end of the evening."

The mood shifted again, running from light to dark to lighter, back to the darkest of all. A full scale of emotions that encapsulated the past. Sadness, curiosity, anger, wonder, regret, delight, guilt, revenge, and fear.

Always fear at the crux.

"Do you blame me for Jesse's death?" she asked.

"No," he said. "I never did. It was my family that blamed you and I'm sorry for that."

"I'm the one who is sorry. You couldn't go against your family. Not under the circumstances."

"Neither could you. If anything, I was to blame."

She took his head in her hands, turned it so he was looking straight at her. "Neither one of us is to blame. It was my cousins who pulverized you."

"And it was my brother who crashed while driving drunk coming to avenge me."

"And yet fifteen years later, the guilt is still an anchor around our necks. If we'd never kissed . . ." She trailed off.

"But we did."

"That's what kept us apart. The guilt."

It was the wedge that time would never erode. Things had been so much easier between them in New York, why was it so much harder here?

Why? Because here the stakes were so much higher. In New York they were free of their families, free of the past. Here, they were haunted. He understood now why she'd left. It simply hurt too much to stay.

"It's all dried up," she said sadly, gazing out at the dusty lake. "Gone."

"It'll be back."

"Maybe not. It's the longest drought on record."

"It'll be back," he reiterated.

"Everything comes to an end," she murmured. "Everything."

"The key is to enjoy what you have, while you've got it." His voice came out hoarse and scratchy.

"That's true." She nodded. "I took my life in New York for granted. I thought I would always be there."

"You'll go back."

"Luke." She ran her hand up his arm.

"Yeah?"

"Why are we here?"

"Is this a philosophical question? Because I'm not the one you should be asking it of."

"No, literally, why are we here? What do you want from me, Luke?"

She had to ask? She couldn't see it on him? His desire. His abject longing for her.

"I want you, Melody. Like I've never wanted any woman."

"I want you too, Luke, but this is only going to work if we don't fall in love. Promise me that you won't fall in love with me."

His pupils narrowed, the irises darkening. "I can't promise that."

She put her palms on his chest, pushed back from him. "Then we can't do this."

He tightened his arms around her waist, holding her in place. "I might not be able to promise that I won't fall in love with you, but I can promise that I will never hold you back. With me, you're always free to be yourself, Melody, and if that means you have to fly away, back to New York or wherever it is that your ambition takes you, then I'll accept it."

She plucked at his collar. "You make it sound as if I'm going to break your heart."

"Honey," he said, "you already have."

Her eyes widened in distress. "What do you mean?"

"When we were teens," he rushed to add, not wanting her to know exactly how vulnerable he was. "It broke my heart that I never really got to talk to you again after that night."

"Oh. Yes, that was a heartbreaking time, but can you handle a strictly sexual relationship? I don't want to enter into this if there's going to be —"

"Sex is good enough for me," he lied. It was better than nothing. And one night with her was more than a lifetime with anyone else.

"Really? Is it?"

"That's what I wanted to talk to you about. For as long as you're in town, I want to be with you."

"Just sex?" she reiterated, looking deeply into his eyes.

"Just sex," he echoed.

"No one can ever find out. It's not worth the fallout to the community. To our families. To us."

"I know."

She slipped her hot little palm up underneath his shirt, splayed it over his chest, setting off an instant hard-on. Classy, Nielson. Real classy.

"If we get caught . . ." He glanced over his shoulder but there was nothing around except sand and cactus and they could see any oncoming cars.

"But we're not going to get caught," she said with so much certainty that he fully believed her. "You're my dirty little secret."

He didn't know if he liked that, but then she put her mouth to his throat and did some kind of sexy maneuver with her tongue that made his eyes roll back in his head and yanked a groan from his throat.

"We can't make love here," she said. "And we can't use our condos either. Too many people around who know us. If they see us coming and going from each other's places, they'll know something is up."

"We can't even use a local motel. Not in this town. People know our cars."

"Marfa?"

"And risk running into Carly?" He stroked his chin.

"It's the same with all the small towns around here. Everybody knows everybody."

"We can't go to my ranch," he said. "My dad is living in the original farmhouse. He would have a heart attack if he knew what we were up to."

"Your father hates me."

"He hates all Fants."

"He blames me."

"Melly, he's bipolar. He's got emotional problems."

"Don't we all," she mumbled.

"We could drive to El Paso," he suggested.

"It's two hours away."

"I'll think of something, but for now —" Luke didn't get to finish his thought because his cell phone rang. He didn't want to answer it, but it was late at night. What if someone he knew was in trouble? What if it was his dad?

Melody pulled the phone from his shirt pocket and handed it to him, and looked at him wide-eyed.

The name on the caller ID flashed: Jeff Davis County Sheriff's Department. His blood froze. He was afraid to answer it.

Melody nudged him with her elbow.

He hit accept and put the phone to his ear. "Luke Nielson."

"Mayor, this is Deputy Calvin Greenwood."

Luke steeled himself for bad news. "What is it?"

"Your office has been vandalized and graffitied with hateful slurs directed at your family name."

It took a second for the words to sink in, for Luke to realize that the news was unfortunate, but not tragic. "I see."

"I decided not to wait until morning to call because I didn't want this thing to escalate," Greenwood said. "I imagine it's got something to do with you winning that Sand Fest trophy."

"Really? Who the hell is that petty?"

"You're asking me? We've both got jackasses on our side of the family. It's probably just kids, but you never know. People get liquored up and do dumb things all the time."

"I'll be right there," he said, and switched off the phone. He looked over at Melody, told her what had happened.

"That call is so much better than it might have been." She fingered the thin gold chain at her throat.

"I know."

"I'll go with you."

"Not a good idea."

"You're right. What was I thinking?"

"That you wanted to be with me." He chucked her lightly underneath the chin. "I appreciate it, but we have to be careful."

"There goes our tryst. This secret affair is going to be harder than I thought."

"Rain check? Let me handle this and I'll get back to you on a rendezvous time and place."

She pointed a finger at him. "Don't leave me hanging."

"I'll text you when I come up with something."

She cast a sly glance at his crotch, winked. "Looks like you already have."

With a heavy heart Melody watched him go, memories of the night that changed the trajectory of their lives washing over her.

She and Luke had been sitting on this very picnic bench, having slipped away from their families' respective Fourth of July celebrations. They'd held hands and watched the fireworks exploding over the water, feeling their teenage hormones rising, pushing them headlong into trouble.

He'd leaned in. She sank her head against his shoulder.

He murmured her name. The smell of gunpowder tinged everything. His lips brushed hers. She sighed. He tasted of watermelon and warmth. His arm went around her.

Her heart was beating so fast she could scarcely breathe. It was the sweetest moment of her fifteen-year-old life. Kissing the boy who made her blood sing. Knowing how dangerous this was, the thrill making it all the more compelling. Need and want and desire overtaking her.

She hugged his neck and he laid her back on the cement table, the stone cool against her heated back. Over his shoulder, rockets burst into brilliant flames — blue, green, yellow, red. Life was love. Love was life. She'd never experienced anything so intense.

They'd been sneaking off for weeks, meeting each other to go horseback riding or climbing through the mountains, alone, away from families and their prying eyes. They could have kissed on any of those outings, and while they'd been nudging closer and closer to it, they had not.

No, stupidly, they'd waited until the Fourth of July, and in a public place they had finally succumbed to the unstoppable force that consumed them. They were so wrapped up in each other that they had not heard the footsteps until it was too late.

Her cousins were upon them, pulling Melody from Luke's arms. Beating him. Hitting him and hitting him and hitting him. Three of them against one, while a fourth cousin held her and called her vile names as she screamed for Luke.

But the popping of fireworks drowned out her cries. They left him bloodied on the ground. Wounded, broken. She tried to go to him, fought the cousin holding on to her, but the other cousins, snarling cruelly and covered in Luke's blood, had grabbed her and forced her into their car. They took her home and when her mother had seen her, all hell broke loose. The names her cousins had called her were nothing in comparison to her mother's wrath.

Melody closed her eyes. The sheriff had appeared on their doorstep, looking for her cousins. Luke was in ICU.

Of course, her mother and father had forbidden her to see him, but she'd gone anyway. Yet when she tried to see him there had been so many angry-faced Nielsons in the waiting room that she hadn't had the courage to face them all by herself, so she'd slunk away, discouraged and heartbroken.

It was only the next day that she learned that Luke's older brother, Jesse, had gone after her cousins in an attempt to avenge his brother. Jesse had been drinking, celebrating the holiday. He was so livid, so full of rage that he'd lost control of his car on the dark mountain road, flipped over twice before it landed in the ravine, crushing the life out of him.

Such a dreadful waste.

A brackish taste filled her mouth and she dropped her head into her hands. What was she thinking? An affair with Luke could only end one way. Was the fun they would have worth the inevitable hurt they were bound to feel? And what if they weren't lucky enough to keep their fling private? If their families found out it would only make things worse.

She couldn't do this. Couldn't go through with it.

Resolved, she took out her phone and

wrote him a text. *Sorry. Changed my mind. We can't do this. Too much at stake.*

For the longest time, she stared at what she'd written, then finally, she took a deep breath and pressed send.

The vandalism bothered Melody.

Not because the damage to Luke's office was so awful. She saw it the next morning when she drove past City Hall. One sanitation worker was busy replacing the glass in the pane that had been knocked out, another was painting over the black graffiti on the outside of the building proclaiming: "Nielson's Sucks." The culprit didn't know when to pluralize and when to use an apostrophe. Or else they'd been intoxicated when they'd spray-painted it. Either way the vandalism was minor, pretty run-of-the-mill.

No, it wasn't the damage that bothered her so much, but rather the act of vandalism itself. Someone in her family was responsible for this. And that someone had lashed out at Luke.

It was a stone thrown in the subterranean pool of animosity. The ripples had started, ripping the wounds open again. Something had to be done.

Last night's resolve not to enter into an affair with him strengthened; she tightened her hands on the steering wheel and instead of continuing on her way to the Chamber of Commerce, spun the Corvette in an unauthorized U-turn and headed for the Sheriff's Department.

Her cousin Calvin was coming down the steps as she was headed up them. His eyes were bleary, his uniform rumpled. He paused when their gazes met.

"You've been up all night," she said.

Calvin nodded, even though her observation had been a statement, not a question.

"Our cousins are keeping you busy."

"We don't want to see this mess get out of control again." He readjusted his Stetson.

"What are you doing about it?"

"Repairing the damage from the vandalism as quickly as possible. Beefing up patrols on holidays and weekends."

Melody sank her hands on her hips. "In other words, sweeping things under the rug."

"Sheriff Reardon and Mayor Nielson agree it's what's best for the town."

"So no charges pressed?"

"We don't know who did it for sure."

She snorted. "But you're not investigating it."

"It's not worth the man-hours. The vandalism is minor. A new windowpane. A fresh coat of paint." He kicked the side of the steps with a toe of his cowboy boot, but did not glance up. "It's just kids letting off steam."

"It was just kids who beat Luke to a pulp fifteen years ago."

"This is an isolated incident. Someone was pissed off because Luke won the side-by-side race. We have these Fant-Nielson dustups from time to time, cousin. You just haven't been here to see it. Nothing has gotten out of control since what happened to Luke. It isn't going to escalate. It'll die down."

Heat burned her chest, spread up her neck, and it wasn't from the morning sun. "And yet, it's been ninety years since the feud started. When do you estimate it'll start dying down exactly?"

"I hear you, Mel, but it's not my call. Besides, you'll be gone soon enough. It's not really your worry anymore."

"Excuse me? Cupid is my hometown. Why would you assume I don't care?"

He held up both palms. "Sorry. I didn't mean to offend you. I'm going home to get some sleep. If you want to buck the system, I suggest you take it up with either the mayor or the sheriff."

She clutched her hands to her shoulders,

stacked elbows in front of her, and watched Calvin walk away. Yeah, she could do that, but she doubted it would do any good. What would be the point? If she let herself get within ten feet of Luke, she'd start rethinking her position on their affair. One smile from him and she'd be butter. Butter had no backbone. No resolve.

He'd already responded to the text she'd sent him last night with *??? U sure?* Her answer had been a solid *YES!* And that had been the end of the digital conversation. She'd been relieved, but she hadn't trusted his silence. He could be planning to show up in person and convince her otherwise.

And those lips of his could be very persuasive.

Besides, it was an election year for Sheriff Reardon, and he'd do his best to keep things peaceful. Plus she already knew Luke's stance on the family feud. Keep things quiet. Don't push.

To her way of thinking, they should be pursuing opposite tactics. The feud should be publicized. The participants in it shamed. And anyone committing criminal acts should be held accountable. Yes, taking that stance might make things worse in the short run, but the town had been sticking its head in the sand over the feud for far too long.

Luke thought he could quell this grudge by keeping the peace, but sometimes you had to break a few eggs to make an omelet.

Question was, how best to handle the situation?

She had to be careful. A creative solution was needed. Something visceral, emotional, and universal. Something that would take all the skills she'd learned on Madison Avenue.

Even if she had to bend the rubbery truth to do it.

CHAPTER 16

Dear Cupid,

The worst has happened. Our families discovered our love and it has ended in the gravest of disaster. Blood has been shed. Ugly words have been said. There's no going back. No undoing what's been done. How can we continue to love when our families hate each other so much? To bring peace, all we have to do is break up. But he is the other part of me. Without him, I will never be whole. But can I be responsible for bringing pain and suffering to others simply so I may have happiness? My beloved says we have to do what is right. Why does that mean we have to let each other go?

— Tearfully yours,
Modern Day Juliet

"Wow," Lace said the Monday after Cinco

de Mayo and the financial failure that was Sand Fest. "How are you going to answer that one, Melody?"

Melody fingered the letter she'd written and dropped into the letterbox Sunday morning after she confronted Calvin. It might have been fictional, but reading it out loud to the group, she felt the sharp, awful pang of loss that she had felt on that long-ago Fourth of July. Fiction came from truth, after all. Now she understood why Michael Helmsly had been so frustrated with her honesty. The literal truth was often a stumbling block to creativity. A figurative truth could be more sincere than the real thing.

"I don't know. Any suggestions?" she asked.

"Tell Juliet it's for the best," Melody's mother murmured. "Love does not exist in a vacuum. There are other people in your life. Other loves."

"But what if Juliet's love for her beau could actually heal the rift?" Melody posed the question. "If only their relatives would give young love a fighting chance."

"I don't ever see how that could happen," her mother said. "Not when it comes to a family feud."

"Your family should know." Junie Mae scooted back her chair. "They've specialized in perpetuating grudges."

"It's not me." Her mother looked around the table. "Auntie Delia, you were at the heart of this. You're the one who remembers when the Nielsons burned down Cousin Zeke's house. What was that like?"

"Actually," Great-Aunt Delia said, "it was never really proven to be Nielsons. You know Zeke did like the whiskey a bit too much and he was a chain smoker. He could have lit the house on fire himself and blamed it on the Fants. Back in those days they didn't have arson investigators around here. Mostly, folks took things at face value. If it looked like a duck, walked like a duck, quacked like a duck, they called it a duck."

Her mother looked startled. "Are you saying that the Nielsons might not have burned down Zeke's house?"

"I'm saying there's all shades of truth, depending on where you're standing." Great-Aunt Delia unwrapped a Werther's candy and popped it into her mouth. She offered the package around the table. "Butterscotch?"

"So what do you think I should tell Juliet?" Melody asked.

"Tell her to move away. Get the hell out of this place. There's no reason to live in a nest of crazy. Tell her to save herself while there's still time." Great-Aunt Delia snorted.

"Excuse me," her mother said. "Are you calling me crazy, Aunt Delia?"

"You've got your feelings hanging on the outside, Carol Ann. I was talking about that there Juliet and her family. Not you. Not this Fant-Nielson mess."

"You know Juliet is a Fant or a Nielson." Her mother got to her feet. "She has to be."

"Now don't you go looming over me. Just because I'm not as spry as I used to be before I bunged up this hip, doesn't me you can sass me. I'm still the matriarch around here. Sit back down."

Her mother did not sit. "I've heard you light into your share of Nielsons over the years. Now that you're old you've suddenly turned saintly on us?"

"Me? A saint? No more than you are, Carol Ann. I'm just tired of seeing people fightin' when they could be lovin'." She shot Melody a pointed look. "So go ahead. Tell that Juliet to leave the place that's got her so tore up, with or without her fella. She deserves to have a peaceful life."

Melody took Great-Aunt Delia's advice and on Wednesday posted a reply to the second Juliet letter, telling her to get on the plane to anywhere, just as long it was away from the feuding families. Although she had to admit that it was sort of weird being both Juliet and Cupid, asking advice and giving it to herself.

When she posted the reply to the Cupid Web site blog and used social media to get the word out about the blog, she was startled to discover the site had gotten a thousand hits in less than two hours. Much of it due to traffic from her people retweeting the Twitter feed from her personal account. She had more clout than she realized. Her reply generated controversy, many of the readers taking her to task for her advice.

"Why should Juliet run away?" one reader asked. "That's cowardly. She should stay and fight for love."

"All those people involved need to have their heads examined," wrote another. "Why can't they see how their hatred is harming their children?"

"Tell Juliet to get pregnant. What are the parents going to do then? If they want to see that grandbaby, they'll have to learn how to get along."

It was all so easy to say what you'd do in that situation, but walking a mile in someone else's shoes was never easy. Most people simply couldn't step outside themselves long enough to put on someone else's skin. She'd picked up a few empathetic skills in advertising. In order to sell stuff, you had to figure out what the consumer wanted. Advertising was based on emotions. That's why anyone bought anything. Selling insurance? Make them feel fear. Selling cars? Make them feel sexy. Selling food? Make them feel hungry. If people believed the products would in some way make them feel happier, healthier, freer, richer, safer, or more loved, they'd plunk down cash. It all came down to that.

Feelings.

Emotions.

Of course a good advertising copywriter knew how to take advantage of those needs. It was manipulative, no doubt. But it did put you in a position to consider what other people wanted.

What did Luke want? What made Luke feel better? How could she meet his needs, meet her own needs, and still meet the needs of her family and community?

Ha. Like that was even possible.

But the brisk activity on the Web site told her she was on to something.

That something was confirmed when she took her Corvette in to Pat to have the oil changed and Pat told her that she'd just fixed a tire for a tourist who came through wanting to know if this was where Juliet was from. Melody couldn't deny that the story was piquing interest. It might not amount to anything in the end, but she'd been right using the letter as a sales tool to bring more tourism into Cupid. Too bad she'd had to go about it in an underhanded manner.

She wondered how Luke would feel if he found out.

Guilt ate at her. She should tell him that she was the one writing the letters. He'd be mad at her, yes, but it wasn't right, keeping it from him. He was affected by the feud, same as she was.

These thoughts were dancing around in her head when she saw Luke pull into Pat's garage and get out of his pickup.

"What can I do you for, Mayor?" Pat asked, tucking a wrench into the back pocket of her coveralls and wiping her hands on a red grease rag.

"I'm here to talk to Melody," he said.

"Go to it." Pat waved at Melody, who was sitting in the waiting area surrounded by cracked vinyl chairs and a dusty table laden with outdated copies of *Popular Mechanics.* "I'll have your oil changed in a jiff," she hollered at Melody and popped her head back underneath the hood of the Corvette.

Luke came inside the small room.

Her heart rate spiked.

"Can I have a word?"

She stood up. "Sure," she said calmly in spite of the blood pounding loudly in her ears. "What's up?"

He took off his Stetson, turned the brim in his hands. "You've got to stop posting those Juliet letters on the blog."

"Why's that?"

"They're causing a ruckus."

She jutted out her chin. "In what way?"

"You received over a thousand comments on that story."

"Which is a good thing. It proves I'm right. Calling attention to the family feud is the way to go."

"It's a way to disrupt our community. I've been getting complaints."

"From whom?"

"Fants. Nielsons. Greenwoods."

"What do they have their noses out of joint over?"

"They say your Web site casts Cupid in a negative light."

"Their stupid grudge is what's casting Cupid in a negative light, not those letters."

"People are concerned."

"What about?"

318

"Juliet. They're worried she'll get hurt."

"She might. But publishing her letter isn't what's going to harm her. It's the reaction of the feuding families."

"You cherry-picked this letter. Feature some other letter to Cupid on the Web site."

"Mayoral edict?"

"Yeah. Mayoral edict."

She sank her hands on her hips. "May I ask you a question?"

"Go ahead."

"How do you expect me to do my job when you keep shooting down every viable option I come up with for increasing tourism?"

"I haven't shot down every option. We had Sand Fest —"

"Which lost money."

"We've got the masquerade stargazing party at the observatory. Your efforts would be better served making sure that event is a moneymaker."

That pissed her off. "Are you suggesting it's my fault that we lost money on Sand Fest?"

"I didn't say that."

"You implied it."

"Look," he said. "I didn't come here to start an argument."

"Didn't you?"

"No. I'm just asking you to stop printing the letters. Can you promise me that?"

"Fine. If that's what you want."

"It is."

They stood looking at each other. She could tell he wanted to say something more. Probably something about the text she'd sent him backing out of resuming their affair, but instead of speaking what was on his mind, he settled the Stetson on his head, pulled sunglasses from his front pocket, stuck them on his face, and walked away.

To keep the man from driving her around the bend, Melody threw herself heart and soul into preparations for the stargazing party, pinching pennies wherever she could while still keeping things elegant for the VIPs. She was determined to make a profit on this event. She involved as many of the local businesses as she could — the florists, the restaurants, the air charter service to shuttle dignitaries in and out. She stuffed gift bags with coupons from places like Pat's garage and Junie Mae's hair salon and spa and Natalie's B&B.

But her enemy was against her. On Saturday, the day of the stargazing party, a hot, relentless wind blew into town. The temperature climbed to a hundred and two, an extremely rare occurrence in the Davis Mountains.

Melody got on the phone, had swamp coolers trucked in and set up outside to cool off the area. Hopefully, by the time the party started an hour before dusk, the wind would settle down and the temperatures would slip back to their normal May range of the low eighties. It was the best she could do. The rest was in the hands of fate.

She'd promised Luke she wouldn't print any more letters from Juliet, and she would keep that promise. But she hadn't promised that she would not dress up like Millie Greenwood for the masquerade party.

She arrived at the observatory an hour before the guests to oversee the preparation, dressed in a replica flapper's dress in the style that her great-grandmother wore during a dance marathon she attended with Great-Grandfather John before they were married.

Just before the party started, Melody slipped on a gilded emerald mask that matched the dress. Cars began arriving at seven-thirty. Limos pulled up depositing the rich, famous, and well-heeled. Melody's film crew was busy interviewing the costumed guests as they arrived on the red carpet that had been rolled out to greet them.

Caterers had set up an outdoor buffet, and delicious smells filled the air. Mysterious mood music was piped in through the sound system — select classical pieces, the themes to *Star Wars* and *2001: A Space Odyssey.* The amphitheater had been decorated for the occasion and masked attendants gave out mini-flashlights as party favors, so that the guests could safely find their way back to their cars after the party was over. There were no parking lot lamps at the observatory. Darkest pitch black was needed for deep stargazing. Scientists milled with the crowd, giving personalized lectures about the heavenly sky above them.

Melody had to admit, you didn't get this kind of sky in Manhattan. For that matter, you didn't get this sky anywhere but the Trans-Pecos. That's why they'd built McDonald Observatory here in the first place. It reminded her what was special and unique about her home.

Waiters moved through the throng, balancing silver trays laden with flutes of fizzy champagne. The air hummed with excited voices. Everyone was in costume, masked, their identities hidden. A thrill ran through her. This was more invigorating than she had anticipated. What fun.

She shook hands with VIPs and made idle

chitchat, but all the while, she was watching, waiting.

For Luke.

But he was nowhere in sight.

She reached for a glass of champagne from the tray of a passing waiter and took a swallow to quell her nerves. Considering how drunk she'd gotten the last time she drank champagne, maybe it wasn't such a good idea.

How weird seeing her costumed friends and family looking like strangers. Novel. New. She supposed that was part of what was making her feel so giddy. She put down the champagne. She needed to keep her wits about her. This was her event. She was the hostess.

The eyeholes of the wide mask that covered half her face were too narrow and she was having problems seeing much in her peripheral vision. The sun had not yet set and the desert air was still exceptionally warm. Many had gone inside the building to enjoy the air conditioning until the stargazing began.

And that's when she saw him.

Rudolph Valentino.

There, on the other side of the pavilion was the woman Luke had come looking for. She was the reason he'd donned the silly sheik costume. This was the desert, after all, why not come as the most famous silent-film lover of all time?

He could feel her eyes caress his face from beneath her mask, and a powerful sexual stirring tugged his cock. Another excellent reason to wear voluminous robes.

Coyly, she tossed her bobbed, dark brown hair. The wig looked good on her. She licked her lips and winked.

Luke winked back.

She smiled a quick, come-hither smile and then ducked her head.

Here we go. The thrill of the chase.

Masked guests were all around him, talking, laughing, joking, drinking, but he could have been stranded on a deserted island or trapped in a timeless vortex. The real world was muffled, far away. He was that focused on Melody and Melody only.

His gaze strayed down the shapeless shift dress to take in her long shapely legs encased in sheer silk stockings, and he just knew a garter belt was holding them up. He could easily imagine himself tugging the silky material down over the curve of her calf.

She lifted her head again, angled him a long, lingering look. This time, her smile was filled with amusement, leaving him with the image of her soft, pliant lips.

Then she retreated, turned on her heels, and walked off.

Every nerve in his body flared to life, alert, vibrant, clamoring for attention.

She made her way through the crowd that was moving along the cement walkway to the amphitheater as the sun disappeared below the horizon. She tossed him a glance over her shoulder. Even in a group of people dressed in mysterious garb, she was the most provocative person there.

Follow me, her eyes whispered.

She pursed her lips, slowly blew him a kiss, and then crooked her index finger.

This way.

Luke felt the impact of her gesture catch him low in the groin. Simultaneously, hormones and endorphins lit up both his body and his mind. He gulped, shook his head. His tongue was cemented to the roof of his mouth. His eyes were transfixed on her lithe form. His nose twitched, suddenly sensitized to the scent of seduction in the air, and his ears filled with a blinding white roaring noise.

She strutted off.

Mesmerized, he watched her hips sway. He went primeval and lumbered after her.

Must have woman.

By the time he reached where she'd been standing when she'd blown him the kiss, she had already disappeared in the darkness. He searched the crowd in the amphitheater, but the sunlight was gone and everyone was in costume. Pierce Hollister stood at the podium in his Dallas Cowboys uniform welcoming the guests and introducing the astronomers who would be showing them the stars that evening.

And then he saw her in the distance, near one of the domes that housed the high-powered telescopes. The flapper paused again, but she did not look back. Had she just assumed he would follow?

She was correct. He would follow her anywhere.

Tossing her head, the brown bob swinging against her chin, she pried open the door of the smaller dome.

Luke followed, his body pulsating.

She vanished inside the dome, the door closing behind her.

Edging closer, he cast a glance around to see if anyone had noticed him. Everyone's backs were to him as they focused on the speaker who was talking about meteors and light-years and milky emissions.

A minute ticked by. Then another. And

another.

Was she coming out or was he supposed to go in?

He wanted her so badly he felt scorched. Unable to stand it a second longer, he opened the door of the dome and stepped inside.

A pleasant, erotic scent hit his nose. His body reacted, shoulders tensing, cock hardening. He would remember this smell until his dying day.

The mouthwatering fragrance of Melody's full-blown sexual arousal.

CHAPTER 17

Luke twisted the dead bolt on the heavy metal door, sealing them inside. The click echoed loudly in the metal dome.

The room was pitch black. She couldn't see him, but she could hear his ragged breathing. She gulped and contemplated switching on the flashlight clutched in her hand, but she couldn't seem to make herself move.

His boots scraped against the cement, coming closer. She smiled, remembering how he looked dressed as Rudolph Valentino. The great lover.

Slowly, his footsteps came closer and closer, her muscles growing tighter as the seconds spun into minutes and then he stopped, so close she could feel heat radiating off his body, but she could not feel a thing.

The darkness felt both intimate and anonymous, heightening the tension. A hand touched her elbow and she jumped back, breath rushing from her lungs in a startled whoosh. Her fingers uncurled, sending the flashlight crashing to the floor.

Luke's arm went around her waist, pulling her close while at the same time dancing her backward until her butt hit the cylindrical wall of the dome. His scent was in her nose, soap, spicy cologne, and masculine male.

His hands manacled her wrist and he pinned her arms overhead, pressed his hot body flush against hers.

Melody couldn't believe she was really doing this. Making out with him inside the dome when a hundred guests waited outside, not two hundred yards away. It felt so naughty, so wicked, so *wrong,* and thrilling her like nothing she had ever before experienced.

He was so receptive, so responsive. When she curled her fingers around his forearm, he actually quivered.

She was trembling too, uncertain but hungry for him. The risk heightening the experience, the costumes making their encounter just that much more enticing.

She gasped, but before the sound fully left her lips, his mouth was on hers, claiming her hard and long and fierce, nothing casual or laid back about this kiss. She responded in kind, nipping his bottom lip up between her teeth, tasting him with a hungry sound. She could feel every inch of his hard arousal, leaving absolutely no doubt as to how much he wanted her.

Wildness spilled from him into her and they were teenagers again, caught in the throes of youthful recklessness. The flavor of his desire filled her mouth and he tasted of secret rendezvous, broken rules, and naked lust — full-bodied red wine, earthy oysters, smoky barbecue, pilfered strawberries dipped in dark chocolate. His surging testosterone smelled of hot race car engines, leather backseats, and musky black truffles — rich, decadent, yet oddly comforting. He made her think of roads not taken, faded snapshots of a former life, the stirring of long-abandoned dreams, husky midnight laughter, and the mysterious feel of a lover's skin.

He broke the kiss, leaving her aching and panting, and taunted her by dangling his tempting lips just above hers.

"What?" she whispered, the sound coming out thick and rough in the empty room.

"I want you," he gasped, his voice as ragged as hers. "If you need to say no, I understand, but you better do it quick because I'm reaching the point of —"

She went up on her toes, snaked her arms around his neck, shoved off the sheik headdress, jammed her fingers through his hair, and yanked his head down to seal her mouth over his. Yes, she got that he was giving her a chance to call a halt to this before it went too far, and while she appreciated his gallantry, she wasn't the least bit interested in it.

Now.

She had to have him now and the consequences be damned. This didn't have to be complicated or fraught with strings. Nothing wrong with enjoying the moment. They were both consenting adults who knew what they wanted. She wasn't expecting happily-ever-after.

"No regrets," she muttered against his lips and speared her tongue past the teeth he parted so readily.

His arms tightened around her and a harsh groan rolled from his throat. "Melody," he murmured.

He tugged off the wig she was wearing, tossed it aside, then plucked at the pins holding her hair back, dislodging them. Tendrils fell about her face. His hands moved to cup her cheek, holding her still while he kissed her again and again.

Nothing had ever felt so good. No man had ever made her feel so desired, so cherished.

Whimpering, she ripped the robe over his head and threw it into the darkness to join her wig, then worked the buttons on his shirt he wore underneath, desperate to get him out of it.

Is this smart?

Hush! It didn't matter. She didn't care. If her heart got broken, she'd deal with it. Later. For now, there was nothing in the world as wonderful as his mouth, those fingers, that long hard body.

He pulled away again.

"No!" she cried and reached for him, only to realize he'd stopped just long enough to wrench off the shirt she'd unbuttoned.

He flung it off into the darkness, with the robe and the wig, revving her engines and leaving her panting and weak-kneed.

Her palms flew to his bare chest, spread across those hard beautiful muscles. While the darkness escalated the mystery, she wished she could see him. He busied himself with the zipper at her back, sliding it down, exposing her bare skin to the warm air.

"I want you," she whispered. "Now."

He responded by drowning out her words with a kiss so powerful it took her breath.

He wrapped one hand around her waist, his palm rhythmically squeezing her buttocks.

God, what a great kisser he was.

"Nibble on my neck," she murmured.

He complied. The minute his sharp teeth sank lightly into the tender skin at the hollow of her throat, she moaned softly.

Quiet. She had to be quiet. People might hear.

But she couldn't even think straight, much less fret about the potential for public humiliation. His palms were skimming up underneath her flimsy getup, his hands scorching against the bare skin of her belly.

Her knees bobbled.

Sensing her weakness, he pressed her back against the wall of the dome, holding her in place with the pressure of his hip.

He didn't speak.

Golden silence. Good. It made things even sexier.

Not hearing his voice made her feel as if he was pure fantasy and it escalated her arousal.

She felt daring and alluring and incredibly adventuresome. This was exactly what she needed.

His movements were measured, controlled, but at the same time relaxed and easy. He'd unhooked the clasp of her bra and his fingers were now trailing circles around her nipples, teasing them into taut peaks.

In the dark, in the masquerade, he was a creature of the night. Sleek and primal, sexual in a way that quickened her breathing and slicked her palms. The air in the dome was heavy with the sound of their rough, synchronized breathing. It smelled of the musk, of their throbbing bodies.

He kissed her again. The glide of his tongue was rich and smooth.

Her blood moved recklessly through her veins. There was that thrill again, rolling through her like an electrical storm, searing and stark and scary.

His mouth was skillful. Gentle when she needed him to be, firm when she needed that too. He was taking his time. She enjoyed his unanticipated leisure, but at the same time it added to her anxiety. The longer this took, the more likely they were to be caught.

Isn't that the point? The danger of discovery.

His arms were so strong. She wished it wasn't so dark, wished she could see his face and gaze deeply into his eyes.

She had intended this to be a clothes-on quickie but it wasn't turning out that way. She was pressed up against the wall, wearing nothing but black silk panties, stockings, and stilettos.

His hand was a hot pressure as he reached out to trail it across the soft silk between her legs. He stroked her gently, his fingertip executing a slow, deliberate circle.

Mewling softly against the pleasure, she grasped his arm for support. He kissed her again while his fingers explored. A warm, soft kiss of satisfaction.

Desire spread through her. She ran her tongue around his lips and he made a masculine noise of enjoyment.

He dropped to his knees, slipped off her panties, and then she felt the touch of his lips against her inner thigh. Slowly, his mouth inched upward.

Her body tensed. What was he doing?

She put a hand to the back of his neck. He raised his head.

"I want to feel you inside me," she whispered. She heard him rustling in the darkness. "What are you doing?"

"Condom."

There was a slight tearing sound like a small package being opened. Always prepared. That was her Luke.

She touched him down there, heard his sharp intake of breath. He was so hard. So big.

"Hurry," she insisted, growing suddenly scared against a nameless sense of dread.

He entered her carefully and then he began a slow, meticulous thrusting.

Swept away, she matched his tempo, arching her back, pushing against him, increasing the tension. The rhythm between them was quite extraordinary. They were so in tune with each other. He thrust, she parried.

It was almost mystical.

Biting need flowed through her body. She needed this intimacy, needed him. Her legs were wrapped around his waist and she held him tightly in a clench.

The orgasm rose in her, in a hot, loud knot. She bit his shoulder to hold back her screams of ecstasy.

He gave one last thrust and his body twitched with the power of his own climax. The sound of his breathing was rough against her ears.

She came as she'd never come before, wave upon wave, an entire ocean crashing through her. He held her gently as she shuddered in his arms.

Then after a while, after they had recovered, he dressed her in the dark.

Aided by the cloak of darkness, Melody left

the dome first. The speaker was just finishing his lecture, and no one had even noticed she was gone. She slipped into her seat at the back of the stone amphitheater beside Lace.

"Everything okay?" her cousin asked.

"Sure. Great. Why wouldn't it be?"

"I don't know. You sound breathless."

"Just stumbled in the dark."

"Where did you go?"

"Checking to make sure the domes were unlocked for the telescope viewing."

Lace cast her a sidelong glance.

"What is it?" she whispered.

"I've got nothing to go on except the light of the stars, but it looks to me like your dress is on wrong side out."

Melody reached up, touched the seam of her dress at the shoulder. So it was.

"You might want to slip over to the building and turn it the right side out before someone else notices." Lace grinned. "I'll make your excuses."

"Thanks."

"You're welcome. I understand what it's like to have the hots for the guy who seems all wrong for you." Lace gave her arm a companionable squeeze.

"I —" She closed her mouth. No point denying it. "I appreciate your help."

"That's what cousins are for."

Melody went into the main building to correct her wardrobe malfunction, and when she came out, the astronomers were assisting the guests as they used the telescope to track the moon and stars. It took her several minutes to find Luke among them and it required every strength of willpower she had in her not to go up and slip her arm around his waist. She wanted to be with him, touch him every single minute.

To distract herself, she turned her attention to her job as hostess, making sure everyone was enjoying himself. By the end of the evening, she had lost track of Luke and had no idea when he left the observatory. She stayed until everyone else was gone and the janitorial staff came in.

It was one in the morning by the time she got home. She was getting ready for bed when there was a quick rap on her door. She peeked out the peephole to see Luke standing on the front stoop. Quickly, she opened the door and dragged him inside.

"What are you —" She got no further because his mouth took hers hostage.

She wrapped her arms around his neck and the next thing she knew he was carrying her into the bedroom. "You shouldn't

338

be here. It's too risky."

He laughed low in his throat. "Oh, you're a fine one to talk about risky. Who was it that lured me into the dome with a hundred people right outside?"

"I didn't really mean to do it. I was just checking to make sure everything was set up for the viewing and you followed me inside."

"Best accidental seduction I ever had."

"That *was* pretty thrilling," she said.

"You're telling me. Good thing I had a robe for a costume. I've had a stiffy all evening and it's all because of you."

"Show me," she said.

He clicked on the bedside lamp, throwing a rectangle of yellow over the covers. "We did it in the dark," he said. "Now let's go for the light."

Slowly, he disrobed for her and she watched with fascinated eyes. He had the most amazing body. She held her breath in anticipation, watching the silky material of his costume drape and fall.

He did a little bump and grind that made her smile.

"You could be a professional," she teased.

"Only for you, darlin'," he drawled. "Only for you."

He crawled up on the bed with her, and

giggling, she lay back against the pillow as he kissed his way from her foot to her knees to her . . .

In no time, she was wriggling beneath his hot, wicked mouth.

He seemed to be everywhere at once. His mouth on the inside of her thigh, one hand trailing over her belly, the other lightly tickling the soft flesh on the underside of her arm. His touch was amazing, experienced. Everything he did was designed to elicit a response from her. He'd stroke one spot and she'd groan. Another spot made her whimper. Still another made her beg for more.

His kisses both robbed from her and gave back tenfold. He left her breathless, and yet feeling stronger, more complete than she'd ever felt in her life. His hands roamed over her body, an avid explorer eager for sensation.

Fifteen years might have gone by, but it felt like yesterday. Everything that passed between them was so poignant, so intense. They'd been young together, suffered horribly together, survived and found each other again. It felt like a miracle.

She tried not to romanticize their joining too much. Tried to appreciate what it was right now. Savored every single second because she had no idea if she would pass this way again. It was a time to be cherished. Treasured. And for this night, it felt ordained. Right. Perfect.

"I missed you," he whispered against her ear. "I missed you so much."

It frightened her how much his words touched her. How he made her feel. As if she was the only person on the planet. As if a million naked women could walk by and he would never notice because he was transfixed by her.

He covered her with his body, looked down into her face, his hazel eyes clear and bright. "Melly," he whispered her name like a lullaby. "Melly."

Her throat tightened. Pleasure swept up her in warm, delicious waves.

His hard-muscled chest was pressed against her soft breasts.

She was acutely aware of everything. His touch. His scent. The sound of his breathing. The acrid burn of her own desire.

She kissed him then, as she'd never kissed him before. Poured everything she had into it. Showing him without having to tell him how unique this moment was to her, what a special guy he was.

"I see you," he whispered. "I know who you are inside and out."

A calm serenity came over her, an odd counterbalance to the wild, out-of-control longing beating through her blood.

In Luke's eyes she glimpsed her authentic self and knew that she was fully accepted for who she was, flaws and all.

It wasn't some romantic notion. It wasn't a flight of fancy. It had nothing to do with private sex in a public place or the thrill of the forbidden or the intensity of teenage fantasies. It was a concrete, unshakable knowledge. A deep-down, abiding faith in him.

And it baffled her profoundly.

"Is that wide-eyed look for me?" he asked.

It was only then that she realized she'd been staring at his penis and it was a sight to behold. "You do have bragging rights."

Luke lay back against the pillows, reached for her, and pulled her over beside him. Cradling her in the crook of his arm, he smiled softly. "You make me feel like a superhero."

"You are one in my book."

He kissed her with exquisite tenderness, stroked her skin with the back of his hand. Slowly, leisurely, they explored each other with all five senses. Massaging, caressing, licking, tasting, finding the spots that made each other sigh, moan, and whimper.

"Give me your hand," he said.

She placed her hand in his and he guided her palm to his chest. She felt his heart thundering underneath his breastbone. Curiosity fused her hand to his skin. She couldn't pull away.

Mesmerized. They stared into each other.

Magic. It felt like simple magic.

It hit her then, what she was doing. Going down the wrong path, romanticizing this moment. Romanticizing him. She knew better, but the slow tempo he'd set had drawn her into the magic of the moment. She had to break the spell.

Only one way. Sex. Not love. Not tenderness. Not emotional intimacy. Just sex.

Hard and hot and real. Powerful orgasmic sex to blow away the mist of fantasy.

She captured his mouth with hers, pulled his bottom lip up between her teeth, and bit down lightly.

He groaned.

She pulled away to slide her mouth down his neck one hot kiss at a time. She tracked a path from his throat down the middle of his chest — with a quick detour to his nipples — before resuming her trek over his muscled abdomen, past his navel, to his pelvis and finally ending up at his most impressive erection.

He shuddered when her lips touched his hot, moist tip.

"Mmm," she murmured. "You taste delicious."

Up and down, around and around until they were both moaning and writhing, consumed by mutual pleasure.

On and on they played. He on her, she on him. Licking, sucking, tasting. Glorious sensations rippled through her body, turning her inside out. They increased the tempo as the pressure built, rising to the inevitable crescendo.

Melody whimpered soft whenever he did something she liked, squirmed when he made a wrong move. He picked up her rhythms, figuring out what she liked and giving her more of it.

She took him deeper until she felt him pressing against the back of her throat, juicy and slick. She rolled her lips back, stretching wider to accommodate his bigness. She wanted to swallow all of him.

Finally, Luke broke away, pulling her mouth from him. "I can't stand it anymore. I have to be inside you."

"Condoms," she gasped, so addled by passion she was impressed that she remembered. Thank heavens she'd remembered. An unplanned pregnancy was not a complication she wanted to deal with.

"I'm on it." Luke stumbled from the bed, searched for his pants, found them, retrieved a condom from the hip pocket, and already had it on before he got back into bed.

He was so damn beautiful. Hard, lean, a fine spray of dark hair between his nipples. Her hips twitched against his, the muscles between her thighs clenching.

And then he was inside her, big and hard.

Their breathing changed, getting hoarser, raspier. Their coupling was primordial. Ferocious and famished. He thrust into her. Again and again. As if he could never get enough. Shoving them closer and closer to the limit.

They were almost there. Both of them. Ready to come together.

Melody made a ragged noise of encouragement. More. More.

He kept up the steady rocking, driving her deeper and deeper into the savage yearning that was changing everything she had ever known about herself and what she was capable of.

Luke thrust into her again and again. His entire being seemed to slide deeper and deeper into hers until she could not differentiate where her body stopped and his began.

Something earth-shattering happened. Something she'd never experienced before. It was as if his soul had leaped from his body and shot straight into hers along with his orgasm.

He cried out as his essence poured out of him, imbuing her with streaming currents of his masculine energy.

Together, they soared.

Just the two of them.

He cried out, jerked, just as she contracted her muscles, pulling him into her very center.

A second orgasm sprang up from inside her, flooded her body, drowning her brain. She was numb, wrung, spent.

Luke's body shuddered, then went limp.

They clung to each other, helpless, as wave after wave of energy rippled through them. Gasping, he rolled over, sinking onto his back and taking her with him. He held her close as her chest heaved and quivered.

Wow.

They lay together for a long time afterward, drifting, coming down from the endorphin high. She flipped over onto her stomach and he curled up beside her, his head resting on the small of her back. She liked the feel of his hair against his skin. Liked the intimacy.

"I love this cute little birthmark," he said, and pressed his lips to the area on her left butt cheek at the juncture of her thigh were she had a deep brown stain the size of a quarter. Because she couldn't see it, she mostly forgot it was there.

"My mother calls it a stork bite. Theory is the stork bit me there while delivering me. You know the concept. Flying stork carrying a baby in a diaper. The image is an ad agency icon."

"Where did they get the idea of babies coming from storks in the first place?" He paused to kiss his way up her heinie to the small of her back. "When the kiddies ask where they come from, and their folks are trying to think of a good lie, how did storks as the culprit leap to anyone's mind?"

"Who knows." She chuckled, enjoying the feel of his lips on her bare back. "Someone in creative smoking weed?"

"And this scar on your shoulder." His lips were there now, tracing the jagged edges of the scar with his tongue. "I love it too. How did you get it?"

"I was in a skiing accident when I was nineteen. Christmas break. Park City, Utah. Night skiing. I don't recommend it."

"I never knew that."

"Why would you? I was living in New York

at the time."

"I hate that you were hurt." He massaged the scar, his body heat seeping into her muscles. "What happened?"

"I'd taken a spill, and another skier jumped over a mogul onto me and I took a ski pole in the shoulder. It could have been much worse. A few stitches and I was good as new."

"But scarred."

"An indelible reminder. A permanent souvenir. I'll never forget Park City." She turned halfway to look at him over her shoulder. He was leaning above her, his chin at the top of her head.

"You're pretty damn resilient, Melly."

"Aren't most people?"

"Not really. A lot of folks have trouble letting go of old hurts."

She poked her tongue against her cheek, thought about the family feud. "Point taken."

He pulled her around as he fell over onto his side, until they were facing each other on top of the quilt. "But you know what I love most of all?"

She propped her head on her bent arm, elbow sunk into the pillow, stared into his face. God, he had such gorgeous eyes. Part brown. Part green. One hundred percent mesmerizing. "What's that?"

"That crooked little tooth." He reached over to run a finger over her lip above the tooth.

Immediately, she tucked her upper lip down over her teeth, hiding it from him. "What's wrong with you? All the things you like about me are imperfections."

"But they're not," he said. "They're perfectly you. Anyone else could have straight teeth and unmarked skin and no scar at all, but only you have all three."

"Oh, I'm certain someone else in the world has a shoulder scar, a big ugly birthmark on their butt, and a crooked tooth."

"Not like yours. Only you have that special combo."

"Lucky me."

"You are lucky."

"I know," she said. "I'm here with you."

"But not as lucky as I am." He kissed the nape of her neck. "I got the better end of this deal."

"How do you figure?"

"I'm in bed with a Madison Avenue advertising executive."

"Not anymore," she said, surprised to discover she didn't feel badly about that.

"Why? You kicking me out of bed?"

"No," she laughed. "I'm not an ad executive anymore."

"You'll be back."

Honestly, she wasn't sure she wanted that anymore.

"Do you miss it something terrible?" he asked.

"I miss the challenge of it, but you know what? I don't miss the pressure."

"Really? I thought you thrived on pressure."

"I am a deadline junkie," she admitted. "Pressure gets the best out of me, but it also takes a lot of me too. Since I've been home, I've realized all the things I've been missing."

"Like what?" he asked, toying with her hair.

"Time with family and friends." She rolled over, looked up at him. "Great sex."

"You didn't have great sex before?"

"I was always in such a rush to meet deadlines that sex became just something else to check off my to-do list."

"Stick around, darlin', we're just getting started," he murmured.

"Mmm," she purred.

And then they were making love all over again.

CHAPTER 18

Luke studied her in the morning light filtering through the curtains. God, but she was beautiful and sexy and irresistible.

And it wasn't just lust rousing him, although she stirred plenty of that, Luke genuinely liked her. She was quick-witted and professional, eager, goal-oriented, a real go-getter. Of course, that was part of the problem, wasn't it? There was nothing much to go get here in Cupid. Everything he'd ever wanted was here.

But Melody? This town couldn't hold her dreams. They were simply too big.

She stretched her arms over her head and smiled at him, guileless as the girl he'd once known, but different too — more beautiful and self-confident in maturity. Multifaceted. His Melody.

She's not yours.

Crazy. He'd never had thoughts like this about any other woman. Wanting to brand her, make her his.

Yeah, maybe she wasn't his permanently, but for right now? Yes, she was.

"Why are you looking so serious?" Hair falling over her sleepy eyes, she reached over to trace a finger over his cheek. "I'm usually the serious one."

He lifted one corner of her mouth, gave her a half smile. God, she was gorgeous. He raised himself up on one elbow, hovered over her, those big brown eyes taking him hostage.

She sank her top teeth into her plump bottom lip. An invitation? Or was she feeling insecure?

Compelled, he leaned in for a kiss — light, tender, testing to see if she was interested in doing more than kissing.

"Nice," she murmured and slipped slender arms around his neck, pulling his head down, parting her teeth, darting out her pink tongue in open invitation.

A groan of pleasure rose up in his throat as he slipped his tongue inside her, while simultaneously slipping his hand up the nape of her neck and spearing his fingers through her wild, thick hair.

She wriggled beneath him and he was instantly hard enough to cut sheet metal with his dick. He was in so much freaking trouble and she was killing him, but man, what a way to go.

He nibbled her bottom lip, and then moved down her chin to her throat. She moaned softly, arched her neck. He smiled against her skin. Ah, he'd found a sensitive spot.

"Do you have any idea how damn sexy you are?" he whispered.

She laughed.

Of course she did, the seductive wench. Just for that, he playfully bit the sensitive spot on her throat again, before flicking his tongue over her jaw and following the firm, smooth line up to capture her earlobe between his teeth.

"Oh my." She breathed.

He went back for a second helping of that delicious mouth. Face it. He was a greedy bastard, devouring her as if she was his last meal, and she didn't seem to mind in the least. In fact, she seemed just as hungry as he. Giving as good as she got. She ran her palms over his back, stroking him in all the right places.

Things were getting too heated. He wanted to savor this.

"Whoa," he said, breaking contact. "We better slow things down if you don't want this over in twenty seconds."

Her breath came out in short, hot gasps and her eyes widened and he simply could not resist. With a groan, he pulled her into his arms, rolled onto his back, taking her along with him. She ended up straddling his waist, her knees planted on either side of the mattress.

Mischievously, she rocked back causing her buttocks to bump against his erection.

He ran his hands down her spine, stopping when he got to her slim waist.

How had he gotten so lucky?

Enjoy it while you can. It won't last.

He knew that. Had told himself from the beginning not to expect too much, but damn if he hadn't already gone ahead and fallen head over heels in love.

They spent that entire Sunday in bed, getting up only to shower, eat, and go back to bed again. It was the most perfect Sunday she'd had in recent memory. By the end of the day, Melody was raw, achy, and happier than she'd been in a very long time.

Who knew? Great sex was a wonderful tonic for what ailed you. Too bad there wasn't a way to bottle the stuff.

In the dark of night on Sunday evening, Luke left their love nest and crept back to his own condo, after making sure no one was out and about in the complex when he made his stealthy move.

The minute he was gone, the place felt desperately empty. To keep from dwelling on it, she immediately threw herself into the final preparations for the events she was overseeing for the Memorial Day weekend, including the bachelor auction and the Sadie Hawkins dance.

She ventured out on Monday morning, dropping by the radio station to record a commercial spot about the events. While she was there, the DJ asked her to stick around for a short interview. She did so obligingly. In the listener call-in Q&A session that followed, she was surprised to find that most of the questions she fielded were about the Cupid letters she'd put up on the Web site the previous weeks. A lot of people wanted to know if Juliet was a Nielson or a Fant. Melody said that she couldn't speculate on Juliet's true identity, but quickly pointed out how universal the issue was from the Hatfields and the McCoys to the Capulets and the Montagues to Scotland's MacDonalds and Campbells. Juliet could be from anywhere.

Afterward, she headed back to the condo and she'd no more than gotten inside when the doorbell rang. Her pulsed leaped. *Luke?*

Of course not. He knew better than to show up on her doorstep in the light of day. She opened the door to find a delivery boy holding a box of flowers. Fresh flowers? In a drought?

"Shipped from Houston," the delivery boy said, reading her mind. "Flown in this morning."

She tipped him, shut the door, and brought the flowers into the kitchen to find something to use as a vase. The bouquet was roses and stargazer lilies interspersed with baby's breath.

The card inside read: *A night of stargazing I'll never forget.*

Melody put three fingers to her mouth, closed her eyes. "No, Luke. No, no."

She paced, wrung her hands. Things were getting out of control. She couldn't let this slide. She had to say something. After putting the flowers in a vase — he'd already sent them, she might as well enjoy them — she picked up her cell phone and called him.

"Hello," he answered in that deep, sexy voice of his that never failed to turn her upside down.

"What are you doing?" she asked.

"Is this the part where I'm supposed to tell you I'm sitting on the couch in my underwear?"

"This isn't a phone sex call."

"No? Damn."

"I'm serious, Luke. Why are you sending me flowers?"

"Who says I sent them?"

"Who else would it be?"

"You underestimate yourself, Melly. Every eligible man in town, and some that aren't so eligible, drools whenever you walk by."

"Look, we agreed, just sex. No dating, no romance. This is supposed to be a secret affair. Flowers are romantic and the delivery boy now knows someone sent me flowers and you know how gossip flows in this town. If someone really wanted to find out who sent them to me they could."

"Hey, what if you thought of it as a thank-you for a good time."

"If you're going to send flowers and do romantic stuff then we have to stop sleeping together."

"You're overreacting."

"I'm serious about this. From what I've heard, you've never had trouble keeping things casual before."

"I give flowers. I'm a flower giver. It's my thing."

"Flowers are how men try to get women into bed. You already got me there. No need for flowers."

"You're right. It was an impulsive gesture. My bad."

"I don't mean to sound bitchy," she said. "They are nice flowers."

"I did have a great time this weekend." He lowered his voice. "You were sensational."

"You were pretty good yourself."

"Can we get together tonight? I promise no more sending of flowers or gifts of any kind."

"Well, you can bring food. Food is okay. Everyone has to eat, right. As long as it's not romantic food. No asparagus or oysters or anything like that."

"Where am I going to get oysters in the desert?"

"Where did you get flowers in the desert?"

"How's this? You come over to my place tonight for another midnight rendezvous. I'll have supper ready. Nothing romantic."

"Oh, you can't cook it either. A man cooking for a woman is romantic."

"But if I get take-out for two won't that be suspicious?"

"Hmm, you're right. Okay, you can cook for me."

"I'm so happy. See you tonight." Luke hung up.

Leaving Melody to realize she'd just made

a date.

With each passing day the drought grew worse. Old-timers lamented that they'd never seen a time when it was so bad. No matter where you looked, there wasn't a sprig of green in sight. Temperatures soared during the day and everyone stayed indoors. People murmured in hushed tones about leaving the valley. Melody worried. How arrogant it had been of her to think she could save the finances of a town in the midst of the worst drought in recorded history. Even the die-hard Cupidites were talking about leaving. How could she hope to bring tourists to the town?

But she couldn't let the Chamber of Commerce see her doubt. She had to put the best spin on things that she could, but as she stood in the meeting room at the converted rail station, watching the board members file in with dire expressions on their faces, she knew she faced a daunting task. It was like being the captain of the *Titanic* trying to convince the passengers that the ship wasn't sinking.

And she'd been hiding out in bed with Luke. She wished she were there now. Oh man, she was in so much trouble.

"Good morning everyone," she chirped.

"What's good about it?" Pat asked. "You know how many cars I fixed this past weekend?" She held up a finger. "One. Exactly one. And the customer couldn't pay me outright. I had to agree to installments."

"I'm so sorry to hear that," Melody soothed.

"You're not doing such a hot job of bringing in the tourists." Pat frowned.

"I'm trying and I do have some encouraging figures to share about the stargazing party."

"Hmph." Pat settled herself in a chair.

"Woman's got a point." Guy plopped down beside Pat. "I've only sold three cars this month. No one can afford a new one. This is getting freaky scary. I'm thinking about moving the dealership to El Paso."

"El Paso is involved in a drought, the same as we are," Melody pointed out.

"Yeah, but they've got the population to support a dealership. We're screwed out here." Guy grunted. "I'm ready to hear what other ideas you have up your sleeve, 'cause what we've tried so far ain't working."

Melody nibbled her bottom lip. Truthfully, she was out of ideas. The only idea that kept circling her head was about reenacting Cupid's history, complete with the Greenwood-Fant-Nielson feud. It was the only thing in town that seemed to have stay-ing power. And the letters from Juliet she'd printed on the blog seemed to support that theory, until Luke made her stop.

"We'll discuss all that today," she assured them.

Luke walked in and every eye turned to him. "Eloise isn't here to take the minutes," he said. "One of her barn cats died from heat exhaustion and even though it was a stray, she's really torn up about it. Could someone take the minutes?"

"I'll do it," Junie Mae volunteered.

His eyes met Melody's. She hadn't seen him since four o'clock that morning, when she left his bed to slip back over to her place. Remembering, her cheeks heated. She ducked her head in case anyone saw.

"You ready to start?" he asked.

"Yes."

He sat down at the head of the table, swept a hand at her. "Go ahead and take the floor."

Five pairs of anxious eyes fixed on her. She kept the smile pinned to her face and stood up. "I have some good news."

"I have some bad news," Ricardo said. He'd been sitting off to one side, watching and listening as everyone else had expressed their concerns, but not speaking up until now.

"Give us the bad news first," Walker said. "I prefer to end on an up note."

Ricardo ran a hand over his scalp, leaving his salt and pepper hair standing up in tufts. "I have tried to think of a way around this decision, but there is none."

"Maybe we can help," Melody ventured. "Tell us what's troubling you."

"I am beyond help," Ricardo said. "I have seen a lawyer. In order to save my personal funds, I must file for bankruptcy. La Hacienda Grill will be closing at the end of the summer. I'm only keeping it open that long, because August 31 is the seventy-fifth-year anniversary of when my grandfather first opened the place."

"Oh no, Ricardo!" the group exclaimed in unison.

"I have had a lot of local support, and I've been very lucky," Ricardo said. "But without tourists, there simply isn't enough business to keep the restaurant open."

Walker laid a hand across his belly. "What will I do without my breakfast burrito?"

"Joe proposed to me at La Hacienda," Junie Mae said. "If he were alive, he would be so sad about this."

"The place is a Cupid icon," Pat put in.

"Movie stars ate there."

"How much do you need to keep it open," Luke said. "Maybe we can help you get a loan."

Ricardo shook his head, "Failing money falling from the sky, my lawyer says bankruptcy is my only choice. I mortgaged the place to the hilt to send my *niños* to college. There's no more money to be loaned. I'm at the end of the road."

"This can't be happening," Melody said. She had plenty of fond memories of La Hacienda Grill herself.

"But it is." Ricardo sank his face into his upturned palms. "I have failed my family."

Junie Mae rubbed his back. "It's not your fault. It's this damn drought."

"So." Pat straightened, fixed her gaze on Melody. "Tell us the good news."

In light of Ricardo's bad news, her good news was pathetic indeed. "The stargazing party brought twenty-five thousand dollars into the community."

"Spread over how many businesses?" Pat asked.

"Thirteen."

"So that's what?" Walker narrowed his eyes. "About two grand a business?"

"That's a general average, some business made a little more, some a little less,"

Melody explained.

"Two thousand?" Guy snorted. "Is that all? Two grand doesn't pay the light bill at the dealership."

Melody raised her chin. "It's a start."

"It's a drop in the bucket," Ricardo said gloomily.

"A drop is better than nothing," Junie Mae said.

"Not in a drought," Guy countered.

"All right. It's clear we have a situation and we've got to do something to turn things around," Luke said. "But don't forget, we still have the bachelor auction and the Sadie Hawkins dance and the Memorial Day celebrations coming up at the end of the month."

"How are early ticket sales for that looking?" Guy asked Melody.

"They've been tepid but it's still ten days away, I'm doing my best to get the word out. I had a radio interview yesterday in Alpine and Pierce has gotten a Dallas Cowboy to commit as one of the bachelors, so I'm optimistic."

Guy snorted. "I'm glad someone is."

No one said anything to that. What could they say? She'd let them all down and they all knew it. She had failed at her job and her community was paying the price.

■ ■ ■ ■

For the rest of the day, Melody couldn't stop thinking about Ricardo's plight and the look of sorrow in his eyes. Losing La Hacienda Grill, a place with such deep roots in Cupid, was going to be a big blow. A blow from which the town might never recover.

Honestly, she was out of ideas. The only thing that held any promise of bringing in more tourists was those letters from Juliet. She had seen a big spike in comments from the first letter to the second, until Luke had made it clear he didn't want her publishing any more of those letters.

What would it hurt to publish one more? Yes, Luke would be mad at her, but if it boosted tourism he'd have to forgive her.

And if he doesn't?

Well, in their current situation, they didn't stand much of a chance for happily-ever-after anyway.

Knowing she was setting herself up for a lot of potential heartache, she waited until everyone had left the Chamber of Commerce for the day, took out the red silk stationery and started to write.

CHAPTER 19

Dear Cupid,
I would love to take your advice and leave this place. It was a home I once loved but now, it has been ruined by hatred and intolerance on both sides of the fence. I should have left when I had the chance. Now, it's too late. Why didn't I listen to you? Why didn't I leave? Why? It's simple. I'm pregnant with my lover's baby. And my parents are livid. They are insisting I get an abortion. I am only sixteen. Where can I go? What can I do? I love this baby so much already, but my parents have forbidden me to see my baby's daddy again. There are no words to describe the pain inside of me. I want this child. But I'm afraid, so afraid they are going to take it away from me. And if they don't, what kind of world am I bringing him or her into?

A world where people hate and don't ever forgive.

> — Yours in utter despair,
> Modern Day Juliet

"Oh my God," Natalie exclaimed as Melody read the letter in the red silk envelope. "This is terrible. Horrible. Awful."

"Stuff like that happened all the time when I was a girl," Great-Aunt Delia said.

"They had abortions back then?" Natalie asked.

Great-Aunt Delia leveled her a look. "What? Just because it was illegal didn't mean people didn't do it. Mexico's less than two hours from here."

"I never knew that," Melody's mother said.

"What, that Mexico is so close or that there were such things as abortions before *Roe v. Wade*?" Great-Aunt Delia gave her a saucy look.

"That you knew people who went to Mexico to have illegal abortions."

"What? You thought we were all stiff-lipped virgins back in the day?" Great-Aunt Delia snorted. "People are people the world over. They laugh, cry, have sex, feud, get pregnant, fall in love, get old, die. It's a tireless cycle."

"To my way of thinking," Junie Mae said, "the real question is who is Juliet? I think we should see if we could find her. Reach out to her and her parents. Talk some sense into them."

"Do you think she's a Fant or a Nielson?" Natalie asked.

"She might be neither," Melody offered, feeling guilty now that everyone was getting so worked up over poor fictitious Juliet. "She could be from somewhere else. Marfa. Alpine. Marathon. You never know."

"Anybody heard of any feuding families from those towns?" Junie Mae asked.

No one said anything.

"Most of us in this room — Junie Mae excluded — are Greenwood-Fants." Her mother met her gaze. "Our family has enjoyed a prestigious place in Cupid. The Nielsons have always come up second place. There are less of them for one thing. They're the second richest family in town and no matter what they do they can never seem to match us in money, skills, or talent."

"That's from a Fant point of view," Melody said. "Ask a Nielson and I imagine they'll have a different story to tell."

"So." Great-Aunt Delia rubbed her palms together. "How are you going to answer Juliet this time?"

"I'm going to ask her to reveal her true identity to me in a private letter and I'll try to intervene between her and her parents." The weird thing was, Melody was starting to think of Juliet as a real person too. How did the saying go? You tell a lie long enough and you'll start to believe it? With this move, she was reaching the end of her plan to convince Luke to stop sweeping the family feud under the metaphorical rug. Next step after this, come clean publicly that she'd written the letters. That put a knot in her stomach. He was bound to be mad about what she'd done. But she'd known that when she'd started this.

"Sounds like a busybody move," Great-Aunt Delia said. "I like it."

Five minutes after Melody posted the third letter the phone began to ring off the hook at the Chamber of Commerce.

"Boy, you sure lit a fire under them folks by publishing those letters on the Internet," Emma Lee said. "All ten lines are blinking and I got more backed up. They all want to talk to the woman who answers the Cupid letters to Juliet. I told 'em it was a bunch of volunteers that do it, so they want to talk to the person who's been putting the letters on the Web site. That's you."

"I'll field the calls." Melody picked up the phone.

"Abortion is wrong!" the caller hollered.

"Thanks for your opinion," Melody said and got rid of the angry one quick.

"That poor girl," said the next caller. "I just want to put my arms around her and hug her. If I come to Cupid can I meet her?"

"No one knows who Juliet is," Melody said. Well, except for her. Juliet was a conglomeration of Fant and Nielson women throughout the last ninety years. Or so she told herself. But it didn't really ease her conscience.

"Where's that young man in all this?" the next caller asked. "He deserves a vote in what happens to his unborn child."

Melody plowed through a total of twenty-five calls, every single one of them fired up over Juliet's dilemma. Wow. She was a better marketer than she realized.

"Melody!" Emma Lee called from the reception desk. "You're trending on Twitter."

"What?"

"And the blog has gotten three thousand forty-six comments. Let me check Facebook. Omigod!"

"What is it? Melody left her office to go stand at the reception desk.

"Holy mushrooms." Emma Lee's eyes met hers. "Juliet's gone viral."

Braced for an angry call from Luke for breaking her promise about not publishing any more letters from Juliet, Melody shut down her cell phone to avoid the inevitable. She had a good excuse for her cowardice. After Emma Lee took off for school at ten, she stayed busy fielding inquiries about Juliet's well-being and selling tickets to the bachelor auction, Sadie Hawkins dance, and Founder's Day picnic. The phones did not stop ringing. There were people buying tickets from Houston, Dallas, San Antonio, Austin, El Paso, and Santa Fe.

By the end of the day, all the Memorial Day weekend events had sold out and all the lodging in town was booked. The power of the Internet stunned her. People cared about Juliet. They cared a lot.

Making Melody feel guilty about the lie. *It's all for the greater good,* she tried to convince herself.

At four o'clock, Luke stalked into the Chamber of Commerce. "Melody!" he bellowed.

Uh-oh, time to pay the piper. She smoothed her skirt and came out of her office to find him standing there.

"I've been trying to call your cell and it keeps going to voice mail," he said. "And the line here is constantly busy."

"I've been busy myself."

"I know. Everywhere I went today, I heard about it. The town's buzzing." He came toward her, his expression enigmatic.

"You don't say?"

"You disobeyed me." He closed in on her. "And printed another Juliet letter anyway." He waved the greensheet in front of her face. "This could have been you. It could have been us."

Her palms went instantly sweaty. Did he suspect something? "But we never got that far, did we?"

"Because of our families."

"Because you were too afraid to rock the boat."

"No," he said firmly. "Because I knew that if I rocked the boat I couldn't depend on you to stay in it with me."

Punch to the gut. Ouch. She forced herself not to move. "The girl was in such despair, Luke. I had to print her letter."

"If this ends up causing trouble for the community —"

"How can it cause trouble?" she interrupted. "All the empty beds in town will be filled on Memorial Day weekend. The events are sold out. All over the Internet they're talking about Cupid. I did my job, Luke. I brought tourists back to town in the midst of the worst drought in history."

"You did at that," he said and lowered his eyelids. "The mayor part of me is damn proud of you."

"And the lover part?" she whispered, leaning in.

"Well, he's going to need some placating."

Melody couldn't stay away from Luke. No matter how hard she tried. Time and time again, she found herself drawn across the courtyard to his condo, where he'd started spending every night since the stargazing party, her body on fire for him. It was the fourth time that week that she'd gone to his place or he'd come to hers.

This relationship wasn't going to end well in the long run, she knew that, but here she was, standing on his front stoop, wearing nothing but a raincoat.

Stupid to wear a raincoat in a place that hadn't seen rain in over eighteen months. If anyone saw her . . . but it was midnight again and quiet in the sleepy town. The nosy neighbors were sound asleep. Or at least that's what she told herself.

Blood churning, she wet her lips, raised

her fist to knock on his door, but it swung inward before her knuckles had a chance to rap and Luke pulled her inside. Sexy music played on the sound system.

"I've got a bubble bath waiting for you," he soothed, and guided her to the master bath, untying the belt on her raincoat as they went.

Okay, she'd admitted. She was addicted to being with him. So sue her.

The sex play just kept getting better and better. On Monday night, they'd watched an erotic movie together and acted out the story line. Whee! On Tuesday night, she tied him to his bed with silk ties and read Anaïs Nin poetry to him before doing the things described in the book. On Wednesday, he'd given her a pedicure, a foot massage, and then blown her mind by sucking her toes, unearthing a minefield of erogenous zones she had no idea she possessed. She paid him back with a massage of her own. And now, tonight they were taking a bubble bath together complete with vanilla-scented candles, champagne, and Barry White crooning sex songs.

"You know," she said as Luke washed her back. "I'm going to be really busy this entire weekend with the upcoming Memorial Day events. We're going to have to take a break."

"I know," he said mournfully and kissed the nape of her neck. "I'm going to miss you."

"I worry that we're growing incautious." She ran her fingers through the hair on his arms. "We're so hung up on each other that we're not paying much attention to what's going on in the community."

"We're very good not to show it when we run across each other in public. The other day at the board meeting, when you looked right through me, it sort of hurt my feelings until I remembered you were just playing it cool."

"That's what I mean about incautious. This is just about sex, Luke. I haven't changed my mind."

"Is it because you're scared?" he murmured as he nibbled her ear. "Because I'm scared too."

"I know. It's scary. It would be so easy to cross the line."

"Remind me again why that would be such a horrible thing?"

"Your family hates my family, my family hates yours. I'm only here temporarily. Long-distance relationships rarely work."

"Oh yeah, that."

"I'm not sure —"

His mouth found a sensitive spot on her

ear. She moaned and sank deeper into the tub. "What's that?"

"Huh?" She shivered.

"You were saying?"

"I dunno. When you do that thing you're doing there every thought just flies right out of my brain."

"Well, here. Let me do that again."

"Okay, but after tonight, we have to cool it for a while. All right?"

"Whatever you say, darlin'," he said, and tugged her under the water with him.

Somehow, she managed to stay away from Luke on Friday. Small victory, yay! But honestly, it was because she started work at six A.M. and didn't fall into bed until after midnight. During this entire week she'd probably slept a total of thirty hours. They had to take a break from each other or collapse from lack of sleep.

On Saturday morning, Melody dressed for the heat in a red sundress and matching sandals and pulled her hair up in a loose chignon to keep it off her neck, put on a pair of silver earrings, and picked up her handbag. As she went out the door, she noticed that Luke had not spent the night at his condo.

That was good, she told herself. Never

mind the disappointment lodged in her belly. He needed to take care of his ranch, just as she needed to focus on her business. Making sure the Memorial Day weekend was a financial success. While tourism had picked up a bit because of the activities she'd advertised and orchestrated, and the stargazing party had been a success, it wasn't enough. They needed a big influx of people and the sooner the better.

She could do her job much better without the mayor underfoot distracting her.

The sun was peeping over the horizon as she drove into town, parked in the Chamber of Commerce parking lot, killed the engine, and reached for her purse. It was already furnace-hot and in just those few seconds after the air conditioner shut off, perspiration stuck tendrils of hair to her forehead, but the minute she got out of the car, the arid air evaporated it.

"It's going to be okay," she told herself. "Somehow you'll pull this off."

The parade started at eight, followed by the bachelor auction, a community picnic, and in the evening, the Sadie Hawkins dance to be held at the community center gymnasium. And she was in charge of it all. Never mind. It's what she was getting paid to do.

People were passing by, most of them headed for the area where the floats were parked.

"Good morning, Ms. Spencer."

She turned to see a grinning Luke coming toward her. He was dressed in his usual cowboy attire, but over his shoulder, he carried a tuxedo in a see-through garment bag.

"Hello, Mayor," she said coolly, as if she hadn't spent the entire last week learning every inch of this man's naked body. "Preparing for the bachelor auction, I see."

He came closer.

She tried not to react, but that was like saying she tried not to get thirsty in the desert.

"Are you going to bid on me?" he asked.

"What part of 'secret' affair confuses you?" she whispered. "I can't bid on you."

"So you wouldn't bid on me even if Widow Jones is the highest bidder?" he asked, referring to a bawdy local woman who'd once been a Vegas showgirl before becoming the trophy wife of wealthy Jeff Davis Country rancher, Virgil Jones. Senior citizen Virgil had died of a heart attack on his wedding night with a smile on his face, leaving his newly minted widow wildly wealthy and sex-starved to boot.

"Seriously?" she raised her voice. She

didn't want to appear conspiratorial to the casual passersby. There was most likely a Fant or Nielson among them somewhere. "I'd pay to see you on a date with Widow Jones. Maybe we could sell tickets. I'm always looking for a way to bring in tourists."

He narrowed his eyes, a faint grin slightly turning up the corners of his lips. "You've got a cruel streak, Melody Spencer, anyone ever tell you that?"

"You're the first," she said, struggling to make it look like they were not friendly if anyone happened to overhear their conversation.

"And too cool to stoop to bidding in a bachelor auction?"

"That's right."

"You're missing out," he promised.

"On what?"

"My date gets a home-cooked dinner at Chez Nielson."

"You're cooking?"

He puffed out that magnificent chest; she tried not to stare. "I am."

"I'll tell your date to be sure to put the poison control center on speed dial." Of course she already knew he was a good cook. He'd cooked for her. Omelets and waffles. Spaghetti with homemade garlic cheese toast. But it couldn't look like she had any idea he possessed mad cooking skills.

"Hey," he said, playing along. "For your information, I took cooking lessons and I make a mean chicken enchilada."

"*You* took cooking lessons?"

"Of course. Women love a man who can cook." He lowered his voice, leaned in. "You certainly do."

Melody made a show of rolling her eyes as a group of women strolled past. "If you'll excuse me, I have a lot to do to get ready for this event."

"Well," he said. "I better go start the parade. Mayoral duty."

"Yes. You do that."

He turned to go.

"Luke?"

He turned back, his simmering hazel eyes drilling into her. "Uh-huh?"

Why had she stopped him? She couldn't say the words on the tip of her tongue — *I want you so badly I can taste it.*

"Yes?" he prompted.

"Better stock up on condoms," she teased. "I heard Widow Jones drinks Red Bull and takes a lot of B vitamins."

CHAPTER 20

The bachelor auction started at ten, right after the parade.

Dressed in a tuxedo and feeling like a side of beef, he waited backstage with the other bachelors. Yes, the whole bachelor auction thing had been his idea, and he would do anything to help his hometown, but dressing up in a monkey suit hadn't been his idea.

Melody had insisted on the tuxedo. "We need to present you in a whole new light," she'd said at Tuesday's board meeting. "Elegance and style."

Yeah. He should have known. Packaging things to look pretty was her stock in trade.

But why was he the only one stuck in a tuxedo? The Dallas Cowboys' second-string kicker, Domingo Diaz, got to wear his uniform, and so did the local fireman. The Chippendale's model was dressed like a construction worker, and a rancher from

Alpine wore Levi's and a Stetson. Why had she insisted *he* wear the tux?

Maybe that was her sexual fantasy. She went for the suave and debonair types. It made sense, but too bad for him. Suave wasn't his style. He was cowboy all the way.

He tugged at the bow tie.

A click of high heels, a tsk of the tongue, the scent of exotic, sophisticated perfume, and there she was, standing in front of him, chocolate eyes, a tolerant smile, long blond hair cascading down her shoulders, a trim but shapely body that would drive him crazy if he let it.

He scratched his palms. Hell, who was he trying to kid? Her body *did* drive him crazy.

Melody stopped in front of him. The bodice of her pretty red sundress molded over the slope of impressive breasts. Wisps of hair curled around her face, softened her high cheekbones, and her mouth . . . oh that mouth!

Damn him, it was the most kissable mouth on the planet — full and wide and welcoming. When he looked at those lips, he remembered . . . one thing and one thing only.

Sex.

Honestly, it wasn't just those hauntingly beautiful lips that made him think about sex, but rather, it was the total package —

from the endearingly bossy, I'm-in-charge-here expression on her face, to the way she carried herself all regal and proud, to the vulnerable glint that came into her eyes when things weren't going according to plan.

Poor kid. Being a perfectionist in an imperfect world had to be hard. He wanted so badly to teach her that it was okay to be ordinary, that she had nothing to prove, that she was just fine as she was.

He longed to muss her hair, to kiss her hard and smear that pristine lipstick, to make her call out his name again in hot, breathless pants. Yep, everything about this woman stirred him.

Did she have any idea what she did to him? Wearing that little red dress held up by strips of material no thicker than a strand of linguini? He imagined chewing those straps right off her body, and licked his lips.

She reached up, and for one blinding second he believed she was going to kiss him in public and he thought, *I'm not going to fight it.* His arms went up of their own accord to slide around her waist and . . .

"Hold still," she scolded. "Your tie is askew."

Ears burning, he dropped his arms. "It's not like I wear one of these things every day," he grumbled.

Her nimble fingers readjusted his tie and she patted his lapel. "There."

The blue-green vein at the hollow of her throat fluttered fast and hard, matching the tempo of his own pulse thundering through his temples.

His dick hardened. The combination of her scent, that thin cotton dress, and those full lips unraveled him completely.

Unable to keep staring at those tempting lips without losing his mind, he dropped his gaze and noticed with a jolt that, God bless her, she was wearing a camisole instead of a bra and he could see the outline of her nipples beaded up hard and taut. A gentleman would look away, but then again, Luke had never claimed to be a gentleman.

He ogled.

And she noticed.

Frowning, Melody crossed her arms over her chest, hiding those lovely nipples from his sex-starved view. It had only been since Thursday that they'd had sex, but it felt like a year.

"Save it for the ladies bidding on you," she teased.

"Huh?" he said, feigning ignorance.

She gave him a chiding look.

"Okay," he acknowledged and raised his

palms. "I'm a Neanderthal. I freely admit it."

"Some things never change." Melody chuckled and moved on to the next bachelor in line. She beamed at the rancher, ran a hand over the man's beard-stubbled jaw. "Love the scuff, Clint. So will the ladies."

A sick feeling came over him, as if he'd just eaten a bushel of raw potatoes. Especially when Clint grinned at Melody and touched her shoulder.

Deep inside, his inner Neanderthal stirred. He fisted his hands, fought the startling urge to punch the guy with a hard jab to the nose and lay him out flat on the cement floor.

She went on to the next bachelor and then the next, commenting on their appearance, giving them auction block tips, smiling and touching and . . .

Luke swallowed back the green bile that scaled his throat. He pictured himself pummeling every single man standing there just for looking at her, leaving them bloodied and broken. He wanted to scoop Melody in his arms and spirit her off. Claim her again. Make her his woman once and for all.

Whoa! Hold up there.

He wasn't a jealous guy. He didn't get jealous. He was laid back and easygoing.

Just ask anyone. That's one reason the damn family feud ate at him so much. He was a lover, not a fighter.

Melody disappeared behind the curtain, getting ready to take the stage and start the auction. The hot rush of jealousy ebbed, but it left him jittery, as if he'd downed too much strong coffee in one sitting. He hadn't experienced this shade of shakiness since pulling all-nighters in college.

The exit door opened, letting in a shaft of bright morning sun. A gaggle of giggling girls appeared in the hallway, clutching autograph books and ballpoint pens. When they spied the bachelors lounging backstage, they let out squeals and stampeded toward them.

He expected them to be all over the Chippendale's dancer and Domingo Diaz, which they were. What he did not expect was a trio of nubile young women sidling up to him.

"Mayor Nielson?" one of the young women asked.

He smiled automatically. "Yes?"

"Can I have your autograph?"

The girl couldn't have been more than fifteen and she gazed at him with adoring eyes. She was the same age Melody had been the first time he'd kissed her. Young.

Far too young. It disturbed him to think she might have a crush on him. He knew the girl's father. They went hunting together.

"Sure thing, Amber." He signed her autograph book and passed it back.

"Thanks." Amber cast a sweet, backward glance at him over her shoulder before she moved on to the fireman.

"How about signing something a little more personal for me," a husky voice oozed.

He glanced up to see Widow Jones sending him a sultry stare. She wore skin-tight short-shorts, a leather-fringed halter top, and matching leather sandals. She puckered her lips, lowered her lashes, and rolled her shoulder forward in a classic Marilyn Monroe gesture.

"Hi, Doreen," he mumbled.

She touched a patch of bare skin just above her cleavage, handed him an uncapped Sharpie; and leaned in close, smothering him in the cloying smell of her gardenia perfume. "Couldja sign here?"

Taking extra care not to touch her ample breasts, he quickly signed her overly tanned skin with the black marker, and handed it back to her.

"I brought plenty of cash." She winked, and for the first time he spied the bankroll of hundred-dollar bills peeking out of her cleavage.

Sweat popped out on his brow. Aw shit. He had an unsettling suspicion he was going to end up spending the day fending off the Widow Jones just as Melody had predicted.

"Don't blow your fortune on me, Doreen. You know Domingo Diaz is up for bidding." Okay, cheap shot trying to shift her over to Domingo, but the guy was a Dallas Cowboy. He had experience handling overly affectionate fans.

Doreen took a step closer. "He's too short for me, sweetie. I like my men over six foot."

"That's heightist," he pointed out.

She canted her head, did another shoulder roll. "So sue me. I've never been very politically correct. If I let people's opinion bother me I never would have married Virgil and I wouldn't have the money to buy you."

She plucked the cash from her cleavage and wagged it under his nose.

Ah Virgil, why did you have to die? Eighty-nine was far too young.

"Just remember," came a teasing feminine voice behind him. "The bachelor auction was your idea."

He yanked his head upright at the feel of warm breath skimming over his ear, swung his head around to see Melody smirking at him. The vixen.

She turned away from him, clapped her hands, and addressed the women crowding the corridor. "Everyone, the auction is about to begin so if you could take your seats we'll get this party started."

Dutifully, the women filed out the door.

"I see you and Widow Jones were getting better acquainted," she said, a twinkle in her eyes.

He tipped up his chin. "Jealous?"

"On the contrary, I'm already counting the money she's going to pay for you. The animal shelter will be so grateful."

"Mercenary."

She lowered her lashes. "That's what the auction is for, is it not?"

"I didn't fully think this thing through."

"Common theme with you."

He grabbed her arm. "Seriously, Melly, you're not going to let her win me, are you?"

She shrugged him off. "Face it. You've got that animal magnetism women can't resist."

"So really, you're not the least bit jealous?"

"Nope," she said cheerily.

"Not even a little?" He measured off an inch with his thumb and forefinger.

"Not even a dust mote." She laughed again, a dismissive sound that cut him to the quick. If her intention was to drop-kick his ego, she was doing a damn good job of it. "Now, let's get up onstage."

He couldn't help raking his gaze over the length of her rocking hot body. In that red sundress, she looked good enough to devour. He wanted her to be jealous. Hell, he wanted *her.* For keeps. No ifs, ands, or buts about it. Even knowing all the trouble that wanting her could bring into his life, he didn't care.

Impulsively he reached out and snaked an arm around her trim waist, pulled her to him.

She sucked in an audible breath.

Cradling her in the crook of his arm, he dipped her low, as if they were dancing the tango. He lowered his head, pursed his lips, and went in to seal the deal.

A hand came up, jammed flat against his chest, holding him off.

"I'm warning you, Nielson," she growled. "You kiss me in public and I swear to God, I'll make sure you regret it."

When Luke let her go without kissing her, Melody breathed a sigh of disappointment. She *wanted* him to take a stand. To stop placating their relatives and just go ahead and kiss her in public already. But this wasn't the time or place, she knew it. Why did she feel so let down?

She straightened and walked away. It took everything she had inside her not to look back over her shoulder to see if he was watching. She had an auction to run.

The auditorium was packed with women, a great many of them out-of-towners drawn to Cupid by the Juliet story. She'd done her job, and while it was a little ego-y, she was damn proud of her accomplishment.

Melody pressed her damp palms against her hips, put on her brightest public relations smile, and stepped up to the microphone. "Good morning! Welcome to the first annual Founder's Day Bachelor Auction. It's great to see you all. I'm Melody Spencer and I'll be your auctioneer today. Before we get started, let's go over the rules."

Quickly, she covered how the auction would be run, including the fact that the event was opened to online bidding. She was proud of herself for coming up with that idea. "Junie Mae over there will be manning that process."

She motioned toward the older woman perched at the computer desk situated far stage left. Junie Mae waved at the audience.

"And now for the moment you've all been

waiting for . . . those delicious bachelors. Let's hear it for our handsome hunks."

On cue, the men lined up behind her onstage and Melody started the applause.

The twenty-four men, most grinning sheepishly in their costumes, took a bow.

Widow Jones stuck her fingers in her mouth and let loose with a long whistle that earned her a stern frown from some of the other women in the crowd.

"Remember, all monies raised goes to benefit Perfect Buddies Animal Shelter. The director, Angi Morgan, wants to tell you about the good work they are doing over there."

Melody stepped back to allow the shelter director to take her place at the podium. Luke's gaze caught hers and she had to admit in that tuxedo, he eclipsed every other man on that stage, even the Chippendale's dancer.

But if she were being honest, it wasn't just the tux. Even in frayed blue jeans and a T-shirt, he possessed knock-'em-dead charisma. As evidenced by the way Doreen had been falling all over him backstage. Just thinking about the way the sexpot woman looked at him set her teeth on edge.

And from the looks of things, Doreen, who was already waving a stack of bills in the air and winking at Luke, was going to be the one waltzing off with him today.

The muscle in Melody's left eye spasmed. Her telltale tic. This was craziness. *Snap out of it.* She resisted the urge to rub her eye, and instead widened her smile, hoping that the affliction was not that obvious.

By the time Angi finished talking about the shelter, the services they provided, and some of the animals they'd rescued, more than a few audience members were misty-eyed.

"Thanks, Angi." Melody resumed her place at the microphone. "We appreciate all that you and the shelter do for Jeff Davis County homeless animals."

Angi left the stage and Melody addressed the audience. "Ready to get this party started?"

The audience let out a whoop of approval.

"First up on the auction block, you know him, you love him, Clint Ridgeway." From the notes she'd made on her cell phone, Melody read off the rancher's vital statistics. "He owns the Rambling J, the biggest ranch in Alpine. He stands five-foot-eleven, weighs a hundred and seventy pounds of pure muscle. Clint raises Arabian horses, loves stargazing and mountain biking. Last year he won the Sam Elliott look-alike contest at the Terlingua Chili Cook-off. He's looking forward to a candlelight dinner with one special lady."

Clint sauntered up to the big wooden oak auction block set up center stage, and the room burst into fresh applause.

The bids flew and a date with the rancher ended up going for three hundred dollars. A thrilled woman rushed up to the stage to claim her cowboy.

They were off to a great start, even though there hadn't been any online bids for Clint.

One by one, the bachelors took their places. The Chippendale dancer came out and did a little striptease when it was his turn on the auction block and the crowd went wild. Dozens of women wanted in on him and online bidding lit up the computer. Melody found it a bit of a challenge toggling from the auditorium bids to Junie Mae, who was texting the online bids to Melody's cell phone.

The local librarian won Chippendale Guy for two thousand dollars. "I'm going to read poetry to him. Just like Susan Sarandon in *Bull Durham*," she crowed, and hauled him off the stage. Just like Melody had read Anaïs Nin to Luke.

Doreen Jones didn't even bid on Mr. Chippendale. In fact, the woman hadn't bid on any of the other bachelors. She only had eyes for Luke.

By the time it was Luke's turn on the auction block, the tic in Melody's eye was jumping so hard that she had to keep her head ducked to camouflage it from the audience. He might hate wearing a tuxedo, but he rocked it like a movie star.

"Next up we have Luke Nielson," Melody said, struggling to keep her breathing even and her voice neutral. Oh, this was ridiculous. Why was she so shook up?

"He's six-foot-two, tips the scales at a hundred and eighty-five pounds," she read from the bio he'd supplied. "He got a business degree from the University of Texas, owns the Rocking N Ranch right here in Cupid, and is the mayor of our little burg. He likes prime filet mignon cooked medium, Kentucky bourbon, ATV racing, quick-moving cutting horses, broken-in cowboy boots, and giving foot massages to lovely ladies. Let's start the bidding at —"

Doreen shot to her feet. "Three thousand dollars!"

Alrighty, then. Melody blinked. It was the highest starting bid — in fact the highest bid, period — all morning. "We have three thousand. Do I hear three-thousand and twenty-five?"

Doreen swung her gaze around the auditorium and glared hard as if daring anyone to bid against her.

Melody met Luke's eyes and he flashed her a silent message. *Help me.*

Hey, since he liked massaging lovely ladies' feet — and she knew firsthand how good he was at it — he should be in hog heaven with Doreen. From the looks of things, she wore at least a size eleven shoe. Lots more foot to rub.

But it was her job to get as much for him as possible. "Do I hear three thousand and twenty-five," she repeated.

"No one else is bidding. He's mine." Doreen moved from her seat, headed for the stage.

"Wait, we're a little slow with this online bidding. Do you have any bids, Junie Mae?" Melody asked.

Junie Mae shook her head.

"No one else wants to bid on this very eligible bachelor? I mean, look how gorgeous he is."

"That's a lot of money," someone in the audience threw out. "If Doreen wants him that badly . . ."

Melody walked over to Luke and swept a hand. She didn't make eye contact with him, but she could feel the tension rolling off his body. "C'mon ladies, you can't tell me he's not worth every penny, and I have it on good authority he's cooking his famous homemade chicken enchiladas for the woman who wins him today."

"Three thousand and twenty-five," a woman from the top of the auditorium called out.

"Three thousand and fifty," another woman yelled.

Doreen's face flushed. "Four thousand!"

Melody glanced at the other women in the stands. They both shook their heads. "It's for charity," she cajoled. "Help us save the animals and get a private dinner with the mayor."

"Hands off! He's mine," Doreen said, and held up her wad of cleavage cash. "I can keep bidding all day."

Everyone looked cowed.

"You've jacked the price up enough. It's time," Doreen wriggled a finger at her. "Do that going, going, gone thing."

She thought about Doreen chasing Luke around his condo. It was funny, really, and it would be great fun to tease him about it afterward, but a rush of acrid bile burned up her throat. As discreetly as she could, she slipped a text to Junie Mae: *4.5K.*

"Okay," Melody said. "It looks like Doreen —"

"Wait." Junie Mae held up her hand. "A bid for forty-five hundred just came through from an online bidder.

"What?" Doreen said. "Who is it?"

"Going, going, gone," Melody hollered, and raised the gavel.

"Oh no, you don't. You ain't shuttin' me out. Five thousand."

"Five thousand," Melody said weakly, "do I hear five thousand and twenty-five?"

No one said anything. Melody had fifty-two hundred left in her savings account. Throwing caution to the wind, she texted Junie Mae.

"We've got another online bid," Junie Mae called out. "Five thousand and two hundred dollars."

"Six thousand," Doreen said. "Seriously, I can do this all day, people. Virgil left me ten million dollars."

Melody was out of options. Luke was on his own. She raised the gavel again. "Going, going, gone, a date with Mayor Luke Nielson sold to Doreen Jones for six thousand dollars."

Gleefully, Doreen raced up to the stage to collect her prize. She took his hand and led him off.

Melody was so busy feeling sick to her stomach and glaring after Doreen that she hadn't realized the next bachelor had stepped up onto the auction block until Junie Mae texted her. *Honey, envy is such a tacky color of green.*

CHAPTER 21

"You took that on the chin," Eloise told Melody after the auction was over.

"Excuse me?"

"Letting Doreen get away with your man."

"Luke's not my man," Melody said.

"Honey." Eloise laid a hand on her forearm. "I've known that man since he was five years old. I can tell when he's in love."

Was Luke in love with her? She blinked at Eloise.

"I have to say I was skeptical when he told me he was bringing you to town to work under him. That family feud thing can cause a big mess and when he reached into his own pockets to pay your salary and fund these events, that's when I had my first inkling just how deep his feelings for you ran."

"Fund my salary? What are you talking about?"

Eloise put a hand to her mouth. "You

didn't know?"

"But the money comes from the Chamber of Commerce."

"The Cupid Chamber of Commerce barely has two quarters to rub together. The board members are all volunteers. You and Emma Lee are the only ones getting paid over there. Luke is the one who fills the coffers."

Melody put a hand to her throat. Why had Luke hidden this from her? *Would you have taken the job if you'd known he was footing the bill for your upkeep?* No, no she would not. Her cheeks heated. "I had no idea."

"I'm sorry if I spilled the beans. Please don't say anything to him. I just meant to tell you that although in the beginning I was against bringing you here, I'm glad he did it. You've been good for him and good for the town too."

"Thank you, Eloise."

"There's just one more thing, honey."

"What's that?"

"You break that boy's heart and I'm going to hunt you down and break your face."

"I'm disappointed," Doreen said as Luke eased chicken enchiladas onto her plate with a spatula. "I thought we were going to be eating at your place."

"My mayoral duties require me to be at the Founder's Day picnic," he fibbed. There was no way on God's green earth he was going to allow Doreen into his condo.

"Well, that's a shame."

They were sitting under the big, open-air tent set up in the botanical gardens. Swamp coolers had been brought in to make the noonday picnic more comfortable. Picnic tables were lined up end to end, and they were all full of families. Kids played tag around the tables. Manned barbecue grills gave off the delicious smell of mesquite wood. A local band played at the back of the tent.

"I was hoping for some privacy." Doreen sighed.

I was hoping not.

"Doreen, I do want to thank you for your generous bid. I know Perfect Buddies will put your money to good use. Think of all the animals you're saving."

"I'm thinking about how delicious you look in that tuxedo." She licked her lips. "Thank you for not changing out of it."

"Anything to please you."

"Do you mean it?" She leered.

"How are the enchiladas?" he asked. "Did I use too much chili powder?"

402

"They're fine. Could we take a walk after lunch?"

"In the noonday sun?"

"I just want to get away from the crowds a bit."

I don't. "Sure," he said. What's the worst that could happen? Doreen would try and kiss him? Ugh.

He dawdled as long over the food as he could, but finally, she got up and held her hand out to him. Not much else to do but get it over with. He had to spend the whole day with her.

They left the gardens and walked down Main Street, the same path he'd traveled with Melody the night he'd found her mailing a letter to Cupid. She'd tried to deny it, but he'd seen her mail that letter with his own eyes and he wondered if she'd gotten the answer she wanted. He couldn't recall any letter in the greensheet that could have been hers. Then again, he didn't know everything there was to know about her and he didn't read every letter to Cupid. Or maybe she intercepted the letter at the committee meeting after he caught her so that it wouldn't get answered.

He smiled, remembering that kiss.

"That's the way I like to see you," Doreen said. "Smiling."

"You want to go to McCleary's for a cream soda?" he asked her.

Walker McCleary's Pharmacy had an old-fashioned soda fountain in the back that was popular with the tourists. It was good to realize they had tourists again. He kept smiling.

They picked their way over the old train tracks running behind the Chamber of Commerce, when the neck strap on Doreen's halter top broke and her boobs came spilling out. Making it clear, in case he hadn't already figured it out, that the Widow Jones was not wearing a bra.

"Oh my goodness, will you look at that." Doreen giggled. "Being a triple-E is such a curse sometimes. I can't go into McCleary's like this."

Luke immediately closed his eyes. "Um, we could go into the Chamber of Commerce. I've got a key and I bet we can find a safety pin in the reception desk. Or a stapler. Or some tape to hold you in until you can get home and change."

"Aren't you smart," she said. "A problem solver. My kind of man."

Oh boy. He hated the thought of being alone with Doreen and her malfunctioning wardrobe, but he couldn't really stand out on the street with her as she struggled to cover up her abundant breasts with her arms.

"This way." He put his hand to her back and guided her toward the rear entrance of the old train depot.

They entered the quiet building and he flicked on the light; the first room from the back was Melody's small office. He opened the door and let Doreen go in first. She stood there, holding her boobs like they were a pharaoh's treasure.

Averting his gaze, he stepped to Melody's desk. It smelled like her. He smiled, and opened the desk drawer.

And spied two boxes of red silk stationery, matching envelopes and several letters in Melody's handwriting with a big X drawn through the middle of each page. He glanced at notepapers. They appeared to be early attempts at a letter to Cupid. Were these renditions of the letter he'd caught her mailing? Could there be a hint of her true feelings for him in the text?

Grin widening, he eagerly started reading, but halfway through his stomach turned. He leafed through the second letter and the third. They were first drafts all right, but they were not heartfelt letters from Melody expressing her feeling for him. They were drafts of the Juliet letters that had been printed in the greensheet.

It took a second for his discovery to fully sink in, but when it did, he felt like he'd been gut-punched.

Melody hadn't been just publishing the letters from Juliet. She'd been writing them.

The last thing Luke wanted to do was attend the Sadie Hawkins dance. Having Doreen on his arm was bad enough, but it was going to be damn hard to see Melody again and not call her out on what she'd done. But the dance wasn't the time or place to air dirty laundry. He had to bide his time.

Faking a smile, he escorted Doreen through the door of the community center. She wore a tight sequined dress to match his tuxedo, but they both looked completely out of step with the theme. That's the way Doreen wanted it. She liked attention and if they were dressed like everyone else, they wouldn't stand out. For his part, Luke felt like a total dill weed.

Melody and her crew had outdone themselves, transforming the gym into a set from *Li'l Abner*. Hay bales, wooden barrels, and scarecrows had been placed among picnic tables with red and white checkered tablecloths. Pink pig balloons floated around colorful streamers that had been hung from the ceiling. Red faux kerosene lamps served as lighting. A "Ladies' Choice" banner was draped above the bandstand where a quartet played a cover of "I've Got a Little Hillbilly in Me."

Teen girls dressed in blue jeans cutoffs and gingham peasant blouses, boys were in plaid shirts and overalls. Children blew soap bubbles with replica corncob pipes or played horseshoes. Parents watched with amused smiles and grandparents reminisced.

Refreshments included apple cider served in little brown jugs marked XXX in white paint, Mason jars of lemonade, pigs in a blanket crescent rolls, cornbread and pinto beans, watermelon slices and blackberry cobbler for dessert.

Through the back window he could see a flatbed trailer strewn with straw, hooked to a tractor, waiting for the night's culmination. A hayride.

Dogpatch had come to life.

Even though he was pissed off at her, he had to respect what Melody had done. The place was packed to the rafters.

The band brought out the banjos. "Foggy Mountain Breakdown" had everyone moving to the music.

He waved and nodded at constituents, made small talk with family and friends, all the time keeping an eye out for Melody.

"You're looking out of place in that monkey suit," said his cousin Pete, hefting a beer in one hand and clamping Luke on the shoulder with the other.

"Well, you know." Luke shrugged. "It's for the ladies."

"Yeah, I see 'em drooling over you. Story of your life."

"I'm lucky that way."

"How come you never got married?" Pete asked.

"Guess I never found the right one."

"You've got a fine one on your arm right now." Pete winked at Doreen and she tittered. "This is a great party, even if a Fant did organize it."

Luke bristled. "C'mon, for one night could we forget about Fants and Greenwoods and Nielsons and just have a good time?"

"Easy to say." Pete took a swig of beer. "Not so easy to do when you've got a teenage son who's intent on chasing girls and half the town females come from John Fant stock."

"Would it be the end of the world if Billy did hook up with a Fant?" Luke asked. "I mean, what's the worst that could happen?"

Pete stared at him. "I can't believe you're saying that. After what happened to you in high school."

"What happened to me in high school is precisely the reason I'm saying this. The need for revenge poisons everyone and everything. Forgiveness is the solution, not retribution."

"You sound like a Lifetime movie. Should I buy you some chocolate and a bottle of Pamprin?"

"Hating violence does not make me a girl."

"Look, I'm just saying, if Billy were to bring home a Fant to meet the family, I'd hit the roof."

"Even if the girl made him happy?"

"How could he be happy with his family aligned against him?"

"I'd be on Billy's side. Peace is the way to go."

Pete narrowed his eyes, puffed out an indignant chest. "What? You some kind of Fant lover now? It's that Spencer chick, isn't it? You always did have a hard-on for her. Can't believe you brought her back to town. Big mistake. You're playing with fire, cuz."

"You ready to dance?" Doreen inter-rupted. She shimmied, shaking her breasts for effect.

"Why don't we wait for a slower song?" he stalled.

"Oh, right, gotcha." She winked. "More romantic that way."

He forced a smile. She gazed at him adoringly. *Terrific.*

The banjo music stopped playing and everyone glanced toward the bandstand. There was Melody, onstage again — God, she could command a room — microphone in hand.

"Hello everyone and welcome to the Founder's Day Sadie Hawkins dance. Have y'all been enjoying yourselves today?"

Someone let loose with a long, loud whistle.

"Yes," chorused the group.

"Woot!"

"Awesome."

"You're the best, Mel."

Doreen squeezed Luke's upper arm. "Honestly, I don't see her appeal. She's too slick, too polished, and too darn skinny, and I bet she'd be hard-pressed to fill a C cup."

"She's damn talented," Luke said. "She won a Clio."

"So? I was a Vegas showgirl."

He bit down on his tongue to keep from saying, *Stripper poles don't count.*

Doreen pushed her bottom lip out. "I bet she's lousy in the sack. Uptight and frigid."

Dead wrong about that, sweetums.

Melody met his gaze across the room.

Smack. Sizzle. Dammit. Every time he looked at her it was like touching a live power line.

She pressed her lips into a thin line and quickly glanced away. Instantly, the smile was back as she addressed the crowd. "Okay, ladies. This is it, your chance to ask the man of your dreams to dance. Don't be shy. Take the bull by the horns. Risk rejection. Channel the spirit of Sadie Hawkins and go to it."

The band launched into a lively rendition of Relient K's "Sadie Hawkins Dance."

Girls sidled up to boys.

Women approached men.

Doreen wrapped her arms around Luke's waist and drew him out onto the dance floor. She was chattering a mile a minute, but he wasn't listening. He was watching Melody, who was talking to the high school girl who worked at the Chamber of Commerce — Emma Lee Gossett, a Fant descendant — and Emma Lee was shooting sidelong glances at Pete's son, Billy.

And Billy was looking back.

Melody whispered something in Emma

Lee's ear. The girl nodded, lifted her chin, and stepped toward Billy.

Billy smiled.

Luke searched for Pete and spied his cousin leaning against the wall, scowling at his son, another beer bottle in his hand. Uh-oh. A nasty premonition tickled the back of his neck and he was jettisoned back fifteen years to that picnic bench where he'd kissed Melody for the first time.

The blast from the past wasn't pleasant. He knew how this ended and suddenly he was backtracking on his earlier comment to Pete that he would be on Billy's side if the boy wanted to date a Greenwood or a Fant. The town wasn't ready for a repeat of that terrible summer.

Emma Lee held out her hand to Billy.

He took it.

Together, they moved out onto the dance floor.

Instantly, Pete launched himself from the wall, headed toward the kids. "Hey, hey, boy, get away from that Fant!"

Billy tightened his grip on Emma Lee.

Pete clamped his hand on Emma Lee's shoulder.

Emma Lee squealed.

A half-dozen Fants sprang into action.

Luke's legs were in motion before his

brain caught up to what he was doing. He jumped between Pete and the converging Fants. Stretching out his body, futilely attempting to hold them at arm's length, but already a brigade of Nielsons, including Luke's father, Gil, were backing up Pete.

Emma Lee clung to Billy like a grass burr.

"Fant trash." Pete spat. "Get your fucking hands off my son."

"Stop it!" Luke commanded. "Stop it right now."

But it was too late. The punching had already started.

Police sirens broke up the fight. People ran higgledy-piggledy, hightailing it for the exits, leaving a mess in their wake.

The minute the first punch was thrown, Melody called the cops. She couldn't believe things had spiraled out of control so quickly. When she encouraged Emma Lee to ask the boy she liked to dance, she never dreamed it was Billy Nielson.

Talk about déjà vu. Her heart flew into her throat.

Luke sat on his butt on the dance floor, his tuxedo torn and bloodied, his right eye swelling shut, his bottom lip cut and bleeding. Doreen was on her knees beside him, smoothing his shoulders with her palms.

Melody raced over, but her heel caught on a streamer that had been pulled from the ceiling and lay tangled on the floor. She tripped, stumbled, almost fell, but managed to regain her balance.

"Are you all right?" she asked breathlessly, coming to a stop beside Luke.

He peered up at her with his one good eye and tried to say something, but immediately he put a hand to his lip. "Ow, ow."

"Oh, you poor baby." Doreen stroked his head. "Don't try to talk."

Law enforcement came through the door, but by then the instigators had dispersed. One of the deputies was Calvin Greenwood. Hand resting on the holster at his hip, Calvin sauntered over. "What happened?"

"Fant-Nielson crap."

Calvin sighed. "Ah shit. I knew it was coming after your office was vandalized and Melody kept putting up those damn Juliet letters. When are people going to get over it?"

"It'll never be over until we have an open dialogue about it," Melody said. "Both families have been sweeping it under the rug for generations and nothing ever gets solved. We need to own this feud before we can do something about it. That's why I published those letters from Juliet."

Luke glared at her with his one good eye. She knew what he was thinking. His way was the best way. Yes, she might have brought tourists into town with the letters, but at what cost?

"I saw everything," Doreen said. "Luke was trying to break up the fight and look what happened to him."

"Seems like you were the primary victim, Mayor." Calvin eyed him, tension evident in the stiff set of his shoulders. "You wanna press charges?"

Luke shook his head. "Putting those men in jail will only make things worse."

Calvin pushed his Stetson back on his head. "You sure about that?"

"I'm certain."

Calvin glanced around the room at the few people who'd stuck around. He raised his voice. "Anybody else want to press charges?"

No one said anything. A few shook their heads.

"Could I speak to Luke in private?" Melody asked.

Calvin held up his palm. "Go ahead."

"You don't need my testimony?" Doreen looked hopeful.

"No," Luke said, wincing. "Go home,

415

Doreen. I'll have to give you a rain check on our date. We'll start fresh."

Disappointment crossed her face, but she nodded. "Okay."

Melody motioned for Luke to follow her to a private corner of the room. Seeing his battered face cut her to the core. "You should press charges."

"Against your cousins?"

"They assaulted you."

"It's not the first time a Fant has assaulted me. Pressing charges would only make things worse. I want to end this damn feud once and for all. Filling out a police report would have the opposite effect."

"They're just going to think you're a coward."

"Do you think I'm a coward?"

"We should talk this out."

"Not here. Not now. Not with your cousin glaring at me."

Melody glanced over her shoulder to see Calvin scowling. He was still a Greenwood, even though he'd been sworn to uphold the law and do what was right, ultimately his sympathies were with his family.

"It's his decision, Mel," Calvin called out. "If the man doesn't want to press charges, honor his wishes."

She turned back around to her cousin.

416

"So just let him get the hell beat out of him again at the hands of our family?"

Calvin didn't answer that. "You want to go to the hospital and get checked out?" he asked Luke.

"It's not the first time I've had a black eye and busted lip," he said. "I'll live."

"In that case, there's not much I can do. Are you absolutely sure?"

"Yes."

"All right then." Calvin shrugged and motioned to the two deputies who'd come into the building with him. "We're heading out. Unless you want to file charges for destruction of property, Mel."

Should she?

"Don't." Luke shook his head. "There's not enough cells in the county jail to hold everyone who was slinging punches tonight. Besides, the effects of this are probably rippling throughout the town right now. Instead of messing with filing police reports, the deputies need to be patrolling the streets to nip hostilities in the bud."

He had a point.

She glanced around at the gym. It had taken a punishing. Her decorations were ripped to shreds, blood streaked the floor, chairs were knocked over, food spilled. It was a mess, but no serious damage done.

"Luke's right," she said. "People are out there seething over this. You need to keep a lid on that."

Calvin nodded. "Let me know if you change your mind."

The deputies departed.

Melody sighed. "What a mess."

A hand touched her shoulder and she looked over to see Natalie and Lace standing there. She hadn't even realized they were still in the room.

"You go on home. You've had a long, trying day. Lace and I will clean up. We've got the guys to help us." Natalie indicated their husbands, Pierce and Dade.

"Besides," Lace murmured, "someone needs to doctor Luke's face."

Relief moved through her taut muscles. She was lucky to have such a loyal, understanding family. "Thank you," she whispered. "I do appreciate you."

Her cousins both gave her a hug.

Melody retrieved her purse from where she'd stashed it behind the bandstand and went over to Luke. "Come on," she said. "I'll give you a ride home."

CHAPTER 22

The ride to the condo was silent. Feeling uncertain, Melody cast a sideways glance at Luke. What was he feeling?

She pulled to a stop in her parking spot. "Can I come in and tend to your wounds?"

"The way my face is hurting, I'd be a fool to say no." He got out of her Corvette and led the way up the stairs to his condo, but there was a difference about him. Something she couldn't decipher.

He unlocked the door, held it open for her.

She stepped over the threshold, accidentally brushed against his shoulder on the way in. His muscles tensed, and she heard the air leak from his lungs in a quiet hiss. Was he upset with her? Did he consider this whole thing her fault?

Was it?

Reaching around, he flipped on the light. He motioned her farther inside, tugging at the bedraggled bow tie at his neck and yanking it off.

She followed him deeper into the room. He shrugged out of his jacket and slipped it over the back of a chair and proceeded to roll up his shirtsleeves.

"We need to get you taken care of," she said. "Sit down."

He slumped heavily onto the kitchen chair. He was wearier than he wanted to let on.

She went to the refrigerator and opened the freezer.

"What are you looking for?"

"Something to ice that eye with. Do you have any frozen peas?"

"Hate them."

She spied a bag of chopped bananas. They would do. She rummaged in the drawers, found a kitchen towel, and wrapped the bag of bananas in it, and then took it to him. "Put this on your eye. You look like you've gone fifteen rounds with Mike Tyson."

"Twelve."

"What?"

"Title fights are twelve rounds. They don't fight fifteen rounds anymore."

"But I bet it feels like fifteen."

"Yeah, it does."

Silence fell over them. The only noise was

the ticking of the kitchen clock and the hum of the refrigerator. He looked pristinely disheveled in his torn tuxedo. His white shirt was dotted with blood, his collar torn.

He took a deep breath. Winced again. "Damn, it hurts to breathe. I think I might have cracked a rib."

"Luke, why didn't you say something? We should get you to a doctor."

"No need. There's nothing they can do for a cracked rib, a black eye, and a busted lip."

She fisted her hands. She could punch someone herself right now for causing him pain. "They could give you some pain meds."

He shook his head. "I don't want to dull the pain. I need it as a reminder."

"Of what?"

"The kind of suffering this feud causes. And this is small-scale stuff. I need to remember."

"I never forgot."

His eye met hers. She saw something disquieting there. "I know. I can't forget. Believe me, I've tried."

"Luke?"

"Yeah?"

"Why am I here?"

"You were going to tend my wounds."

"Not that. Why am I in Cupid?"

He swallowed. "We needed you."

"No you didn't. Anyone could be doing the things I'm doing."

"Not with your originality and flair. Besides, you were jobless and homeless when I found you."

"But you didn't know that when you came up to New York. What was your real motive?"

He swallowed, blew out his breath through puffed cheeks, winced. "I've thought about you a lot over the years."

Her throat seized up and she couldn't say what she wanted to say. *Me too.*

"I'm ready to get married, settle down, Melody, and you were the first person I thought of."

Panic shot through her. "What are you saying? That you want to marry me?"

He gave her a one-sided smile, sparing the side that was cut and bruised. "That's not what I meant." For a long moment, he didn't say anything else.

"What did you mean?" she prompted.

He shrugged, grimaced. "I realized I couldn't be a good husband to anyone until I dealt with the past. Our past."

She folded her arms over her chest. "So you were actually tired of sweeping it under the rug yourself."

"Talking about that night. Finally coming to peace with what happened. Learn from those mistakes. Hell, Melody, I'm scared I'll get married and have kids and the same thing that happened to us will happen to them."

"Why not just move away from Cupid?"

"The Rocking N is part of me. It's been in my family for five generations and if I leave there's no one to take over. Carly's got her own family and her life in Marfa, and she's not interested in ranching. Jesse's gone. My dad is in no shape to handle the responsibility. It's all on my shoulders."

Responsibility.

That she understood. She couldn't look at his damaged face any longer. She turned away. "Where do you keep the antiseptic? That lip needs to be cleaned."

"I don't give a damn about the lip, Melody. I want to talk about this."

Her heart beat against her chest, a wild bird trying to break free. "Why? I still don't see how talking about it is going to change things."

He got up from the chair so forcefully it tipped over and hit the floor. Bam.

She cringed.

He came toward her, wrapped an arm

around her. "Because I want to be with you, Melody. Don't you get it? That's why I agreed to the sex-only thing. I was hoping to change your mind."

"Luke." She shook her head, backed up.

"I loved you," he said.

Melody caught her breath. He'd never said the words to her back then. "You did?"

"More than you can ever know. What happened between us destroyed me. How could I love you when my love for you caused my family such great pain? Because of the fact that I loved you, Jesse died."

"We're always going to be haunted by that night, aren't we?"

"Until there's peace between our families. Now do you understand why I try so hard to keep the peace around here?"

"I do."

"So why did you defy my wishes, *Juliet*?"

Dread flooded her body and she couldn't move. He knew. That's why he'd been acting so odd with her. "How . . . how do you know?"

"I found first drafts of the Juliet letters in your office desk."

She gulped, knotted her hands, didn't breathe.

"What I can't figure out is why you didn't destroy those drafts?" He shook his head.

Why hadn't she? Had she secretly been hoping someone would stumble across the letters and she'd be found out? "Luke, I can explain. I —"

"You deceived me," he said. "Plain and simple. But I'm sure it's not your fault. That's just advertising, right? Just the way they do things on Madison Avenue."

His sarcasm cut her slick as a whetted knife. Her stomach turned to stone and a white heat spread throughout her body like a pathogen. "Excuse me? I deceived *you*? Better climb down off that high horse, Mayor. Eloise told me you paid me from your own pocket. That's not exactly on the up-and-up."

"That's different. I was trying to help you."

"And I was trying to help the town and oh, oops, it looks like I did. My deception brought tourists into the town. It filled the motels and the restaurants. It got people talking about Cupid. Face it, Luke. You were wrong about what it took to end this feud and I was right. We have to own it because it's our story. Secrecy gives the feud power. Feeds the ugly emotions."

"Um, yes, because your method worked so well tonight. Thanks to your nifty little plan, *Juliet,* I look like this." He tossed the bag of bananas across the room. It hit the wall with a resounding *thump* that made her jump. "And if you're so eager to 'own' the feud, why don't you tell the truth? Make an announcement. Admit to all your online friends that there is no Juliet. Announce that you lied and deceived them too."

"If people find out Juliet was fictional there'll be a backlash against Cupid. We'll lose all the gains we made with tourism."

"Well," he said. "You should have damn well thought about that before you wrote those letters. Now, if you don't mind, I'd like very much to go to bed. Alone."

Luke was right about everything. Her lie had caused more problems than it solved.

Why had she strayed so far from her principles? Why had she let what happened in New York affect the way she'd conducted herself in Cupid? Why had she bought into Michael Helmsly's assertion that the truth was rubbery? The success she'd enjoyed here was a lie, and now, when the truth came out, the people of her hometown would be the ones to suffer.

Feeling miserable to the core, Melody couldn't even bring herself to eat the delicious breakfast she'd ordered at La Hacienda Grill.

Ricardo came bopping from the back over to her table, his eyes bright. "Miss Melody," he said. "You are a goddess. I want to worship at your feet. Because of those letters you published from Juliet, I made more money the past three days than I've made in the last two months. It's incredible. Unbelievable. If this keeps up, I will be saved from bankruptcy. Thank you. Thank you. Your breakfast is free from now on."

She barely managed a smile. False praise. How could she ever tell the truth when it had the power to destroy good, honest, hardworking folks like Ricardo? "No," she said. "I insist on paying for my breakfast."

"Please." He held up his palms. "It is my honor to serve you."

"All right," she said, but after he walked away, she left a twenty-dollar bill on the table to cover the seven-dollar tab.

She walked into the Chamber of Commerce. Emma Lee was behind the desk looking pale and unhappy.

"What's wrong?" Melody asked.

"My parents think I'm Juliet. They think I'm pregnant with Billy Nielson's baby. They want me to give it up for adoption. I'm a virgin, but they don't even believe me."

"Oh, Emma Lee, I'm so sorry you're going through this. Get them to take you to a doctor. That will convince them you're telling the truth."

"It won't convince them to let me date Billy," she said woefully.

Not knowing what else to do, she patted Emma Lee on the shoulder. When she'd written those fictitious letters, she hadn't thought about all the ramifications they would have in the lives of others. She'd been rash and shortsighted.

The door to the Chamber of Commerce opened and they looked up.

In the doorway stood a serious-looking, ebony-haired girl dressed in black and wearing dark-framed glasses. She looked like an English major from an Ivy League school, and Melody knew at once that she was from New York.

"Hello," she said. "My name is Laurel Tucker and I'm an intern for the popular soft news TV program *One Hour.* I'm looking for Melody Spencer."

"I'm Melody Spencer."

Emma Lee's eyes went wide. "*One Hour*? Wow. My dad watches that show all the time."

"Glad to hear it," Laurel said. "We were in the area, considering a follow-up story on a segment we did about Marfa last year.

428

Did you happen to see it?"

"I did," Melody said.

Emma Lee wrinkled her nose. "I don't much watch *One Hour* myself. It's all newsy with old people on it."

"The episode is up on YouTube if you want to catch it," Laurel told Emma Lee. Then she shifted her attention back to Melody. "Anyway, our chief interviewer, Jory Striver, just fell in love with the area when he was on location here and he was alarmed to learn about this terrible drought. When we heard about the letters from Juliet and how they turned the economy here in Cupid around, we were intrigued. We asked around town and learned you were the volunteer who answered Juliet's letters. Is that correct?"

Melody nodded. "Yes."

Laurel consulted her tablet computer. "My research has turned up that you used to work for the Tribalgate ad agency on Madison Avenue. Do you mind me asking why you left?"

Saying she got fired wasn't the smart thing to do, so Melody went with the positive spin. "I missed my hometown."

For a second, Laurel's face shifted, softened. "I'm originally from Goose Neck, Idaho," she said. "I understand what you mean. Sometimes the city can be so intrusive."

"You don't really appreciate your hometown until you've left it."

"No indeed. If you're willing, we'd love to interview you."

"On *One Hour*?"

"Yes. Oh, and Miss Spencer, do you have any idea who Juliet really is? We'd love to interview her as well."

It was on the tip of Melody's tongue to tell the young woman the truth. That she had invented Juliet for publicity and as a means to try to put an end to the family feud.

But before she could get to it, Emma Lee spoke up. "I'm her. I'm Juliet."

Two days later, Jory Striver was sitting in the Cupid Chamber of Commerce while the *One Hour* crew buzzed around them setting things up for the interview, while half the town of Cupid waited outside.

Melody had not seen or talked to Luke since the night of the Sadie Hawkins dance. He hadn't shown up for the last Chamber of Commerce meeting and it made her miserable. She would have called him, except *One Hour* had given her a perfect opportunity to redeem herself.

She and Emma Lee waited in her office. The makeup artist had just finished with them and they were alone.

"Are you sure you really want to go on camera and tell a lie, Emma Lee?" She had already asked her a half-dozen times over the last two days.

"My parents already think I'm Juliet," she said. "Why not get some mileage out of it? This could be my big break."

"Just so you know, I have to tell the truth on camera. I should have told the truth the minute Laurel asked, but I was just so taken aback by your lie I didn't have time to think it through. Plus, I wanted to give you a chance to come clean yourself."

The girl looked truculent. "You're gonna tattle on me?"

"People are going to find out soon enough that you're not really Juliet."

"Who cares? By then I will have already been on TV." Emma Lee tossed her pretty red hair.

Melody rubbed her forehead with two fingers. The girl was complicating things. *Hey, things have been complicated ever since you decided to spin a tall tale.*

Laurel came to the doorway. "You guys ready?"

"Yep." Emma Lee jumped to her feet.

"I have a request," Melody said. "May I be interviewed first?"

Laurel pursed her lips. "Sure. Why not? We'll edit to suit the piece. Come with me."

"Aw man," Emma Lee said. "I wanted to go first."

"You'll thank me later," Melody whispered, and followed Laurel to the interview chair across from one of the finest journalists in the business. She was feeling pretty intimidated.

Jory Striver — who looked shorter in person than he did on TV — started off by asking her about why she'd left Madison Avenue. She meant to give him a pat answer about that, but it dawned on her if she was going to tell the truth, she had to tell it all.

"I was fired for being too honest."

"I could see where honesty could get you into trouble in advertising." Jory chuckled. "So tell me what it was like coming back home to Cupid and discovering your community was on hard times because of the drought."

"I was horrified."

"Understandably so. Your new job here was to revive the town by increasing tourism."

"That's correct."

Jory spoke to the camera, telling about

how the letter-writing tradition in Cupid began, and then he turned to her again. "Did you have any idea that when you published the letters from Juliet that it would have this kind of impact?"

"I hoped," she said. "But I wasn't certain. Because you see, Juliet isn't a real person. She's represented in spirit today by my young cousin Emma Lee Gossett, but I invented Juliet from an amalgamation of women I've known throughout the years."

Jory looked taken aback. "You wrote the letters? Pretending to be Juliet?"

"I did," Melody confessed. "And let me tell you why . . ."

Ten minutes later, as she finished telling about how Juliet came into being, including the whole story about Luke and her and the night Jesse died, there was a great commotion from the people outside the building. Whooping and hollering. What was up? A flash of electric blue lightning streaked the sky, and shortly thereafter a loud crack of thunder.

"Praise the Lord," someone said. "It's finally raining."

The *One Hour* segment aired on Sunday. Melody sat watching it with her extended family gathered at her parents' house.

433

"That was really brave of you, daughter," her mother said. "I'm proud of you."

"You're not mad that I lied about Juliet?"

"Are you kidding?" said her father. "It took a lot of guts to get up there on national TV and admit your mistakes."

"It was a brilliant idea." Natalie leaned back against her husband Dade's arm and he cradled Nathan against his other side. "And as you said, Juliet is any woman who's been caught in the crossfire of a family feud."

Melody blew out her breath. She'd been so worried about how her family was going to take the news. She hadn't expected them to understand, much less approve of what she'd done. "But I lied."

"It was for the greater good," Great-Aunt Delia said. "And in the end, you came clean."

"And it rained while you were doing it," her mother said. "I consider that a sign that God approved."

Well, Melody didn't know about that, but it felt good to be accepted for who she was, imperfections and all. But she couldn't help wondering if Luke had seen the program and if he had, what did he think?

Her cell phone rang. Luke? She plucked the phone from her pocket, held her breath when she saw the caller ID.

Tribalgate.

"Hello?" she said tentatively.

"Melody, Michael Helmsly here."

It took her a full second to remember who Michael Helmsly was. She was so caught up in what was going on in Cupid, her old life felt a million miles away.

"I just saw you on *One Hour,*" he said. "I have to say, brilliant work."

"What do you mean?"

"A fictitious letter about a family feud, a letter that ended up saving an entire town? I have to say, I'm impressed. I didn't know you had it in you."

"Thanks," she said. "I think."

"Listen, the reason I'm calling is that the person we hired as your replacement simply isn't working out. She doesn't have your work ethic."

"I thought my ethics were troubling to you."

"Ah," he said. "I should have expected you to bust my chops over this. Go ahead and get it off your chest."

"Actually, Michael, I have to thank you."

"For what?"

"Showing me the error of my ways. You taught me how to lie and look what happened. Poof, I'm on *One Hour* and you're

435

calling to suck up."

"Firing you was hasty. I admit I made a mistake. Will you come back?"

"Not for my previous salary."

He paused. "All right. How about a promotion to creative director with a twenty-five-thousand-dollar yearly bump up."

"Seriously?"

"You can't tell me that you're making anything like that kind of money where you are and I sure as hell know you won't have the prestige."

"The cost of living is much cheaper in Cupid. I don't have to make that kind of money here. Besides, I've got all kinds of opportunities. I could go anywhere."

"Fine." He sighed. "Thirty thousand more a year."

"No dice."

"Thirty-five," he said. "But that's my final offer. No one else is going to pay you that color of green."

"Michael, I wouldn't work for you again if you offered me ten million dollars a year. My integrity is worth more than that."

"Really? You're going to insult me?"

"Nope. I'm simply telling the truth," she said, and hung up the phone.

CHAPTER 23

Luke was rounding up cattle with his ATV when he spied her.

The slender young woman in short, tight, cutoff blue jeans, bright red cowgirl boots, and a red blouse with the hem tied into a knot underneath her breasts, exposing a smooth, flat midriff as she ambled across sandy pasture toward him.

Luke blinked. Was his side by side a time machine that had transported him back fifteen years?

She stopped. Raised a hand. No. Not a mirage. It was Melody. Looking even lovelier than she'd looked at fifteen.

One singular thought thrummed through his brain. *I love this woman. Always have. Always will.* But just because he loved her didn't mean that they were good for each other.

He cut the engine and the cows immediately started drifting from the tightly packed group he'd herded them into. Beautiful, flat, white-bottomed clouds rode the electric blue sky. It had rained for three solid days, bringing the desert alive with color. It was a perfect day.

She was still several yards away. He swung off the ATV, headed toward her, his heart knocking erratically inside his chest. What did she want?

Hope kicked him in the lungs. Stupid hope. How many times had hope disappointed him? He refused to hope, to set himself up for another massive letdown. He already missed her more than he thought it possible to miss someone. She was the first thing he thought of every morning when he woke up and the last thing that crossed his mind every night when he closed his eyes.

But there was no way it could work out between them. He tried every angle he could come up with, trying to make the puzzle pieces fit. They just didn't and that's all there was to it. She deserved the world, and all he had to offer was his little rugged corner of the Trans-Pecos. She needed someone sophisticated she could show off at parties, someone who knew how to use the right forks when they ate at fancy places. And he just wasn't that guy. He was cowboy through and through and that's all he would ever be. All he ever wanted to be. He was happy with that and he accepted who he was.

"What are you doing here?" he asked tersely.

The bright smile she offered wavered, but then in typical Melody fashion, she hoisted it back up like a flamboyant sail. Ah, damn, he was a sucker for her resilience.

"I came to tell you that my former boss offered me a promotion and a thirty-five-thousand-dollar-a-year raise," she said.

Needing something to hold on to, he rested his hands on his belt buckle. So she'd come to gloat. He tried to sound sincere. "Congratulations. You must be real happy about that. I suppose you'll be on the next plane out of here."

She canted her head, studied him a long moment. "Well, that all depends."

"Is this the place where I'm supposed to say on what? Because I've got a lot of work to do and I'm not in the mood for guessing games. If you've got something to say, Melody, just spit it out."

She didn't flinch. "May I read you something?"

He blew out his breath. Why was she torturing him like this? Why didn't she just go back to New York and leave him alone?

"If you feel like it's something you have to do. Go ahead."

She pulled a folded paper from her back pocket. It was a copy of the love letters greensheet. She unfolded it, cleared her throat.

"More fiction?"

She gave him a look that managed to say a dozen things that set his heart reeling against the wall of his chest, including, *I want you, I need you, you're being a bit of an ass.*

Panic grabbed hold of him and he had no idea why. "No, you know what," he interrupted. "Don't read it. Just take that job in New York. Go back to where you belong."

Melody crumpled the greensheet, threw it on the ground, and ran back to her car. He wouldn't even listen to what she had to say. He didn't want her. She had to accept that.

Blinding tears obscuring her vision, she threw the Corvette into gear and went flying down the mountain. The same mountain road that Jesse Nielson had gone flying down that dark night he'd died. It had been raining then too.

Once the heavens had opened up, they seemed determined to pour down all the rain they'd stored up for eighteen months.

Fat drops spattered the windshield as she left the Rocking N, now it was pure deluge, sluicing over her hood in sheets.

She swiped at her eyes with the back of her hand, turned her wipers on high, but she could still barely see the ribbon of road in front her.

Slow down, slow down. You're going too fast.

But her foot wasn't listening to her brain. Neither was her heart.

He'd sent her away. He'd told her he loved her the night he'd broken up with her, but he hadn't forgiven her. She thought if she showed up dressed as she had been the first time they'd kissed, he wouldn't be able to turn her away.

How wrong she'd been!

Oh God, it hurt. It hurt so damn bad. He wasn't going to forgive her. He did not want her.

The curve up ahead was steep. She shifted her foot from the accelerator to the brake, but the road was slick. As soon as she applied pressure, the Corvette fishtailed wildly. She fought the steering wheel, trying desperately to keep the car on the road, but the rain conspired against her, and the next thing she knew the Corvette was tumbling off the side of the mountain.

The rain hit the greensheet with big splats as Luke picked it up from where Melody had dropped it. He unfolded it.

Dear Cupid,

I know these letters are supposed to be anonymous, but there are a lot of people I need to apologize to, not the least of whom is the man I've loved since I was fifteen years old. Circumstances tore us apart, making it impossible for us to be together. I moved away and forgot about him, or at least that's what I told myself. But the truth is, I never really stopped loving him. In order to deal with losing him, I became a workaholic, and for years, that sustained me. I lived to achieve goals — a great job, prestige, an important boyfriend. I was happy. Or so I thought until I saw him again and oh, Cupid, there I was, aching like time had never passed.

Except the family problems that separated us all those years ago have not gone away. We were still at a crossroads. So, with the very best intentions, I told a lie in an effort to shine a spotlight on our feuding families and put an end to the anger and hatred and fear. And it looked like it might work.

But dishonesty is dishonesty and a lie is a lie. The end does not justify the means, even if the motives are pure. For you see, I thought that I wasn't good enough on my own, that I had to be perfect in order to be loved. Success at all costs. That ended up being my motto. Here's the paradox; the more I strived for success the further I got from what I really wanted. For deep in my heart, the one true thing I desired most was to be loved unconditionally.

And now, even though my knees are quaking, here I am, laying it all on the line in this letter, showing everyone who I am, warts and all. Will I be accepted, loved, and forgiven for my imperfections? Or have my lies condemned me to a loveless life?

Remorsefully yours,
Melody Spencer

Gobsmacked, Luke stared at the paper coming apart in his hands as the rain poured down. Could she honestly believe that he had stopped loving her because she'd made mistakes?

He had to go after her. Tell her what a scared fool he was. Beg her to forgive his mistakes as he forgave hers.

Because he loved her, loved her with everything he had in him, and he couldn't bear to think of life without her.

Melody's face hurt so badly that she couldn't think. She was hot and cold and wet. She lifted a hand to wipe the moisture from her eyes, but her hands wouldn't move and she tasted blood.

Where was she? What had happened?

She tried to raise her head, but the minute she did, her vision winked out.

"Hang on!" a man called out from somewhere above her. "I'm coming after you."

She smelled gasoline. Oh crap, she wrecked her car, her beautiful white Corvette convertible. Courtney was destroyed. No, no. Maybe it wasn't too bad. Maybe Pat could knock out a few dents, change the tires, do an alignment, and Courtney would be okay.

What seemed like hours later, after she passed out and woke up several times, she felt strong, masculine arms go around her. Her eyes fluttered open. "Luke?"

"No, it's Gil. Luke's father."

Gil Nielson, the man who hated her guts.

"We've got to get you out of here," he said. "The car is leaking gas. It could blow up at any moment."

"Let me see if I can walk," she said, but her legs were numb.

"I've got you," he said. "Don't worry."

She tried to put her arms around his neck, to make it easier for him to carry her, but they just flopped helplessly at her side. Was she paralyzed?

Panic swept through her.

"You're okay," Gil kept chanting. "You're okay."

Funny. She didn't feel okay.

He started up the ravine, but slipped on the rocks, almost fell, and muttered a curse.

"I'm sorry," she apologized, and opened her eyes. His face was blurry. "So sorry."

"Shh, stop apologizing."

She closed her eyes again and winked out until a jostling roused her. She blinked. They were on the edge of the road. Sweat was pouring down Gil's face. The veins in his neck bulged blue.

"Here." He grunted. "We're almost back to the road."

She saw a white pickup truck just ahead of them. Only a short distance away, but it was all uphill. "Let me try to walk."

"You're in no condition."

"Honestly, Gil, neither are you. You look like shit."

"You're not so pretty yourself right now."

Her face was hurting again, particularly her chin. She reached up a hand.

"Don't," Gil said. "Just don't."

He sounded so much like his son when he said it that tears sprang to her eyes. Would she ever see Luke again? She dropped her hand. "I love him, you know."

"I know, and I'm a hardheaded old fool for holding a grudge so long. He's been with a lot of women. Most of them wanted him for his name or his money, but you? You just wanted him for who he was."

"He doesn't want me."

"Of course he does, girl. Don't be as dumb as me. He's loved you since he was seventeen and he's never stopped." Gil's breath was wheezing in and out as he struggled to crest the edge of the ravine.

Finally, he reached the top, and laid her down on the asphalt. She looked up into the sky, dark gray with rain thunderclouds. She was dizzy again and the baling wire was so tight around her lungs she wasn't sure she could take another breath.

And then Gil Nielson clutched his heart, cried out in pain, and toppled over beside her on the wet, lonely mountain road.

Luke was barreling down the mountain when he came upon his father's truck, with the door hanging open. He glanced to the right. Down to the very ravine where Jesse's car had gone over, and there laid the white Corvette, broken into half a dozen pieces.

"Melody!" he cried.

It wasn't until he parked and got out of his truck that he saw the other car. A silver Toyota Camry. He rushed around his father's truck to see what was going on.

There lay both his father and Melody on the ground. Melody's eyes were closed, her face gashed and bleeding, her skin the color of ashes.

And kneeling beside Gil, giving his father CPR, was Melody's mother, Carol Ann.

"Miss Spencer, can you hear me?"

Melody opened her eyes to a brown-skinned man in a white coat. On the pocket of his lab coat, his name was embroidered in blue thread. Dr. Raj Patel. "Yes."

"Very good." He beamed. "There are many people here that want to see you. May I let them in?"

"Please do," she croaked. She was hooked

up to IVs and a heart monitor. An electronic blood pressure cuff was attached around her arm.

"You were a very lucky young lady," he said. "From the way they describe the wreckage of your car, you should be hurt much worse. As it is, you have a mild concussion, a broken toe, and two lacerations, one on your forehead and one on your chin. You will have some scarring but in the grand scheme of things, you are extremely fortunate to be alive."

"Gil Nielson," she said. "How is he? Did he have a heart attack?"

The doctor nodded. "I cannot discuss the specifics of his case with you, but thanks to your mother, he will live."

"My mother?"

"Yes. She performed CPR in a timely manner and saved his life."

A Fant had performed CPR to save the life of a Nielson? Unheard of. And not just any Fant or Nielson, but her mother and Luke's father.

"I will allow your family to come in now." The doctor gave a slight bow and disappeared.

A minute later, the door opened and a flood of people poured into the room. Whatever happened to the two-visitors-per-

ICU-patient rule?

The first to come through the door were her brothers, followed by her father and then her mother. Next came Natalie and Lace and Calvin and Emma Lee.

And then the Nielsons started filling the room. Carly and Billy and his father, Pete. What were they doing here? Everyone moved aside, making room.

"The feud?" Melody asked.

"It was over the minute Gil pulled you from that ravine," her father said.

"No, it was over the minute Carol Ann gave Gil CPR." Pete shook his head.

"Really?" Melody said. "Just like that? Ninety years of grudge holding and we're all going to let it go?"

"We have no choice," Carol Ann said. "Now that we're all going to be one big family."

"What are you talking about?" Melody frowned.

"Ask him." Her father inclined his head toward the door.

And in walked Luke.

Everyone told her to get well soon, squeezed her hand, gingerly touched her shoulder, waved good-bye, and slipped out, leaving her alone with Luke.

He moved to her bedside, took the chair drawn up beside the bed that her mother had been sitting in. "Melly," he whispered, and squeezed her hand.

"Is it really true?" she asked. "Is the feud really over?"

"It is and you're the reason why. You were right all along. Bringing the grudge into the light, facing the problems head-on instead of covering them over and hiding from the truth was the way to go. Granted, we had some resistance at first, but there's always resistance when you change the status quo. That's what I failed to realize. I was so busy trying to keep the peace and prevent problems that I forgot sometimes you have to break a few eggs to make an omelet."

"That's my saying."

"I appropriated it. Do you mind?" He stroked her arm, peered deeply into her eyes.

Unable to get enough of looking at him, she peered right back. "Not at all."

"I was wrong. I was too damn scared to consider that any way besides my own might be valid."

"But my way caused so much trouble."

"No, your way got people used to thinking about how the feud made our lives less than what they could have been."

"So you forgive me?" Her voice climbed an octave on the last word.

"There's nothing to forgive."

"I'm not perfect," she said. "I've made a lot of mistakes."

"Nobody's perfect, darlin', and that's just the way it should be. Imagine how boring life would be without any bumps and blemishes. You wouldn't have your scar." He touched her shoulder. "Or your stork bite, or that cute little crooked tooth I love so much."

"Dr. Patel tells me I'm going to have a couple of new scars."

"I'll love them too," he said. "Because they are part of you."

She reached up a hand to finger the bandage on her chin. "If you love my imperfections so much, why did you send me away, Luke? Why did you tell me to take the job in New York?"

"Because I can't be the one to hold you back, Melly. You have to stay in Cupid because you want to be here, not just because I love it here and you love me."

"How do you know I love you?" she teased.

"I read your letter in the greensheet."

"Oh, that." A warm flush spilled over her. He leaned over to kiss her gently on the cheek. "When you get out of here, we'll celebrate properly and then I'll ask you to marry me. On bended knees, with flowers, home-cooked meal, a ring, the works."

Tears blurred her eyes and her pulse beat painfully against her veins. Her whole body shook from the effort of trying to wrap her mind around too much all at once. She was terrified she was really unconscious and hallucinating the whole thing.

He slid onto the bed with her, and gently drew her into his arms. He was solid and real. She pressed her face against his chest, inhaled his scent. She clung to his hand. Never wanted to let him go.

They were alive. They'd made it through both the drought and the family feud in one piece. And most importantly of all, they were together.

Her gaze locked with his and she fell into the pool of his eyes. "Did you ever think we'd get to this point?"

"We had to," he said. "You're the only one I ever wanted to be here with."

Then he kissed her carefully and her whole world narrowed to this one man, this one beautiful moment in time, where despite all they'd been through, it was imperfectly perfect.

The taste of his lips and the thump of

their synchronized heartbeats created an unbreakable bond, secure, safe and strong.

"I love you, Melody Spencer, now, forever, and always, and don't you ever forget it," he whispered against her ear.

In that sweet bliss, life was absolutely perfect.

EPILOGUE

Luke and Melody were married on the Fourth of July. Even though they had to rush to get the preparations done quickly, neither one of them wanted to waste another day. The Fourth of July seemed so fitting since they could have their wedding date on the anniversary of their first kiss.

And even though it was also the same day that Luke's brother had died, by honoring Jesse's death with their wedding, it helped seal the tentative bond of their two families. Because of the *One Hour* program, so much success had come to their community that the town was able to hire Melody as the president of the Chamber of Commerce. She would have a new job to come to after their honeymoon in Manhattan. And of course, they were staying at the Hilton.

If Millie Greenwood could have lived to see her great-granddaughter get married, she would have been very proud, because she too had once dared to love someone who was forbidden to her.

As they said their vows on the edge of Lake Cupid, now full of glistening blue water, their family and friends in attendance, there wasn't a single soul in town who doubted that this was, indeed, a union to last a lifetime.

And the legend that Millie Greenwood and John Fant started all those years ago lived on.